LAND OF DRUNKEN PHARAOHS

High Table Hijinks Book Three

CHRISTOPHER JOHNS

MOUNTAINDALE
PRESS

This book is dedicated to my readers suffering through those silent battles that others may never know or even begin to understand. I hope you find solace and care in these words, because you matter to me and all these characters. We raise our hearts and glasses to you in solidarity and unity.

ACKNOWLEDGMENTS

I would love to thank my wife, and our daughter, my son and his mother, for all of their patience and perseverance as I work through all of the fantastical stories stuck in my head. This work takes me away from all of you for so many things, and through all of it, you support me how you can. I can only hope that in the times you have me to yourselves, you guard that time and treat it as special as it is for me. Because every anchor to this reality is precious and you keep me floating safely.

I love you all.

THE STORY SO FAR...

We saw Marcus Bola, Marine, returned to Columbus to hide from some shady dealings that took out his unit while stationed overseas, then got involved in some crazier and shadier dealings himself. The supernatural world is real and there are people out there trying to maintain the tenuous peace between humanity with their ignorance and the supes in their incessant boredom.

Those good people happen to be employed by an organization called the High Table and, with branches all over the world, they keep the monsters who go bump in the night bumping to good music with good booze and service.

At least, that was until the wanna-be-drug-cartel-kingpin Seelie Fae, Ascal Qin Moira, decided he didn't want to wait for natural progression to give him power and instead decided to try to flood the streets with a new drug. This drug was liquified mana that had been chemically added to and then further altered to make it highly addictive. It gave a wicked boost to the already powerful supes who took it, but it even gave humans a boost as well, allowing them to see the supernatural aspects of the world and flow of mana too. But the cost for the supes using it was just as intense—to the point that it would eat the natural mana supply of the user after a while and make them a mana funnel before killing them if they couldn't find more magic.

Marcus, with his new girlfriend Cassia, an oni with a big heart and a penchant for fighting, stumbled onto the scene and couldn't leave well enough alone. To help with the growing crisis Marcus had Arden, a flame jinn, and Galaxy, the amnesiac goddess who resided within him and drove them all to grow stronger, join his increasing crew to stop this all from going down. In the fray which ensued, they encountered Merlin, a young Warden in training who had been assigned to a nephilim junkie, and took him in under their wing when things went south for his former trainer. You know, six feet south.

With the help of his new friends at the High Table, Marcus was able to rescue his son and stop the production of the magical drug in time for the different Warden orders to clean up the mess and really buckle down on the area.

But with their involvement came the need to scrutinize Merlin, who had been ordered to attend a tribunal and face judgement for his actions. At the same time, Marcus was given a seemingly-impossible task by the High Table Council. He and his newfound family and friends would need to go out and reclaim the Huntsman's Mantle in order to be of even greater service and use to the High Table, ensuring this would help keep his crew together, and Marcus safe from any possible Seelie reprisal should he fail.

Merlin's outcome was a sentence to perform the rite of passage for the Order of the Sword, which necessitated Merlin having to join with Marcus, Galaxy, Cassia, and Arden on their trip into Grestal to hunt for the Mantle. But this was never meant to be an easy thing. The entire place wants to kill and consume, but the Wardens couldn't just leave the group alone either. Driven and hunted on all sides, the group commandeered/rescued a young lady by the name of Amabala who could sense portals around her and had trained to be able to see and find them her entire life by her abusive Matron.

After being there to help support Merlin in passing his rite of passage, the group went to a city in the humanoid portion of Grestal in order to try to gear up for Marcus's portion of the mission. There, because the Wardens are asshats and can't leave well enough alone, they are set upon by said Wardens. After the fight, the group takes off into the Forest of the Fel, where even the monstrous creatures that make up the myths and legends of Earth, who call Grestal home, refuse to go. The search for the elusive Huntsman's Mantle takes days, after which they find a city of small cat people who end up sacrificing them to their god of death in a massive ziggurat of blackened stone.

While trying to figure out a way to escape, the group is beset by a drake, who calls for another that the group had previously injured and forced to run off.

Thrown into the temple of the cat peoples' god, the deity reaches out and offers to help Marcus with the fight to save his friends from the monsters outside.

It helps with the depleted power of the Wild Hunt.

After the fight goes their way, Marcus takes the black-scaled drake as his mount, a requirement to bond with the Huntsman's Mantle.

Skipping the showdown with a certain mohawked, sword-wielding Warden, they all end up home after having accomplished the mission. Normally, we would stop there, but when it rains, it pours and Marcus and his friends find out that Merlin had been abducted and go to find him after needing to put down Manny the Mantle's conscious mind.

Xehano had been the one to abduct Merlin, and there was no way that was going to stand for long. Marcus battled the boy's former mentor from the Order of the Staff as Cassia and Arden fought the jinn that he had somehow managed to enslave. The group saved the day, rescued the damsel in distress and made off with the jinn to free him and learn more about Arden's bottled family members who appeared to have been scattered to the winds. One of them in the sands of the desert close to Egypt.

Already preparing to embark for Cairo as their first job acting as the Wild Hunt, Marcus and his friends better get a move on…

CHAPTER ONE

My phone chirped and whirred on the stand next to my bed, the light filtering from it blinding to a still slightly drunk and exhausted me. I lifted it to my ear and grunted, "Hello?"

"Marcus?" I recognized Luca's voice and my heart instantly began to race.

"Is Connell okay?"

He chuckled, the sound of me falling off the bed to try to find some clothes likely going through the receiver before he could reply. "Yes, the boy is fine. I called because I got word that you had returned from Grestal, and thought that you would like to meet with Conellar some time soon?"

I smiled, grateful for the other man's presence just then, relief notwithstanding. "I would love that. I'll be heading to Cairo in a couple days, but is there a time that would work better for you? I can put off some prep time to see him."

There was a pause and then I heard, "So it's true? You truly have become the Huntsman?"

I grunted and cleared my throat. "Uh, yeah. Yeah, I have."

"I see." He paused and his voice became muffled enough

that I couldn't hear it. He was gone long enough that I worried that he would have to hang up. Which reminded me, how had he gotten my number?

His voice returned. "We would not want the Huntsman's missions to be delayed over much, but if you would like, I can bring him to see you for a short time today? Maybe there in an hour or so?"

"You'll do that?" I asked, more than a little shocked.

He laughed again, deep and throaty. Finally, he said, "I meant what I said about him getting to know you. He wants to know who his father is, and I am inclined to facilitate this. I think it best that a boy knows his father."

I nodded and then realized he couldn't see me. "Thank you, Luca. That means a lot."

He added softly, "I have only just gotten his mother to agree to this. Sorry it could not have been sooner, forgive me."

"Nothing to forgive." I grinned. "You guys wanna meet at the High Table? Have some breakfast?" I looked at the phone in my hand; it read early afternoon closer to one. "Make that lunch?"

He laughed again and then I heard giggling in the background which had me grinning even broader as he said, "That would be nice. See you soon."

I stood up and stretched, casting my gaze back to the bed to see Cassia staring up at me with a handheld game system in her hands and a grin on her face. "You gonna see your son today?"

I nodded at her and looked down at Galaxy who was cuddled into the crook of Cassia's arm and nestled closer. Her dark skin with specks of light strewn across it could have been a mosaic to the stars and skies of the heavens, her elvish features cute while she slept with her dangerous curves hidden from us both with a blanket. Cassia wore nothing but a pair of basketball shorts and watched with a grin still on her face.

She caught my gaze and gave me a slow wink that could have made any battle-hardened man blush and I sure as hell wasn't about to be the exception. But my mind was elsewhere.

"Can you take care of munitions for my Fae Frame and Silvaero?" She blinked at me, slightly crestfallen, but nodded. "And could you check in with Jayvali to see if he has Thumper up and running yet?"

"I'd have to go in and see him. Probably gonna take a huge bribe to get him to part with another rifle like that." She frowned then smiled. "Though Magdalena will want to talk to Merlin about her little *project*, so I imagine that could buy us a little sway. Arden and I can take him shopping and finish out there for you. Is there anything else you want?"

I grimaced at the memory of the sword the dwarves and goblins had concocted, phials of mana filled with the ambient magic in the air or from things he killed with it, connected to it to give additional magical power to strikes. I wished there was something I could do for guns, but even though gunpowder was a Grestallan thing, it was pretty much useless there. That whole thing confused me as it was some kind of mixture of Grestallan and Earth materials, but it acted differently *only* on Grestal. I wanted to call bullshit, but it wasn't in me to risk a weapon if I didn't need to, so I trusted Cassia and my friends. Though I was jealous of it in a way, that didn't help me thinking about how Thumper was still out of commission.

One of the last surviving Seelie had doped himself with Divinity and attacked me, my only manner of staying relatively uninjured being to use the Dwarven rifle as a makeshift shield to block the strike. She'd crumbled and Jayvali still hated me for it.

"Pop for the flight." Galaxy yawned and opened her vivid green eyes up at both of us, snapping me from my revery. "I desire much of it."

That made both of us laugh, then I pointed to her. "You know, that stuff will rot your teeth."

She blinked at me and replied pointedly, "I am a goddess, Marcus. I am unused to being teased, and I think my teeth will retain their enamel just fine should I will it to be so." I blinked at her, a little deflated until she grinned back at me. "I like this teasing thing. Are you going to take a shower?"

I nodded as Cassia snickered and fought not to laugh at my confusion outright.

"I'll join you, if you don't mind?" My eyebrows shot up and I glanced to Cassia who shrugged. Galaxy grabbed my chin and her voice rang out in my mind. *This is my right as your girlfriend, as well. It is only the two of us, Marcus. No other woman is needed and Cassia is fine with it.*

Was she? I raised my eyes to her and she caught my gaze.

"If you don't go take a shower with her, I will." Cassia smiled at me and I just shook my head before I turned and went to the bathroom with Galaxy.

A short time later, I came out of the bathroom clean shaven for the day and dressed, Cassia looking up from her phone with a smile. "Jay's pissed, but he's said that he has to listen to Magdalena in this matter and will try to get you something close to the majesty that was Thumper."

"He hasn't been able to fix it?" She shook her head and I grimaced. "Man, I really fucking feel bad about it."

"It was outside your control; I wouldn't worry too much about it." She grinned and got off the bed, standing so that she could move to stand in front of me. "The big crybaby will get over it eventually. Despite how he acted last time, he does still like you."

I frowned, uncertain if she was being honest or not, then again, she'd never lied to me before. "You sure?"

"He called you a beardless fuck stick, of course I'm sure."

"Cass, I don't think that's a sign of someone liking me." I stared at her and she just rolled her eyes. "What? What don't I know?"

"When a dwarf insults you, it means that they're more likely to forgive you for something." She patted both my shoulders at the same time and let her arms fall to her sides. "I'm his favorite, so I should know."

Galaxy burst into a fit of laughter in the bathroom that caught us both by surprise. She poked her head out the door, her hair still wet from the shower. "You broke *how many* of his weapons?"

Cassia looked bashful for a heartbeat, the tips of her index fingers touching like she was some adorable anime girl as she answered, "'Bout twenty-three?"

"Holy fuck!" I almost fell onto my desk with the shock from it but she looked really embarrassed. "How did you break so many?"

She groaned and grimaced before she finally answered, "He kept trying to ask me on a date and when I refused, he would challenge me to a fight. He let me pick the weapons and I broke the majority over his head."

I laughed so hard that I saw spots in my vision after a while. After a minute or two wheezing, I finally managed to say, "Why?"

"I didn't want to date anyone at the time, and he thought I was just a Touched human. I showed him I was an oni and we've been friends ever since." She crossed her arms and kind of smirked. "It's because of me he's one of the most feared fighters that the Forge has, you know?"

I snorted as she tried to explain herself. Finally, she tired of that and went off to look for Arden and Merlin to save her from Galaxy's and my chuckling at her past with the surly dwarf.

"I think we should make it a point to reach out to Servant and Chris to ensure they know that we will be out of reasonable reach should anything happen for an undisclosed amount of time," I muttered to Galaxy as I pulled my boots on and laced them up. "You know, just in case Servant can't keep him safe from whoever could potentially be a threat to him, and all that? Still don't understand what kind of threat that could be, really."

She nodded as she dressed, and her figure faded and shifted until she was inside of me where she belonged, as I was her vessel in the mortal world. *That would be a good idea.*

"Well, let's go and see Connell." I threw my dirty clothes onto the floor at the foot of my bed and raised my voice. "Seamus, I'll be back in a little bit and I'll bring some stuff for you too."

I heard a snuffling laugh from the reclusive brownie and closed my door, locking it before I moved away.

CHAPTER TWO

I stood outside the High Table for a few minutes before Luca, decidedly human-looking, and Connell walked down the sidewalk from the direction of the parking lot.

Connell was the same scruffy-haired boy with almost golden-toned skin that I had just rescued a few days ago from the Seelie court drug cartel in the making. Maybe I would pay clan Moira a visit as the Huntsman and see what the young master had to say for his actions?

"Marcus." Luca had eschewed his battle leathers for that of a motorcyclist and carried himself as such. I couldn't find any discernible weapons on his wiry frame, but that didn't mean much. I'd seen the Fae fight; he was capable, and I was damned sure he could hide a weapon in his leather jacket if he wished to.

"Luca." I stared him down, and then offered my hand with a sincere, "Thank you for this."

"It was as much his idea as it was mine, believe me." His smile was genuine and the mirth in his gaze and tone was believable. He turned his gaze down to Connell as we shook hands, "Connell, I have to supervise this visit merely to assuage your mother's guilt and conscience. I want you to have fun with your father and even if it is only for a little while, know that I won't be upset by anything said. You know the rules as well as I."

That brought a slight frown to my face as I glanced from him to the boy. "Rules?"

Connell nodded stoically. "There are things we aren't supposed to say concerning matters of… court."

Luca smiled proudly at the boy and ruffled his hair. "Well said, my boy. Well said."

A pang of jealous rage reared its head when I heard Luca call my son that, but Galaxy's voice quelled it. *He helped raise him, and he's here with Connell now offering an olive branch. Take it, Marcus. Don't let your human pride get in the way of a relationship with your son.*

I took a slightly stifled and stilted breath and blew it out carefully. *Thank you.*

Luca caught the sound of that and tilted his head, then must have realized that something was off, but kept it to himself. "Lunch?"

I nodded and moved us toward the diner that Uncle Yen had taken me to when I first returned to Ohio. Though the walk there was short, Connell told me all about his soccer stats for the team he played for. Luca grumped that they didn't keep score—which made me and Connell both laugh—but that the team was doing much better after the new leg drills that the coach was implementing.

We sat down and ordered some burgers and in addition I ordered all of us milkshakes, which excited Connell to no end. Luca spoke up then, "Connell, I know you love them, but why is it such a mainstay in the hum—*American* diet?"

I blinked at him and frowned, leaning forward. "Have you never had a milkshake?"

The elven prince seemed embarrassed, and I nearly fell out of my seat laughing at that. After I calmed down a little, he spoke again in a low tone, "I'm hundreds of years old and drinking the milk of another seems base. I know that it's meant to be healthy, but I just never had an interest."

I shook my head and chuckled again before saying, "These aren't healthy, my friend; they're delicious. That's the reason."

The burgers came a few minutes later and with them the milkshakes. They were like you would see in the movies, glass cups and all, topped with whipped cream and a cherry on top.

Connell and I waited to enjoy ours in favor of watching Luca tentatively put the straw to his lips as he had his first taste of the concoction. He blinked and his cheeks reddened slightly as he took another sip.

Connell and I shared a look and I offered him my fist. He grinned and bumped it with his own before both of us joined in.

We made short work of the meal and spoke for a brief time until Connell had to get up to use the restroom. This time, Galaxy separated herself from me and padded into his shadow to join him on the way so that she could keep tabs on him for me.

Once he was out of earshot, Luca spoke with his head dipping closer to the table. "How's the hunting?"

I paused and leaned back from him but kept my voice just as soft. "It hasn't happened yet, but we have plans as I mentioned over the phone."

"Do you mean any harm to the Unseelie?" He asked the question with no preamble and to be honest, it caught me by surprise.

I shook my head and he frowned. "Is something wrong, Luca?"

"Several Fae have defected from the Unseelie Court, disappearing from Grestal and the human realm, and the neutral Fae are in an uproar over something that makes no sense." He sat back and frowned even more before he gathered control over his bearing. "At first, I had thought that they had a way to sense that the Hunt had reformed and risen again, but now that I know that you haven't been interfering, this is cause for great concern."

"Is Connell in danger?" I leaned forward without thinking about it, the shadows in the room deepening with my concern. I blinked as he stared at me in fascinated horror and I asked, "Is it the eyes?"

He nodded and I took a long moment to pull myself together. "Sorry."

"Do not apologize for being concerned with your son's safety." He offered me a sympathetic smile. "I know I would be. No, he's not in any danger and I know that should I call on you, you would come running to aid in protecting him."

He closed his own eyes and shook his head. "We will have to investigate further and look into things that are just rumors so far."

"Are the Seelie moving against you?" He grimaced and shrugged. "Is that an 'I don't know' shrug or an 'I couldn't say even if I knew' shrug?"

The war between both factions of the Fae still confused me. I'd had Galaxy teach me a bit more from the meager bit that I knew, but all I could really reliably come up with was that they had never gotten along, and if one could end the other, there would be a serious power shift.

"A little of both, I think?" He chuckled and shook his head. "I am glad that you seem to be picking up on our ways a little from your interactions with us."

"How's Aeslyn?" My sudden question threw him off a bit and I held up a hand. "I know you're married, and as much as it may sound like I'm lying, I am so over that. I could never think about her the same way after what she did, not even now."

Do not forget that there are two women pining after and already sharing you, Marcus, Galaxy chided playfully, but there was another undertone there that said more than it didn't. If I found another woman, she would flay me. It was a tad concerning that she was listening in to my conversation instead of watching my son, and as soon as I thought that she cleared her throat. *Sorry.*

"I'm pretty full up on my dance card to boot," I added before he spoke which made him snort.

He just raised a hand and smirked. "She will likely ask after you when I get home with Connell. All I will say is that it took some doing to get her to agree to this and I have earned many an ear chewing." He stared at me for a moment longer, then offered, "Otherwise she is well. And what your friend Arden told you is true—she gave up much to ensure that your child was well taken care of and protected. Much more than most Fae women would ever allow."

"Like what?" He shook his head and I pressed, "What, another thing you can't talk about?"

He fixed me with a glare that I hadn't expected and answered softly, but sternly, "No. One that I will not talk about because the sacrifices she made were not mine to dictate, nor any of your business unless she chooses to tell you. Though she is her own being and Fae—powerful in her own right and a fierce warrior—she is also the mother of your child and must have earned some inkling of respect from you. At least allow her that much."

I opened and closed my mouth, then opened it again, and just snapped it shut. He was right and, as much as it pissed me off to think about, Connell was a great kid even without having known me. He was smart, strong, happy, and curious. Everything I wished he could have been with me.

Did I have a right to be angry and bitter? Yeah. Hell yeah. But at the end of the day, she had given *something* to ensure he was allowed a childhood and safety.

"I mean to begin teaching him how to fight soon." I turned my gaze back to him and he smiled. "I remember our conversation concerning the matter. I will not be cruel to the boy, but he will learn hard lessons."

I nodded and he smiled wider. "I would like for you to take part in some of these lessons, if you are capable and available."

I nodded again and muttered, "Wouldn't miss it for the world."

"I would not ask you to skip your mission in Cairo." He lifted his milkshake to his lips and licked some of the cream off the top, grimacing. "Oh, that is delicious. What is this again?"

"Whipped cream." I found myself smiling at that as Connell rejoined us. "Hey buddy. Everything okay in there?"

"Yup!" He beamed at me and Luca. He nodded to Luca. "You have whipped cream on your nose."

The prince's eyes widened and he lifted a napkin to his nose and wiped as the boy laughed. "Thank you. Why didn't you tell me, Marcus?"

I winked at him and glanced pointedly to my son. "I wanted him to see it too. Not everyday someone older than you messes up."

Luca rolled his eyes and we all laughed together. After a long silent moment, I stared at Connell. "I know things are weird right now, and I have to go away again for a little bit, but I want you to know that I am always here for you. If you need me, all you have to do is call me. Okay?"

Connell nodded, his hair shaking with his head, then he tilted his head to the side as his eyes flashed at me weirdly. "Why do you have a dragon standing behind you and a cat on your shoulder?"

My eyes widened as I whipped my head around hard enough that my neck adjusted and ached almost immediately. Mako rumbled within me, my forearm itching where he nestled in waiting and Galaxy watched in fascination from within me.

I turned to stare at him and Luca turned a slightly shocked gaze toward me. "What is the meaning of this, Conellar?"

"You can't see them?" Connell turned his head toward his stepfather and blinked again. "You're wearing your crown and the mantle of your station right now, as well."

Luca's eyes widened and he grabbed my arm. "We need to get him to safety."

"What's going on?" I hissed as I pulled cash from my wallet and slid it onto the table with a tip that was likely too large.

Luca grabbed Connell into his arms as if he weighed next to nothing, holding him to his chest as he started toward the door.

I followed closely behind them as Luca looked around the street, then toward me. "We need somewhere safe; can you guide us?"

I knew he knew ways to get into the gym and that he was concerned for Connell, so I just nodded and sprinted across the street to the hidden entrance to the gym that the High Table staff used.

The gym was filled with oni and shifters lifting and working out. All of them heard me come in and when Luca came in, they sprang to their feet. One of them called to me, "Bubba Marcus, what's wrong?"

"I don't know," I shouted back and looked to Luca. "What do you need?"

"Space." He continued down the hall in front of us and found a sparring room that was empty and pulled me inside with him. "Hold him."

He shoved the boy into my arms and shouted, "The Court will cover the cost of repairs if there are any needed after this, but I need you to trust me."

He whispered something and the room's temperature dropped and ice began to form as someone I didn't recognize walked into the room. It was a woman who could have been a female Luca, but she was more ethereal and covered in frost. A man stepped through the air after her and he towered over all of us. He barely looked like an elf at all.

"Mother, Father, Conellar is awakening." Luca looked calm but there was a tightness to his voice that sounded like he was barely holding it together.

"What does that mean?" I asked over the din of the whipping wind that rolled through the room.

They ignored me and the woman muttered, "This room isn't cold enough."

"Luca!" I snarled and the man turned toward me, looking like he wanted to punch me. "If you need the cold, I can help, but I need to know what's going on."

He looked to his parents and they nodded, his father speaking in a language I couldn't comprehend, then the words *shifted* and I could understand him. "…Memorial the Unseelie awaken to their various gifts in a rush of heat and power. The cold is to help regulate his temperature so that he does not hurt himself or others. As a halfblood, we are not certain as to what that will mean for him. If we do not cool this room more, he may die."

His little body blushed red and I looked to Luca. "Take him."

"We don't have time for this, Marcus. I have to find a way to—"

I snarled and barked, "Take him, goddamnit!"

His mother appeared beside me and took my son as Luca's father trundled closer with his son as if they were going to try to control me.

I closed my eyes and summoned my will. "Galaxy, you give me everything we've fucking got."

Bonds are opened wide. Pull, but be cautious of pulling too hard. Her voice could have very well been a whisper over the rush of blood in my ears.

My son was probably dying because of his heritage and there was little I could do but this.

"*Raaaaaaaaaarrrrrgh!*" With all the fury in my body I cast Hoarfrost and willed the room around me to freeze. Ice splintered the air, the scent in the room changing to the harsh cold of winter in the span of a heartbeat. My mana depleted, rose as I took from Cassia, then Arden, then Merlin, and finally Amabala as I continued to pour everything into my mission.

Within a moment, I dropped to my knees, spent and barely able to keep my eyes open. Warmth ran from my nose to my lips and over them as I watched the queen holding my son. Luca's eyes were wide on me, his face in my vision as I tried to get him to worry about Connell.

"Connell," I managed as I fell forward and into darkness.

CHAPTER THREE

I woke up immediately in the space inside my being which Galaxy called my mana sea. It was empty but slowly refilling. For as vast as the space felt, the pace it took felt slow, but droplets were coming to fill it bit by bit.

Quite the feat of strength, little cousin. A voice that sounded somewhat familiar rang out around me from nowhere and everywhere at once.

"Who are you?" I looked around and found nothing.

Everything you once were and could become again, the voice said sweetly, sounding like a whispering breeze over my shoulder. *You are so much more than a mere host to some goddess... we can show you the way.*

"I don't need some stranger telling me what to do, thank you." I folded my arms over my chest and glared into the darkness.

Cute, coming from someone who relies on the enemy for power, the voice jeered and left.

I blinked and the light that filtered into my eyes stung slightly, but I appeared to be back on the floor in the gym.

Kenshi's face drifted into view and then back out. "Bubba awake, Prince Luca."

I sat up slowly and grunted, "Connell?"

Luca held out a hand and put it onto my chest. "He is alright, you helped him get through it."

I blinked and looked around, finding him about ten feet from me with the doctor checking his vitals. I noticed that his ears were darker and came to a point.

"What happened?" I grumbled and turned to push myself to my feet. My mana was only in the single digits but it was there, at least, and not rising. I guessed that whatever had visited me had something to do with my ability to gather mana to myself? My stomach gurgled, and I almost thought it could have been tied to me not taking care of my body so soon after a massive use of power. But I wasn't sure.

"Well, you passed out and then his body began the awakening," Luca explained as he rose from his crouch. "Like all children of halfblood descent, there's a chance they will become full-blooded elves, but with him he seems to have awakened his elf blood, and something else."

Connell opened his eyes and from here I could see that they weren't the same brown that I knew, but instead a vibrant and startling orange with an eerie glow to them. He turned his head and glanced at me, smiling. "I still see the kitty cat and the dragon."

Everyone in the room looked at the boy as if he was seeing things, but for me this was a real concern. How could he see them? *Galaxy, come out as a cat, please?*

Once everyone else leaves the room, I will. She watched my son curiously from within me and asked, *Do you know what could possibly be going on?*

Can you read my memories from just before I woke up? She shook her head and I frowned. *I don't think I'm entirely human myself.*

She stared at me from inside and I just continued to move toward my son as best I could. "Doc, he alright?"

The doctor nodded, his eyes focusing on me. "He is, but how are you?"

"I'm fine." I grunted and looked around at all the shifters and Kenshi. "If any of you are in here after I get done counting down from ten, you're going to meet Mako, my mount."

Kenshi seemed fine with it and the doctor did too, but that was only until Luca started to go for Connell and I put out a hand to stop him. "Eight... seven..."

The other shifters hightailed it out of the room and even Kenshi moved toward the door until I finally said, "One. Mako."

A flex of my will sent a shiver into the air and the drake burst forth from where he had been as a tattoo on my forearm. He grunted and huffed at the air, much too large for the room to fit comfortably, which he let me know with a deep growl that made Luca and the other Fae's eyes widen.

"Is this what you saw, buddy?" I was calm in my question, but inside I was in turmoil as Galaxy stepped from my neck onto my shoulder in her cat form as Connell nodded.

"They're real?" I nodded and he tilted his head at the drake. "Is that a dragon?"

"That is a drake, young Conellar," Luca's mother stated, her eyes on Mako and me. "And that you could see the Huntsman's mount while it was hidden is astounding."

The boy turned and glanced at her, smiling. "I can see the crown that you wear too. And the king. What's going on?"

"You are stronger now than you were before," Luca answered as he tried to make his way toward my son. Mako growled deeply and the prince stopped, looking to me for assistance.

"Mako," I said and he touched my shoulder, my body sucking him into my skin so he could become a tattoo once more. "Sorry, he's possessive."

"I am certain he is." Luca seemed rattled but recovered quickly enough as he turned back to Connell. "We are going to help you come into your powers as we can and will begin training straight after we see your mother."

He turned to me and muttered, "I am sorry, Marcus."

"Don't be." I nodded to him as the king and queen of the Unseelie Court moved to the other side of the room. "Connell?"

The boy stood up with Luca's assistance and peered at me through his bangs. "Be brave, okay?" He tilted his head and I stepped toward him, both Luca and the others taking a step back. "No matter what your power throws at you, you keep coming back and try to control it. I'll be around to help you as soon as I can, okay?"

He nodded and held out his hand, fingers splayed. I grasped it and he smiled widely as he said, "Thanks for the milkshake, Dad. See you soon."

He let go of my fingers and I just stood there watching him leave with Luca and the royalty through a portal, stunned that he had called me Dad.

Breathe, Marcus. Galaxy batted me half-heartedly with one of her paws before she hopped onto the ground and took her elven form. "We have other things to do and less time to do them. Not to mention, we need to discuss what it was that happened while you were unconscious."

I closed my eyes and groaned, "Yes, ma'am," before following her out of the room as she held her phone up to her ear.

"Yes, Chris? We need to see you today, if you can make it?" She paused in the hallway, "You're nearby? Wonderful—see you soon."

CHAPTER FOUR

A medium-sized tan and white dog ran around the fenced-in dog park that we had ridden Mako to so that we could meet the aspiring author. Thankfully, we were invisible to Normies and most supernatural creatures, according to Galaxy.

His other dog, the large white Pyrenees, lumbered around with his pal and played with the smaller dogs gently. It was quite the sight. Or would have been, if I wasn't wondering where Servant, the dog's shadow, was hiding.

He's likely on Zeke's person, Galaxy reminded me as the man walked over to greet us with an upraised hand.

This back and forth between Chris and Zeke is getting confusing. Are they the same, or not?

I... don't know. She stayed quiet and I returned to watching.

I noticed that there was something there that I hadn't been able to see before, a ghostly black ring with jewels of seriously beautiful cuts and sizes on the hand he'd raised. Aside from that, he looked normal, but somehow looking at him with my peripheral vision seemed to reveal more. As if something was hiding in the air around him.

"Hey guys!" He smiled and reached out to shake my hand. "How's it going?"

"Good. We actually wanted to meet with you to let you know that we will be leaving the city again for a time." Galaxy's explanation was swift and to the point.

I added, "You'll be welcomed at the High Table if you need anything, of course." I shook his hand and the smaller dog blitzed me. "Woah!"

"Gemma, down," Chris ordered, his tone broaching no disobedience. She fell to her front paws and looked up at him with uncertainty as he rewarded her with a soft grin. "Go play, you little gremlin."

I brushed off my shirt, her dirty paw prints fading only slightly with each swipe. "Cute dog."

He just laughed and shook his head. "Yeah, she's a little shit for sure. Here." His hand barely touched the remaining paw prints, but the shadow his palm made on my shirt deepened to the point that it could have damn well been the void itself and made a wiping motion that left the shirt completely spotless. "There we go, good as new."

I leaned forward and whispered harshly, "What the *hell* was that?"

Chris blinked and pointed down to my shirt nonchalantly. "That?" I nodded once and he just waved me off. "A parlor trick."

I glanced at Galaxy and she just shrugged, uncertain herself. I just opted to ignore it and hope it was as she said, "Well, if you need anything, you have our numbers. But if you go to the Table, ask for Kenshi, I'm certain that he will take care of you."

"I'll do that." He smiled a little wider and leaned onto his back leg, a smaller dog flying by so fast that they bowled over the person on the other side of us. "Where are you guys heading, if I can ask?"

"Cairo, ever been?" He shook his head at me and I shrugged. "Me either, but the desert itself is pretty familiar, I should think."

"Well, good luck out there in the dunes, my friend." He clapped me on the shoulder. "And if you need me for anything, give me a shout, okay?"

I nodded and Galaxy waved goodbye. Once he was out of earshot, I tilted my mouth toward her, asking, "Did he seem different to you?"

She nodded and grasped my hand, my sight changing long enough to see why. There was a vulpine figure around him with multiple tails that loomed over him and carried itself well. He seemed none-the-wiser about it, but it was like the animals around him could tell something was off and moved if he got too close, then wandered back closer if he turned his attention to them. It was shocking.

"What the hell is that?" My voice was shocked, but I couldn't take my eyes off of it even after the vision faded.

"I don't know, and the others are far too busy for me to pick their brains right now to see if they have any clue either. Whatever it is, it's bothering me. We need to leave." Galaxy's hand reached out and grabbed mine, tugging me gently toward the gate to the dog park.

Once we were far enough away, we mounted Mako and made our way back to the High Table far above the city. "He made the dirty paw prints disappear with a swipe of his palm, Galaxy, and I saw the shadows that were there. It was like what happens when my mood shifts with the Huntsman's powers, only more controlled."

"Are you certain that's what you saw?" She had her arms around my waist and it was easy enough to hear her over the wind whipping by us because of it.

"You can read my mind, you know damn well what I witnessed." My retort was a little sharper than it was meant to be.

"I can't trust that right now, Marcus." She sounded uncertain with that confession, but pressed on. "You had some kind of revelation when you had only been out a couple minutes at most, and I can't see what happened at all, even with your blessing."

"It's not purposeful on my part." I sighed and tried to look back at her, but failed, looking forward in frustration. "You know that if I could show you, I would. If I knew what the hell they were talking about, I would happily let you know."

She was pensive for a time and I didn't know what to say to her. Finally, Mako landed on the roof of the gym and I recalled the drake with a thought. When I turned to look at her, I could see the worry on her face, and it tugged at my heartstrings.

"Look, just because they seem to think that you're the enemy doesn't mean that I do." I reached out and rested my palm against her cheek. "Far from it."

"But what if you do?" She insisted and gripped my forearm. "We have no idea who or what I really am—no, Marcus, not truly, just guesses based on half remembered memories and research."

She turned away and threw her arms into the air. "What if it turns out that I'm the ultimate threat to mankind or something like that?"

"So what if you are?" I snorted and she stared at me dumbfounded over her shoulder, not bothering to turn around as I continued to speak. "I am literally wearing the mantle of the being that killed most of the dragons in some ancient war and now I have voices in my head whispering shit to me. Who says *I'm* not the threat?"

She just rolled her eyes and faced forward about to walk off but I shouted, "Seriously!" She stopped and turned around with her arms crossed. "If that was the case, would you abandon me?"

She frowned and looked like the idea appalled her, muttering a soft, "No…"

"So then why do you not trust me now?" I stepped closer to her, ducking my head so that I could more easily gaze into her eyes. "We've been through some shit together, and I know that

I've fucked up before, but I'm all in on this. I need you. I'm here for you."

She stared at me sullenly for a moment longer before she quietly looked up at me and then smirked. "Sure it's not just because you think I'm hot?"

I laughed and answered, "No?"

She put a hand on my chest and then her forehead. "I'm sorry. I just don't know what's going on and I'm scared for both of us."

I wrapped my arms around her shoulders and nodded absently, glad I could at least console her. "I get it. I would be too. But I'm not going to let some bodiless asshats try to con me out of a pretty sweet friendship." She looked up at me pointedly and I rolled my eyes. "Sorry, relationship. You know this is new for me, right?"

She nodded and just laughed at me. "Come on, stud, we have other things to do and I think the others will be here soon."

Thinking about things, I turned my thoughts inward and focused on my mana sea. It was refilling now, but I wasn't sure still if it had been the voices forgetting about me, or if it was because of another reason. I really needed to figure this all out.

Sure enough, while Galaxy and I discussed the possibilities of what Chris could be in my room, Cassia and Merlin walked in with bags of things for us. "Hey, Merlin!" He winked at me and threw Galaxy a bottle of Pepsi. I closed my eyes as her delighted laughter rang out around me. "And so it begins."

Cassia handed me a bag and I frowned at her. "This is from where Masonai works." She nodded and grinned. "Why did you go there?"

Arden leaned against the doorframe with a Switch in her hands. "I keep my promises and figured if we all had a flight to get there, we all might as well be playing something."

I opened it to find my own Switch and shook my head, about to ask about how Galaxy would play when Arden pulled another bag from behind her back. "She's covered too."

Galaxy squealed delightedly and I just rolled my eyes. "How was the visit to the Forge?"

"Eventful!" Cassia's smirk worried me a tad. "Jayvali was still pissed at you for what you did with Thumper. So much so, he tried to fight me on giving you any kind of rifle or weapon to replace her, or ever again. So, I told him that if he didn't play nice, we couldn't keep the armory there and Magdalena would be pissed too."

With a flourish of her hand, she made a similar-looking rifle appear. "He says it's not as good as Thumper, but it's passable. And before you ask, no, Jay wouldn't give you a weapon that isn't serviceable or in good condition."

I took it and broke it down into the upper and lower receivers before pulling the charging handle out and the bolt behind it. I put the larger portions onto the desk behind me and broke the bolt down further. Retaining pin, cam pin, then the firing pin. And around the firing pin was a small sheet of paper that had been folded and taped to it, thin enough that it would fit together, but thick enough that it would keep the firing pin from fully connecting with the chambered round.

Cassia gasped, her eyes widening. "That little shit!"

I just shook my head and pulled the paper off to unfold it and read.

Check your weapons, you beardless asshole, and take better care of this one for a bit.

-Jayvali

I snorted and crumbled up the paper before turning to Cassia. "Nothing to worry about."

She seemed worried but I put the bolt back together before smacking it into my palm and flicking it to make sure things were okay with it. Satisfied, I turned my attention to the lower and upper receivers. Other than a thorough cleaning and some love from me, the rifle would work.

"Ammo?"

"On its way into my SUV now. We also have more on its way up here to us, because I know that you like to have your weapons prepared." Cassia smiled at me and blinked. "Before I forget, Yenasi asked to see you."

I blinked and offered the bag in my hand to Galaxy. "I already know that you'll set this up for me, could you get that started?"

She snatched it out of my hand and hollered, "Yes!" She tilted the nearly emptied bottle of brown liquid into her mouth again and I could see the sugar nearly taking her. "Merlin, come over here so we can get started!"

I laughed and dodged the empty bottle she threw at me for it, weaving around Cassia and then Arden as the latter entered my room.

I glanced down the hallway to see that Uncle Yen's office door was wide open.

I knocked and he grunted, "C'mon in, boy."

I turned the corner around the door and he waved a hand, the door whooshing to a close softly so as not to make any noise. He looked up at me, his face stern even with his normal Hawaiian print button up and khaki shorts on. He stared at me, hard, blessedly looking like he had managed to get some sleep for the first time in days.

"What's this I hear about you heading off to Cairo?" He folded his hands in front of his chin as he watched me carefully.

"The Hunt has been invited to Cairo to investigate the murders and butchering of their patrons." I sat back in the seat that he motioned for me to take. His jaw was clenched and he seemed pensive. "I'll be careful, of course."

"I know you will, Marcus, I know. I lost faith in you once before, but I'll have that to remind me of the capabilities you have now moving forward." He grimaced and looked down at his desk before he stood up and began to pace. "I had hoped that there would be time for this when you got back. I hadn't expected this to be so swift."

I couldn't help the soft chuckle escaping my throat in agreement. "Me either, but things have been fast and loose since I got here, and I really can't complain about it too much." He stared at me as if I had gone daft. "Look, I've made friends, awakened a goddess, and become the boogeyman for creatures who stalk the collective id of mankind. It's insane, but it's what I've got to work with."

"So why go to Cairo before you fully understand what you've become?" Uncle Yen pressed, his voice soft and concerned. "Especially at the beckoning of the council when they would have happily sent you to your doom?"

"They did send me to my doom," I corrected him and he threw up his hands as if to say, *see*?

"I don't have a mission anymore." Saying it out loud made me sound pathetic, even to myself. "Most of my unit is dead or gone into the psych ward while I'm thriving, and I want to know what the hell happened in that temple. As to why I would work with the council, I only do it because it gives me someone to serve in a way that makes sense to me."

"There are VA groups, Marcus. Join the VFW." Uncle Yen slapped the desk and snarled, "Join the damn American Legion if you want to be a part of something where someone understands you—don't let those assholes on the council use you for their ends!"

"What the High Table does is important!" I shot back, then blinked and backtracked. "What do you have against the council?"

"I can't tell you." His seething was evident as he stared at the wall to the left of his desk. "And while I can paint a damn colorful picture with obscenities, we just don't have time for that."

He turned and glared in my direction. "You did them probably the *biggest* favor by becoming the Huntsman, and now there are going to be creatures and beings out there trying to take the Mantle from you so they can be in control. It wouldn't surprise me if that was the plan all along."

"Is Serpath one that I need to watch for?"

He shook his head. "She's always been the quiet and conservative one. That she approached you for help right out of the gate would normally be a cause for concern, but she is also dealing with a potential catastrophe."

"So who do I need to watch for?" He gave me a withering glance that said more than it should have. "All of them, got it."

"All of them and more, and that's all I can say on them before I start to lose hair and more." He sighed and grimaced again as he ran his hand through his short hair. He sighed to himself and looked back up at me. "I just need you to watch your back. We can have people watch the bar, Cassia's beta is doing what she can to keep the staff in check and Jolly is helping, but it's just not us who will suffer anymore should you fall."

I nodded once and tried to think of anything I could say that would help to alleviate some of the stress he was under, but looking at him, it just wouldn't happen. Finally, I offered a sullen, "I came back from Grestal in one piece, didn't I?"

He nodded almost morosely, then stared me in the eyes. "Yeah, and you came back with a nuke that anyone stronger or more clever than you could take and unleash on anyone." He lifted his hands to his face and rubbed the heels of his palms into his eye sockets. "Don't forget that book of spells I let you borrow. That's got some simple stuff in it. If you need more, let me know and I'll keep an eye out."

I took that as a dismissal and stood to leave, careful not to upset the man any more than I already had. I opened the door and stopped as I felt his hand on my shoulder. I turned and found him staring at me with unshed tears in his gaze. "I'm proud of what you've become. But don't be anyone else's weapon but yours, kiddo. Come back safe."

I patted his face and said, "You got it," then opened the door and went back down the hall.

I started to walk down the wooden floor when someone in the room shouted, "Fuck, we forgot Amabala!"

CHAPTER FIVE

We rolled up to the jetway earlier than the dawn the following morning in Cassia's SUV with all of us loaded and ready for the next leg of our adventure, the newest member of our little group securely seated between Arden and Merlin, who tried to coordinate an attack on a monster that the two of them had begun to hunt in a game.

She looked a little motion sick, but otherwise was just watching with curious expressions and the occasional question.

Her human form wasn't as near to the lithe and graceful cheetah she was. She had opted to take a little more of a thicker stature, her reasoning being, "I was always the scrawniest of my siblings, so I want to see what it's like to be a little bigger."

She had chubby cheeks and a small round nose, hazel eyes, and her complexion a darker tan like that of the plains where cheetahs would roam here on Earth. She had opted for a look without hair and I had to say, she was rocking it. Though she didn't look like she liked traveling by car, she was supremely confident outside of the vehicle and the way she carried herself shined through.

The hangar the GPS guided us to was huge, and I could

already see the people who worked there moving through the planes in front of it doing pre-flight checks. I'd seen some of these overseas, and they could be pretty extensive depending on the aircraft. Unfortunately, I didn't see the one that we would be taking out on the tarmac. Serpath had said it was a specific design, I thought. Nothing stood out.

"Maybe it's inside?" Arden spoke out loud, having glanced up from her game for just a moment.

"Look out!" Merlin snarled and she dipped her head as Cassia punched the gas.

"Woah!" I bellowed as she nearly drove through the lowering gate that kept traffic off the lot. "It was for the game!"

She slammed her foot on the brakes so hard that I bashed my head against the back of my seat twice. I could feel the weight of the car shift as she turned in her seat and glared at both Merlin and Arden. "I will kill you both."

Amabala raised a hand in front of her chest and muttered, "I believe you."

A knocking on the window drew our attention back to the fore, and she rolled her window down so the guard could speak to us. "Is there something wrong?"

Cassia just plastered a smile on her face and grit her teeth. "Kids being irresponsible and kicking my defensive driving lessons into gear. We're fine, just a bit shaken and nervous about flying to Cairo non-stop."

He chuckled. He looked down at his clipboard and back up at us. From the glimpse I caught of it, it had our photos on it. "It ain't gonna be that bad. I have you all on my sheet here, I think. Let's get you in and sorted out."

He motioned us to the parking lot inside and to the right of the hangar that was fenced off but hung open for the time being. The guard pulled a trolley from the side of the area and brought it up to us before looking at his clipboard. "Manifest has your aircraft in bay four at the end of this building on the other side. Wheels up whenever you're ready, and all you need to do is walk through those double doors over there and stay within the yellow tape."

He reached into his pocket and pulled out a set of connected ear plugs for each of us to put in quickly. The roar and dull noise of a plane passing overhead made my eardrums throb painfully as I squished them between my fingertips and tugged the top of my ear up to place them inside the ear canal. That helped dull the noise a tad.

Once he was gone, we turned and loaded all the bags that Arden had brought with her to the High Table for us to pack things into. Ammo, guns, and other weapons, as well as clothes and toiletries for the trip.

But mostly my guns and ammo. I would be *damned* if I got caught with my pants down like in Grestal. Just thinking about not having them with me again in a strange place was enough to make me want to fondle the grip of the Silvaero.

Instead, we grabbed our luggage and piled it onto the trolly to push into the building.

Technicians and engineers swarmed the place as they cared for their various mechanical charges and the upkeep to keep them in working order. Dodging them all, their gear and bickering ringing out around us reminded me of the hangars and bays I'd been in when I was still in the loving embrace of the green weenie. How many times had I had to run an errand for my gunny to the MAG on Pendleton that was secretly just a way to teasingly remind a buddy of the other-than-grunt life that he lived?

It brought a smile to my face until I remembered that gunny was probably wasting away in a sand dune that had blown into the temple by now.

Galaxy reached out and grabbed my hand where it rested on the trolly so that she could pull me back to the present with her presence. Silently, she advised me, *Don't let that consume you again. Whatever they were, they will pay and we will avenge them.*

Cassia's hand rested on my other hand and she offered me a wink. "We will be able to fight a good deal soon, I hope."

She means scrap, she's just concerned for you. Galaxy snorted in my head and I just chuckled along. It was good to have them both so happy to distract me from the past.

One of the mechanics accidentally backed into Amabala and almost knocked her over. He turned around, the rakish man in his mid-twenties eyeing her with distaste before he growled, "Stay between the yellow lines, *ma'am.*"

I blinked and the weight of Cass's hand on mine was gone, the woman suddenly standing next to the poor bastard. She grabbed the back of his head and forced him to look down. "Stay out of the yellow lines, *sir,* and we wouldn't be having this issue." Cassia lifted her gaze so that she could look pointedly at Amabala. "Now, if you would so kindly apologize for being so rude?"

Amabala's head hung and she started to open her mouth when Arden put a hand on her shoulder and shook her head gently, motioning to the young man.

"Sorry, I should watch where I'm going." He hissed as Cassia lowered his head some more. "Ma'am."

Satisfied, she tugged him backward and out of the way, then moved herself up to the front of the procession with Amabala, her arm wrapping around the other woman's waist before she began to walk on.

The mechanics and other people in the hangar had stopped long enough to pay attention to what was going on, the man rubbing the back of his neck bashfully.

Someone poked their head out of an office, a balding man with a thick mustache and beady eyes who bellowed, "Where's the sound of all you fucks making me rich?" The workers hurried back to their tasks and he closed his door slowly with narrowed eyes.

Someone began ragging on the mechanic immediately and I heard him muttering, "That bitch was like, super strong."

I just rolled my eyes as he cast his gaze toward her and whistled low. "Hot as fuck though." He grinned and spoke a little more brazenly. "Wonder what the Kung-fu grip can do elsewhere."

Something to my right moved and suddenly the man was on his back as Galaxy hissed and shook out her left hand. He grabbed his nose that trickled blood as she growled, "She's mine, and you keep your rude comments and behavior to yourself, boy."

I laughed. I laughed hard enough that it was hard to breathe. I had seen her go head-to-head with Manny but that had been magical fighting. This? She had clocked him with a mean left hook that I hadn't thought her capable of. I'd have to teach her how to throw a proper punch after this if she was going to keep doing it, though.

"Marcus?" Galaxy looked at me uncertainly. "Shouldn't we be going after our girlfriend?"

I just shook my head and smirked. "Yeah, probably. Anyone else that gets in her way is likely to get plugged like this guy." I looked down at the kid and just hit him with a look that I hoped asked, *Really, kid?*

We left, Galaxy putting a little extra sway into her hips as she walked so the kid would be even more embarrassed. I just appreciated the view myself and kept pushing our luggage.

After another five minutes or so, we reached what looked to be our destination. A dapper-looking pilot waited for us with a pleasant smile on his face. "Good morning, ladies and gentlemen." He motioned to himself and bowed at the waist. "I am Hadish, and I will be flying you all to Cairo today. Please, allow me to take care of your effects for you and we will begin pre-flight niceties soon."

That one was new to me.

The jet was slick, an off-white color with a navy-blue stripe down the side that started just under the cockpit windshield and ran all the way to the rear of the aircraft. The stairway to get into the aircraft was already down and ready for us to clamber up it and into the lavish interior.

The trim inside looked like it could have been golden, but

that would have been far too extravagant, right? The deep black of the cushions and walls was a stark contrast to the white on the exterior of the plane, but the gold trim all over and even on the cushions and pillows allowed one to tell where everything was and helped my depth perception cope with it.

TVs in front of each seat or on the side of shared ones were massive enough that I was somewhat jealous of them. The couch that looked like it could fold out into a bed appeared to have a small wall that could be lowered from above for privacy.

"Is this some sort of party jet?" Arden asked softly, more to herself than to us. She checked the TV's and grinned wildly. "Merlin! We can jack into these and play together!"

"That's really cool!" The boy mage grinned back and then looked around before moving closer to Galaxy and me. He passed us a book. "I got this for you both."

I opened the small book that fit easily into the palm of my hand, but when I opened it up, there was nothing inside. "Dude, this is empty."

He sighed and tapped it with his finger and words began to appear.

This book records your deepest and innermost thoughts magically by contact. All you have to do is touch it twice—even if it's not you who technically touches it.

I blinked and he grabbed my finger, forcing me to tap it twice onto the page.

Words began to appear and I flinched as they read: *This isn't going to fucking work. Oh my God, it works. Puppies. Kittens. Marine Corps! I better stop. Why isn't it stopping…?*

"That's just how it works, so it could be a good balance for when you have those blackout moments." His eyes met Galaxy's and she nodded and he walked away.

"Did you ask him for this?" She shook her head and took the book out of my hand, sliding it into her pocket. "How did he know?"

She frowned and answered after a moment, lips still down-turned. "I don't really know. He's still meant to serve us and our needs. They knew about what happened, because I let them all know. But I didn't know that he had access to something like this."

I nodded to myself, wondering at how the possibilities could be endless with someone like him on our side. Hell, with the entire party we had, truly.

If I could have picked all the Marines in my platoon, how much more prepared could we have been for what happened in the desert?

I closed my eyes again. *What the hell is going on with me? That's twice in half an hour that it came back up. I went almost the entire time in Grestal without it kicking my ass.*

You were also in a completely new place and weren't getting onto a jet to go and revisit the area—cut yourself some slack. Galaxy's staring almost made me roll my eyes. *I mean it, Marcus. You need to let it come and experience it, then let it go.*

But I couldn't. Because letting it go would mean that I was okay with my brothers and sisters dying, right?

Instead of getting into an argument with her, I just gazed out the window in time to see that our pilot had finally decided to board the aircraft. He turned around and pressed a button that lifted the stairs to the side of the plane and closed it completely.

Hadish joined us in the seating area and smiled widely. "Friends of my queen, I welcome you to our humble carriage today. I, Hadish, will fly you to your destination as swiftly as our horses may carry us, and might I pray we have a stiff wind at our backs to send us flying forth faster!"

He snapped his fingers and small green creatures rushed from nowhere, at least three of them for every one of us. I had the Silvaero out and trained on the one that had a bottle opener in his hand and it squeaked violently.

"My friend!" Hadish called and hustled closer. "Please, allow Her Majesty's servants to tend your needs and whims unmolested, thank you."

"What are they?" I whispered to him as I stared at the one I had my gun aimed at. Hadish gently grasped the slide and pressed it away from the small creature.

It had a compact body and nearly no neck, but its arms and legs were long and lanky.

"They are gremlins." Hadish smiled and patted the one with the bottle opener affectionately. "They are some of Her Excellency's most valued servants for their quick wit and stupendous mechanical skills. These ones are but juveniles, but they work hard and are willing to assist you in any way you might require."

Galaxy stared down at them and then finally smiled. "I'm hungry."

Seconds later the gremlins brought out trays of food, and pulled the lids off, flooding the compartment with the aroma of rich spices and delicately cooked meats and beans.

A high-pitched voice pierced the air that almost sounded like a dog's chew toy, Hadish clearing his throat stopped it as he held his hands up. "My lovely dearest friend, please, speak with a little more belly for our guests, yes?"

The gremlin cleared its throat and tried again from its belly, this time the voice less unbearable. "Here we have a lightly spiced breakfast soup called Ful, this is made of fava beans and is seasoned with cumin and olive oil, typically eaten with pita bread. We add a little shawarma to ours to make it a little heartier."

They opened another pan and it looked like stuffed pita bread. Arden hopped up and moved so fast toward it that the gremlin cringed but she just pulled a portion of it to her nose to sniff. "I haven't had hawawshi in so long!"

She took a bite of it and the gremlins drew in a collective breath until the jinn woman groaned and her eyes rolled up. One of the ones by me chewed along with her, his gaze hopeful to the point of almost being adorable. Finally, she swallowed and asked, "Who made this?"

The one close to me raised his hands with a look of near terror on his face, squeaking pitiably.

"This is amazing!" Arden gushed at him and took another small bite. "The onions, chilis, and peppers are all well incorporated, but still have a pleasant crunch to them, and the meat is minced superbly. I might have to steal you away from the queen."

The gremlins cried out in joy, my eye twitching at the volume and piercing screeches, but they hooted and hollered and wiggled themselves until the one who held the lid cried, "Stop!"

All of the gremlins complied and looked up at them. "Our joy is our queen's, and our service is but an extension of her hospitality. Enjoy, friends and guests."

We watched as they hopped off the table and more food of similar make was brought to the compartment for us to enjoy.

Hadish's friendly smile was back in full force and he bowed. "I believe it is time for us to taxi forth onto the runway and depart." He stood and put his right arm in front of his stomach like a servant. "I will be flying us straight there, so please make yourselves at home while you are with us."

He turned on his heel and made his way into the cockpit where a small flap fell behind him to allow us privacy.

Arden was already configuring the TVs so that Merlin, her, and Cassia could play their games while something nagged at me in the back of my mind. I just couldn't quite place.

One of the gremlins waited patiently by my right foot and I almost flinched when they touched me. "Water?"

"Uh, sure. Yeah, that would be great." I smiled and they sprinted off to grab me a rather nice bottle of water from a small hole in the floor, which struck me as odd in an airplane. "Is that hole safe?"

"Plane magicked," the gremlin offered by way of explanation. "Anything else?"

"Could I have a sheet of paper and a pen or pencil?" They sprung away from me again and came back with a notebook and a set of pens and pencils with chalk and stencils. "Wow. That's a lot. No! It's okay, I'll take it."

Their faces rose again and they looked all too happy to hand it over to me.

The aircraft began to move, the shift in the motion of it shaking me only a little.

Amabala had a death grip on the arms of the chair she sat in and looked nervous as hell.

"If you don't relax, it's going to get a lot worse for you." She glanced my way without turning her head. "It's okay."

"I'm scared," she said simply, and all of us looked over at her, the gremlins joining us. "I don't like flying and this thing isn't even a bird. How does it work?"

"I could go into the full breakdown of lift and drag, but suffice it to say that it will work, and the rest of us are going to keep you safe." I stood up and moved next to her, putting my hand on her shoulder. "If it wasn't for the fact that you have to be somewhere first to teleport there, we would have let you stay home to get used to the world before forcing you to join us like this. But we have a mission, and we all have our parts to do."

There was a soft shake as the aircraft shuddered to a halt, likely readying for takeoff. Hadish's voice filtered through the speakers above our heads. "We are cleared for flight, my friends. Please, have a seat and we will be in the air soaring like the eagles and Pegasus."

I frowned, not sure what to do about the woman, then an idea occurred to me. "Cass." She looked up from her game and stood immediately as I began to pry Amabala off the chair and walk her to the couch. Cassia grabbed her other hand curiously as the newest member of the group began to struggle and try to free herself from my grasp.

I sat on the couch and nodded for her to take a seat next to me and Cassia joined us on the couch. "We're going to be right here with you to help you through takeoff, okay?"

She whimpered as the space across from us opened up to an outside view of the aircraft that one of the gremlins made appear as if also by magic. It was like staring out the window and it did nothing to help Amabala other than give her a front row view to her own personal hell.

Cassia growled at the little creature and the window began to fade until it was no larger than the one that had been there first.

Amabala clenched her hands in mine and it wasn't too bad until her claws sank into my flesh painfully as the nose lifted into the sky. She screamed and clenched harder as Hadish cried, "We have lift off!"

CHAPTER SIX

About halfway through the flight, with Amabala slumbering on the couch beside me and Cassia off playing games with the others, I had the root of my problem drawn onto the paper I had been given.

Well, not really the root of it, but what was bothering me about it was drawn—crudely, but with the other things that the gremlin had given me, it was easier to draw it out.

The aura that Chris had around him. It looked like an absolute beast of a creature, the tails and hulking figure. And the ring on his finger too… what did it all mean?

Shadow fell over the paper and I looked up to find Cassia staring at the drawing. "A nogitsune?"

"A what?"

She frowned and pointed to the paper. "It's hard to translate to English, but basically it's a bad fox spirit." She thought for a minute, then pulled out her phone and scrolled through some photos. Finally, she stopped and showed me a photo of a woman who wore nothing but a katana and crouched in the rain somewhere in a forest of bamboo. "This is Raisha, a friend of mine in Japan. She's a kitsune. She and the nogitsune, the bad people of her kind, go to war all the time over the mischief and strife that the nogitsune cause."

"Do you think that's what Chris could be?" I raised my eyebrow at her, then noticed Galaxy looking my way thoughtfully. "I mean, how embellished are those books of his?"

"Those were the remnants of memories that he had from his time in a very real place." She frowned and scratched her head as she put her own hand-held game down and came over to stare at the drawing. "It's entirely possible that the entire thing is very real, but we're only up to about book four? From what I understand, he and his friends had a lot to do in order to stay alive, and his social media presence leads me to believe that he has already started on book six."

"Jesus." I grunted and wondered what his life must be like to put shit out like that. Probably just lonely. That or he had someone writing for him, like Servant? Who knew. Who cared? "Do you think he could be a threat?"

"Based on how powerful his aura alone was?" Galaxy didn't finish the thought; she didn't need to.

"How do we keep him in check?" She shook her head and this time Cassia joined her. "What do you mean?"

"What do you do with someone who doesn't know your capabilities and that you think is strong?" Galaxy smiled.

"Kill them?"

Cassia snorted and began to guffaw with enthusiasm, until Galaxy just rolled her eyes and offered me the answer of, "Invite them to join you."

"You want to see about blessing him?" She nodded and I was almost hurt. "Why?"

"If he's so strong that he scares even you, imagine the power that could come from him?" She leaned back in her chair, rapt pleasure on her face. "If he's half as powerful as the books lead me to believe, he could be a huge asset."

That was true, but at the same time... "Even if that were so, he would have to give up his life for the stuff we're doing. The books he's writing, his social life? All gone. Fucked. You all have almost no choice now but to be here because this shit directly affects you and your safety, but he has no skin currently in the game other than just being powerful that we know of."

Cassia nodded, folding her arms across her chest. "Sometimes the only thing that can matter is being powerful. I mean, look at all the main characters in Shonen anime—they go looking for stronger people to fight and pit themselves up against them all the time. There's going to be someone or something out there that looks at him as their ticket to power, or as a threat to be rid of."

"I just think we should wait until we know what we're getting into with him and see what he thinks later on too." I frowned. "I mean, fuck, he just learned that all those ideas he had were memories like a week ago. That had to screw with his head a little. Let the man mourn and learn how to live with that loss."

"Agreed," Arden tossed over her shoulder and Merlin nodded with her as they played.

He did add, "He could suffer from a traumatic break if he gets into anything unexpected or too similar to what he's done in the past. Having him join us without truly understanding his mental state could be a burden at best and a dangerous experiment at worst."

I blinked at him, confused. "Where the fuck did you pull that out of?"

He shrugged and cast a glance my way. "I've been reading up on the mind ever since Galaxy revived me, trying to figure out what is going on with me mentally and why I feel the need to serve her so much."

Galaxy's eyes widened a little and my heart began to pound a bit more. "And?"

"And acts of service and a hyper awareness of someone else is common when you feel indebted to that someone. But reading up on the mind and human mental state is fascinating." He delivered the killing blow on what looked like a massive green wyvern. "I'd love a book on the mentality of supernatural creatures and gods if there was one."

All of us nodded as his attention wavered on us and returned to his material collection in the game.

I blinked at Galaxy and even Cassia and both of them heaved a sigh of relief. "I suppose we could wait for a little while to allow him to come to us if he feels like he could manage it. Or not at all. It just seems so much a waste to not have all that power on our side."

"You mean at your command," Cassia teased Galaxy, the sulking woman a little less inclined to return the jest.

I just snickered and let the two of them tease each other some more as the gremlins continued to work and check in on us.

After another few hours and a nap, the majority of the gremlins perched around Cassia, Arden, and Merlin as the three of them fought a massive creature covered in flames, their characters wielding weapons way too large for their bodies to be able to swing and maneuver but they were doing it.

The gremlins gasped collectively as a huge wreath of flames washed over the screens, then cheered when their heroes managed to pull it out and heal to deliver the killing blow.

I shook my head and moved over to the other side of the cabin, looking out of the window to see the clouds below us.

I smiled, loving to see the darkness of it all, but I noticed it wasn't full on dark as it would be for night, or at least that's what I would think. In the far off distance, I could still see sunshine, which would account for this twilight aspect. I frowned and looked at my cell phone clock. We had left at around six or seven, and had been traveling for nearly ten hours now. It shouldn't be this dark even if Cairo was seven hours ahead of us. It should still be daytime, right?

Motion outside caught my attention and a feather dropped onto the wing of the aircraft. But that wasn't as unsettling as the size of it. The feather was almost as long as the wing was.

"Something's wrong," I muttered to the others, then spoke a

little louder as the edge of a shadow passed from over top of us and the sky brightened visibly. "Something's really fucking wrong here!"

"My friends, it appears as though we are under attack." Hadish spoke over the speakers in his normal chipper tone.

"At least fucking sound worried about it!" Arden snarled back as she hurriedly packed her things into her bag, then put the bag into her inventory. She glanced at me. "What did you see?"

"Big fuck all shadow that hid us from the sun, and a wing sized feather?" I looked out the window as she mouthed the last thing and her eyes widened. "What?"

"A desert Atilta?" She hissed and came over to shove me away from the window. Then snarled, "No it's that fucking *bitch* and her pets. Shit."

There was a knocking from the window on the other side of the plane and we all turned to find a woman's face peering into the glass with her eyes narrowed. She mouthed something that looked like, *Land now!* a few times, then bared serrated beak-teeth at us.

"We better land." Arden grunted and then raised her voice. "Hadish, land the plane somewhere safe!"

"I am under strict orders to get you to Cairo as swiftly as possible, my friends." He sounded like he was gritting his teeth as he said it, and the plane dropped altitude.

"Hadish, if you don't land in a couple of seconds, Shareef is going to tear this plane apart to try to kill us all." Arden let that sink in before she snarled, "Land the goddamn plane!"

The force of gravity lessened in the aircraft as we felt the plane begin a rather sharp descent. This time when I chanced a glance outside, I might as well have just given in to fear. There were dozens of winged creatures that surrounded us, their faces like birds with some humanoid features sprinkled about and all of them were nude and female. Which meant they had to be something mythological, right?

Arden says these are harpies and that they've been doing this for hundreds of years, Galaxy whispered through my mind. *I am broad-casting this to all of you from Arden—do not fight unless they offer offense first and do* not *let on that you have anything of value on you.*

That last bit was weird, but okay.

We came to a rather stressful landing on a roadway in an area surrounded by desert with nothing visible for miles other than dunes and some tan ground that resembled earth. The plane had to have taken some damage and the gremlins were stressing the hell out over it.

Hadish opened the door to the aircraft and we heard a harsh, almost bird-like voice order, "Get out now!"

We all looked to Arden and she nodded and said, "Be calm."

We filed out, Cassia and Arden walking out first with Merlin and Amabala walking in front of me. Galaxy hid inside me, and Hadish brought up the rear. Instead of coming out, the grem-lins hid and likely began to work on the aircraft to get us moving again as soon as possible.

We faced a veritable army of harpies, their ages ranging from mid-teens to those who looked to be in their early to late forties, and all of them were indeed women.

Were there no male harpies? *Arden says no. They keep male pris-oners to mate with and reproduce every ten or so years.* Galaxy's informa-tive lesson in harpy lore was nice and all, but left me wondering if it was ten years or so since their last prison break.

"Why do you fly the skies of my people without paying trib-ute?" The most ornately decorated of them spoke, and her features were the most human. She must have been the one that wanted us to land. Maybe the leader, Shareef?

Her beak-like nose was pointed and her thicker dark eyebrows rose over hickory-colored eyes. Her high cheekbones lent more to her bird-like personage and features and made her look much more feral than some of the other harpies were. Her thick brown hair blew behind her in the breeze as the scarves and necklaces of precious metals and trinkets jangled over her bare chest.

Arden looked at Hadish who just shrugged. "My friends, I do not lie when I tell you that I had not known that their territory shifted so far into our way."

"My territory is my concern!" Shareef spread her arms, the wings along them fanning out. Weirdly enough, they were truly interesting. Rather than just being an appendage that flared out, they had hands at the portion that could have been considered the bend, or elbow of the wing. She pointed at Arden with the wing hand. "You will pay now, or we will take what we want and leave you stranded or dead!"

"If you aren't in your territory, we have no reason to pay," Arden asserted, her eyes on Shareef as the other harpies around us began to whistle and trill in anger. "I have half a mind to cook you where you stand because we're on High Table business."

"You would not dare harm the Sunset Stone Pirates!" One of the closer harpies, her age appearing on the younger side, sneered. This made Shareef raise her chin defiantly.

"The High Table holds no sway over the skies of my people until closer to the promised land—you pay, or you die." She crossed her arms and it was a mere heartbeat after that when the massive shadow of whatever it was passed over us.

"I see that Shareef Jr. has gotten a little bigger." Arden crossed her arms and replied haughtily before her message came to us from Galaxy, *I'm going to try one more thing to see if we can make them fuck off. If it fails, I'll mention the Huntsman, and then you gear up. Okay?*

A mental nod from me and Arden spoke to the seething woman again. "Listen, I want you to know that this is the last chance we will give you, Shareef. You and all your girls. The Wild Hunt is reborn, and you never know where they are. Let us be on our way to investigate the killings in Cairo, and if we find anything of interest to you and yours, we'll keep you in mind. We do plan on going to a temple at some point. Could be something nice in it for you."

She thought about it for a moment, a shrill whistle piercing the sky before the massive bird above us rocketed to the ground and alit on the ground surprisingly gently. Though the spray of the sand slashing against all of us and the side of the plane was enough to make Mako want to come out and play.

It looked like a giant vulture or condor of some kind, bigger than a three or five story house, and it smelled absolutely putrid. It had human-like skin on its neck and the face almost resembled a human too. Looking at it made me want to puke and gouge my eyes out.

"What kind of temple is this? We have seen no temples," Shareef muttered as she moved closer. Her lower half was covered by feathers that looked soft and downy, but her feet wore talons that speared the sand as she moved. "Temples mean much wealth when untouched."

"I've been there before," I offered, remembering what was there. "There was treasure and much to learn. Many men went there."

A whisper of the word men went through the harpies like wildfire before Shareef raised her chin. "You have seen this?"

I nodded and she came closer, sniffing at me with her beaky nose. Cassia stepped closer so that she blocked me from the approaching woman, her skin mottling red as she said, "This one is mine."

Galaxy hopped out of me and onto my shoulder in her cat form, yowling, *And mine!*

"Fuck," Arden swore under her breath as the harpies collectively gasped. "They hate cats!"

Screeches of 'cat' rang out around us as some of the bird women lifted into the air and dove toward us.

Get them away from the plane! Galaxy roared through our minds as she leaped off my shoulder and bounded away from the group and plane.

I snarled and grabbed the closest harpy, punching her in the stomach, then whipped her into another one that was trying to grab Amabala.

"Amabala, I know you hate fighting, but we need to make

sure they don't get the plane, 'kay?" She snarled and jumped inhumanly high, grabbing one of the bird women by the wings and pulling her down. "What the hell?"

"I'm a cat too, Marcus!" She hissed and her features changed to make her look like the cheetah woman she truly was. "Let's see if they can keep up with me."

She slashed the harpy's wings with her clawed hands, then pulled her wickedly curved daggers from the sheaths at her lower back and roared, "Come and get me!"

"Mako!" My voice was drowned out by the crashing din caused by screeches of outrage and pain around us. The drake exploded from my body and immediately snatched one of the bird-women out of the air with a sickening crunch. "Good boy!"

The harpies began to dive bomb Galaxy and Amabala, both of them dodging, ducking, dipping, diving, and dodging the bird people like there was someone whipping wrenches at them. Shareef got closer to Arden and the two of them began to exchange blows, physical and magical.

The massive vulture Arden called Shareef Jr. spread its wings and a tornado engulfed all of us that looked to only be assisting the harpies in getting off the ground and into advantageous position.

"Guns work on harpies?" I shouted over the howling wind and Cassia shrugged. "Well then, let's fucking find out!"

I pulled the rifle from my ring—loaded with a round chambered, thankfully—and began to unload on the birds around us. The rounds didn't appear to be piercing their flesh, but they did leave nasty welts all over a few of them that were closer where the whipping winds couldn't drive the rounds too far off target.

The massive vulture being dipped her head into the maelstrom and screamed, the sound of it attacking my mind in a way that seemed familiar.

The shadows of the world around me deepened and soared toward me, crawling up my body like water running up me to form the Huntsman's armor. My rifle turned into a massive crossbow in my hands and the rounds fired off with chunks of my mana traveling with them and the effect was night and day.

Where my shots had left welts before, they dropped the harpies now, holes like one might expect from a gun but much bigger than this in its place. Smiling, I made my shots count a little better now. Aiming and firing as opposed to the cover fire style of shooting I had been doing.

Every shot hit something vital, but they wised up and moved out of my range, then tried to come at my back to attack me from behind. Motion over my shoulder caught my attention and I turned to find a blood-drenched Cassia in oni form with a harpy in each hand, her eyes nearly molten black, which was new.

She looked a little more streamlined and wiry. "Worry about the big one, Marcus."

"What the hell is going on?" I blinked and she was gone, the ground where she had been torn asunder and the harpies she'd had laying on the ground with mangled throats. "Mako, to me!"

The drake thundered back toward me and leapt into the air as he bounded right next to me, dark shadows snatching me from the ground to pull me onto his back where the saddle burst forth, cradling my butt. We soared into the air as a concussive *booooosh* leveled the ground near where we had been and traveled outward, the wind dying a little.

"Merlin, where are you?" I shouted and watched as the vulture in the center of the whirlwind looked up at me.

He's with the plane, guarding it from about a dozen horny harpies, Galaxy spat into my mind as the vulture lifted into the air coming toward where I drifted. *Kill that thing!*

I steadied myself and inventoried my mana. Thankfully, I still had about half left, which meant that I could try to drill the asshole with my rifle and hope it was strong enough to do the damage I needed to drop her, or I could go close combat and really hurt her. I knew which I preferred.

Mako growled and roared, striding forward on nothing but air, making my decision that much easier. Instead of casting

Mana Blade, I just took out the sword that I had won from Mohawk when I killed him and tossed it up into the air. Shadows exploded from my hand to grasp and wind around the weapon, bending it to my will to make a deadly-looking scythe.

Time to put your theory to the test, Galaxy! My call was more to myself than to her, but her presence was suddenly here with me. Mako took us higher in an effort to get us away from the bulk of the fighting.

Shareef Jr. flapped her wings up toward me and I howled a call to the air and let go of Mako with my legs, the massive monster colliding with the bulky bird before her beating wings could bring her close enough to strike at me bodily.

My free fall put a lot of things into perspective about life choices and the need to maybe reevaluate some of them. Soon, though, the bird was level with me and I swung the scythe as hard as I could at her shoulder.

The blade bit in slightly, then something slammed into my chest and sent me spinning around the haft of my weapon with the added benefit of landing me squarely on her back. The harpies had caught on to me and here they were to harass and harangue me.

"Mako, come on back to me, buddy." The drake was close enough that he could fade into shadow and slink back into me, injured from his brief tousle with the thunderous chicken I now rode on. *Must not have hurt it enough with that hit.*

Closing my eyes, I took a deep breath and began to take account of my immediate surroundings.

The others were below duking it out with the pirate pieces of shit, and I had probably six of them up here with the queen chicken trying to fend off her attacker to get to me. And here I was with only about half my mana. Okay.

Half my mana meant that I had a good little bit. So about *125/250* left. That meant that I had enough to at least do something fun before things got truly dire.

I yanked my scythe out of the wound and the bird screeched in irritation, but I yelled, "Don't worry, tweety bird, I got you!" I leaned down and immediately cast Fireblast into the wounded shoulder.

The concussion of the blast sent me rocketing into the air over one of the harpies and I lashed out with the scythe in my grasp, cutting her in half and changing my trajectory slightly.

The massive bird screeched in pain and started to plummet toward the ground. It hadn't been that strong of a blow, had it? It turned in midair, and as much as he had taken for it, Mako had dished it out just as well. The wounds on the bird's chest looked to be festering slightly, and I could feel the swell of pride in his chest as he admired his work through me.

The combination of both actions must have been what brought the bird low, and not a moment too soon apparently. The harpies appeared to be retreating with their massive bird protector wounded and floundering.

Shareef screamed wordlessly from below as Arden drove a flaming spear through her stomach, but her gaze was on her massive monster pal, or baby. Whatever she was.

Suddenly Cassia stood beneath the falling bird and me, with her jaw clenched and her eyes wide. Just as the bird should have been too close to get clear of, she stomped on the ground and threw her fists up into the air at the giant injured chicken.

Stone speared it in the chest and neck, cutting screeches of agony short as the stone exploded outward from the force of the landing.

One of the pieces of stone shrapnel sliced my hip and made my leg numb from the knee down, while another piece slammed into Cassia as she tried to run to me. It hit her hard enough that it caused her to roll head over heels on the ground with the end of it catching on the sand-and-blood-strewn earth, when a snapping sound like a chalking crunch was heard.

She cried out and sagged as she came to a stop on her stomach, prone next to the speared bird. "Cass?" She didn't move.

My balance shifted and I pitched to the right as I tried to run, my leg just not moving as I wanted it to. "Oof!" I grunted as I hit the ground and crawled my way to her, grabbing her as best I could and throwing her over my shoulder to crawl away. *Arden! Merlin! Cassia needs help.*

We're coming, Marcus, Galaxy called and she felt far away.

Amabala skidded to a halt in front of me and grabbed us both, only to fall on her butt as she tried to pull us out of the growing cloud of dust and sounds of harpies.

A roar of flames drew my gaze backward and I could see that Arden was fighting her way toward us. Gritting my teeth, I muttered, "Mako, go help Arden."

The drake slunk out of me and limped toward her. The fight with the bird must have hurt him more than I could inventory.

"Take Cassia to the plane and see if anyone there can fix her injuries." I grimaced as Amabala got up and grabbed Cass from my back. "Wrap your arms under hers, then over her chest and clasp your hands. Pull her backward toward the plane."

She nodded and did as I said before stopping. "What are you going to do?"

A soft groan escaped before I could clench my teeth and turn onto my back, summoning the rifle from my ring. "I'll cover you." She hesitated and I just fired a round at a harpy who dove at us both before shouting, "Go!"

Amabala grunted and pulled the injured oni as best as she could while I continued to fire round after round into the air behind her and above me from where I was. There was no magic to it now, just the pain of them being shot and the recoil jostling my leg painfully.

Click. The bolt caught as the last round in the magazine exited the chamber and went dry, the harpies angrily preparing to dive again.

CHAPTER SEVEN

Press the magazine release, Marcus, Galaxy urged me. *I'm almost with you.*

Cycling through the motions was ingrained in me, and I had no trouble doing it all without much thought, usually. But this time those words were just the jumpstart that I needed to initiate those actions. Why was I suddenly so sluggish?

I blinked at the weapon as I fed another magazine into the port, then glanced down at my hip. Blood flowered from my pants onto the ground, the sand all around crimson with it, and the pool only appeared to be growing larger.

Rack it back, devil! someone snarled at me in my mind and I obeyed without question, training easing me back into that fuzzy area where I needed to be to kill. *Engage the enemy!*

Huffing, I tried to see the blurry targets as they swooped low, diving at my friends. My Marines.

"Die, fuzzy bunny, die!" Release the trigger. "Die, fuzzy bunny, die."

Something moved to my right, and I used the buttstock like a spear to try to back it away but the little creature ducked the attack and lunged in. Then it was gone.

Come on, Marcus, keep firing, I'll help you until Arden can get here. Galaxy's voice soothed the edges of my vision and I could see enough to be able to do something about the harpies over Amabala now. The whirlwind of sand finally died down, and I could see the plane in the distance behind her.

Harpies swarmed it and there was little more I could do about them from this distance, but I could help with the ones over her and Cass.

"Galaxy, put me prone." She complied, moving my body for me. "Can you have the shadows patch my leg for now?"

Already working on it.

I grunted in response and propped myself up on my elbows to sight in. I had started with thirty rounds in this one magazine, which I hoped would be plenty.

I unfocused my eye, then refocused and started to cycle my breathing with my shots, taking a short breath between each trigger squeeze. Every third shot, it was a deeper breath as I searched for my next target.

Something grabbed me by the back of my shirt and hefted me up high enough that I lost my shot and fired wide. Amabala howled in pain and I snarled at my attacker, the harpy trying to gore me with her talons, lines of fire racing down my shoulder and arm.

I had *50/250* mana left and instead of doing anything fancy, I just used Hoarfrost. I centered the cold on the harpy above and behind me with every bit of mental acuity available to me and more than a little of Galaxy's help.

A screeching, *"Rearrr!"* stabbed at my ears and ate my mana faster than the spell could consume it, but it did loosen its grip. I slipped and fell to the earth painfully and gasped as my right leg regained feeling. I reached down and grabbed the stone in the wound and dug around, my flesh having tried to close around it but failing for some reason.

My fingers fumbled with the bloodied shrapnel for precious heartbeats until finally I managed to find purchase enough to tear it from my body. I felt faint immediately and my vision flickered.

Marcus, you're dying, Galaxy whispered to me softly. *We need to pull on your bonds with the others, okay?*

No. I gasped and tried to stand, forcing my eyes open.

Marcus, if you don't, I can't bring you back again like I did for Merlin for some time. Not without more power.

I couldn't form the thoughts coherently enough without stopping moving, and there were just too many of them still to stay still. But she knew what was on my mind.

I have to be out of you to take them! Her frustration made her growl and stomp inside me. *Fine, but if you die, we're both gone!*

Her shadow left mine and my motor functions stopped. My wound was healing faster, but it was also draining my ability to think as my stomach began to protest.

As she sped along, the shadows grew around her to include the one on the ground around the giant dead bird, and began to darken and open wide, like a lens opening. The body began to sink, slowly at first, then faster as Galaxy and the Mantle consumed the corpse.

One of the furious harpies ventured closer to me along the ground, and was able to get close enough that I could smell the blood coming out of her injured and broken arm. Until she stopped moving. Her eyes rolled up into the back of her head and Rocky, the stone fox that Merlin had bonded with, bit the back of her neck and savaged it before scuttling closer to me.

He butted his smooth head into me and tried to get me to grab him but I was having trouble figuring out how to move on my own at the moment. Amabala screamed again, followed by Merlin shouting something that was lost to me. They were in trouble. They needed me.

I took as deep a breath as I could and bellowed for all I was worth as I fought my body and willed myself to move. To help them.

I wrapped my arm around Rocky's cool neck and slipped a bit from some of the blood still on my arm and upper body. He was patient, helping to drag me toward Cassia, Amabala, and Merlin. I couldn't feel anything from Arden except heat, and with Galaxy gone from me, I didn't have the ability to really feel our bonds. She was the Mantle now.

With a subtle, soft *pop*, the body of the giant bird began to dissolve. The shadows around the base of it climbed higher and where they touched, the depths of the dark grew into a cavernous void. From it sprang other lines of shadow that touched the shadows of the other fallen creatures around us and *yanked* them inward toward the dissipating corpse.

The bodies disappeared in a sucking sound that, to my addled brain, sounded like someone slurping up spaghetti noodles.

A harpy dipped down in front of me, her eyes on me as her wings pumped harder for about twenty feet before she spread her feathered flaps so that her talons flashed forward like twin missiles seeking my heart.

Mako burst from my left, jaws opened wide, and snatched the bird woman out of the air like a massive, scaled puppy catching a tennis ball. Feathers flew in all directions as the woman screamed, his fangs and teeth spearing through her chest and stomach with ease.

Arden appeared next to him, one of her eyes swollen shut and her mouth bloodied. "You look like shit."

I would have laughed if it wasn't for the six harpies diving toward us with another four circling Merlin as he physically traded blows with one of the women trying to mangle Hadish.

"Six o'clock!" I roared and lifted the rifle, tugging Rocky in front of me to line up my sights as Arden turned and blasted a torrent of blue flame at the monsters above us. Three of them split away with feathers singed, but the others weren't so lucky.

Rather than the circling harpies, I aimed for the one pushing Merlin away from her as she tried to attack our pilot. Pushing the air from my lungs helped me sight in just a little bit easier so that I could squeeze the trigger and fire at her exposed spine. The round struck, her back involuntary arching with the sting of it.

Merlin toppled her and pushed her to the ground as the harpies above screeched in victory and dove down toward them. Another breath, another press, another shot. A round hit one in the wing and made the bird woman flinch and recoil the appendage, sending her spiraling in the wrong direction.

I couldn't get another shot off in time, but a high-pitched shriek of fury joined by other ones drew my attention to the top of the plane.

The gremlins had joined the fight. "For the queen!"

"For her guests!" The others snarled before launching themselves into action. One of the bigger ones grabbed two of their friends who clasped hands and whipped them at the harpy in front of them. The two spun and grabbed the beaked woman by the face and began to claw, bite, and stab with their teeth and feet. Her flailing took her off center and made her slap another harpy who was too close.

They both squawked as the gremlins held on and shrieked in fear and anger where they were. The harpies screamed and the one with the gremlins on her face crashed into the ground and broke her neck with a sickening snap. The gremlins let go upon impact and, instead of being crushed, *bounced* back up at the last harpy who remained in the air, uncertain of what was going on.

The one who was slapped had landed on the ground and her arm hung at an odd angle, but she looked to be trying to make her way away from the fight while the other harpy was beset upon by the juvenile gremlins.

"Mako, help Merlin," I wheezed as my vision flickered again. Something was keeping my wounds from fully healing, tearing them open again.

The drake limped forward as fast as he could and roared his challenge to the harpies before him. All of them screamed and began to try to flee, flying higher if they could or hobbling away if they couldn't.

Rocky whined, the gravelly sound of it concerned as he looked back at me. "I'll be okay." I slumped onto him. "C'mon. Let's go."

A vacuous sound caught my attention and made me turn back to where the massive bird had been to find Galaxy standing there with shadows swirling around her and her head tilted back, face toward the sky.

As she turned her face down to us, the rapt look on her face was enough to make me question if I was seeing this right. Next thing I knew she appeared next to me. Her face next to mine.

Let me show you, was all she said as she dipped her head forward to kiss me on the mouth.

She bit slightly, then I was lost in the sea of stars with her once more watching as she created swaths of planets with a wave of her arms and time passed, then there were others. Powerful others, but none so strong as her. After all, these were the children she had chosen to give life to. She gave them everything.

I blinked and the glimpse was gone and standing in its place was Galaxy, her hands under my arms as she helped me stand, a grin on her face. "I was the first true god."

I blinked at her and she grinned even wider. The pain in my hip was gone completely and in its stead was a sort of cool ease that soothed me. My veins filled with that same easy coolness and as she stared at me, her eyes swirled and she seemed even more herself.

"End them all for me, Marcus Massacre, my Huntsman." Her voice was seductive and tempting. So tempting.

It was enough to drown out my doubts and fears at having almost fallen. I was the Huntsman.

I touched her shoulder and called to the power of it all, muttering, "Commence the Hunt."

The darkness shot through me and down the bonds that spanned the earth between me and the rest of the Hunt. The shadows surged over them and gave them a boost to their own power and the orders from Galaxy and me. "Kill them all."

My scythe flashed into my hand and I whipped it at the harpy I had injured with my rifle just moments before while she was limping away from me on the ground with her wing broken and dragging behind her. The blade pierced her chest and I used the shadows to pull it back to me. My mana replenished faster than it ever had and I swung again, not realizing that her body was still on the weapon.

She sloughed off of it, cut in half, and landed on the ground with a disgusting wet slap. Flames rocketed into the air as Arden mounted her shadow horse to give chase to those in the air. Cassia sat up with the black armor of the night over her flesh and stood up to help Merlin as he managed to pin the harpy he fought against.

Cassia's foot crashed into the harpy's head, splattering it like a watermelon under a mallet. She turned toward me and threw her hand out, spines of earth spearing toward us and falling short, but pulling something from the ground as they rose up. Something humanoid that had been beneath the stone and wheezed careful breaths.

Arden and Amabala circled the skies and dragged back more dead and dying harpies for Galaxy to consume. The stone creature had been something that had just been caught in the crossfire. An innocent that would have likely scavenged the remains if there had been any.

The plane appeared to be in the midst of repairs by the remaining gremlins that had opted not to fight. Though the gremlins who had fought and Hadish watched us with barely-contained horror on their faces. At our approach, the man dropped to his knees. "Please, Greatness, do not kill us. We are but poor servants."

I blinked at him, then down at my hands and found I still wore the ebon armor of my station. "Hunt complete."

The armor faded from all of us and I stood there in front of all of them. "We aren't going to hurt our friends, Hadish." I tried to offer him a soft smile, but his concern was still too great. "You and our heroic gremlin pals are safe from the Wild Hunt."

Cassia grunted and cleared her throat, all of us turning to her as she held her stomach. "You guys have any more food in there?"

———

We spent an hour or two grounded so the gremlins could complete the necessary repairs and checks to get us back in the air. With that time, I checked on Amabala.

"You know, I really didn't mean to shoot you." I grimaced, the thought of my round hitting her making me feel sick.

She stared at me for a moment, then nodded. "I didn't think so. Battle is… chaos. At best. No need to apologize." With that said, she walked away to be by herself and I had no more to do than just think about the fight and dwell on what could have been different for the time it took me to realize that I was starving.

While they worked, we ate in relative silence. The chewing around me not bothering me for once as I focused on the fact that I had almost died, and that somehow we had all come out of it. A couple of us had.

And Galaxy looked and felt a little more… whole. Looking at her, even the stars that dotted her skin now twinkled brighter and she was smiling more even though the rest of us were more subdued.

She grunted and blinked. "Before I forget!"

Level up!

I smiled and looked at the others, all of our faces brightening a little more.

I opened my stats and gasped, Galaxy's smile carrying through her tone as she explained, "You had almost leveled up from all the fighting with the jinn and the Wardens, but that threw you through that threshold and then some. Enjoy."

Checking over my stats, there was no way that I was going to let these two levels go to waste.

Mana would be a damn good investment, so that got five of

my available ten points right away. As to the rest, I was stumped.

Amabala and Arden were capable of speed. Hell, it looked like Cassia could even be a speed demon when she wanted to be. Speaking of. "Cass, what was that speed you showed out there?"

"Yang form." She smiled and winked at me. "Something about Galaxy interfering with my ability to grow and be different has helped me unlock the ability to take a different physical form. It was really unlocked thanks to the 'test' that the former Huntsman gave to us."

"So then the first form is like a berserker form, and this one is more for speed?" She nodded excitedly. "Nice. I guess that leaves me at a loss then."

"What do you mean?" Arden slurped some ramen noodles that the gremlins had made for her. It was part of the emergency food they carried for the queen since she liked them so much, and so did Arden.

"Well, Amabala and you are speedsters in the truest sense of the phrase, but Cassia can dabble in it for a time." I pointed to Merlin and Cassia. "While me, Merlin, and Cass are the heavy hitters. You and Merlin have magic out the wazoo, and I'm just wondering what I should do for myself."

"The Huntsman's Mantle augments your battle prowess," Galaxy offered off hand, and I just shook my head. "No, listen. It augments your ability to fight, but you need to have a better grasp of your bonds. It doesn't have to be that you need to be able to do everything on your own, or worry about possibly draining one of them dry if you pull on the bonds you share— you just need to be able to cultivate and control them better."

"Okay." I blinked and she smiled at me, making me narrow my eyes at her. "What do you know that I don't?"

She snorted and shook her head. "Everything, Marcus." My left eyebrow rose slowly as she said, "I was the one who *made* the Huntsman and his Mantle."

All of us stared at her quietly until I finally found my voice.

"You what?"

"I figured out why it felt like things with me and the Mantle had clicked when I consumed Manny after that fight—I made the Mantle." She grinned at all of us and made a motion with her palm that threw shadows around the room which then deepened and shapes began to form.

Figures began to move and lighten with the light from flickering stars, like Galaxy herself.

"The universe, young and still in need of caretakers and guides, cried out for aid and I listened." With a wave of her massive hands, other beings came into existence, their movements a little robotic and jerky, but otherwise autonomous as they spanned the stars around the room before us. "These beings became the gods of the worlds, overgods and whatnot. They created pantheons to help govern the portions of the cosmos that I gave them."

"But who were they?" My question made her frown. "You don't remember, got it."

"Within those worlds, the peoples they created needed someone to protect and watch over them when the gods themselves could not intervene, and that was where the Huntsmen were created." From the central being came the Mantles of the Hunt that found and chose beings to create the various Wild Hunts. "Some helped protect their worlds from beings who thought to take over, others became the beings that those worlds needed to be protected from. But the majority of the universes and intelligent beings were blessed with the Hunts."

"What happened after that?" Cassia's voice was barely a whisper.

"I don't remember." She frowned, the shadows filtering away to reveal the black paint and gold trim around us once more. "But I do know that the Wild Hunt is mine."

The way she said *mine* was a bit more feral than I had expected to hear out of her.

Arden spoke up. "So what does that have to do with Marcus?"

"The majority of the Huntsman's power comes from the bonds available to them." She closed her eyes as if she was trying to remember something. "One of them could steal power from those who he had a bond with, borrowing their abilities at times. Some of them stole the lives of those bonded to them and used their souls to augment their power."

"That's what I'm trying *not* to do!" I growled and she just made a placating gesture. "If I recall correctly, the Huntsman whose Mantle I found stole the souls of his Hunt to fuel his last stand against a bunch of dragons."

"From what I can recall of that Huntsman's decisions, he didn't do it right and they all sacrificed themselves for the cause." She opened her eyes and there was a new zeal within them. "If I knew more, I could guide you better, but I think I have a path for you."

"What's that?"

I want you to focus on charisma. She smiled at me and the others just looked from her to me, then back, clearly realizing something was going on. "We can talk about it later, if needed."

Disappointed, Arden, Merlin, Cassia, and Amabala turned back to their own screens in front of their faces. *How much of that was you messing with their heads?*

So much. Galaxy returned and stared over to me. *If you dump your energy into mana and charisma, you'll be better off and more prepared as the Huntsman.*

But what about my other stats?

You're already inhumanly strong, fast, and robust, and I'm not saying you have to focus all of your energy into charisma. She put a hand on my shoulder and suddenly we appeared in my mana sea. *But pumping more than a point per level into it would seriously allow you to open up the truest source of your power—the bonds between you and your subordinates.*

What if I hurt one of them by pulling on the bonds too much?

She seemed to think about it for a moment, then finally replied with, *What if you fail to save one of them because you were too scared to operate at full capacity?*

That might as well have been a knife to the gut for how much it hurt to even consider.

I clenched my fist and my jaw, then snarled, *What do I have to do?*

You know what you have to do, Marcus. Galaxy slowly sauntered toward me, hips swaying side to side as she stared me in the eyes. *Take control of the power you hold, and use it all.*

I nodded and blinked, coming back to myself. I touched the screen next to charisma and pumped all five points I had left into it. After that, I checked the spells tab and found that nothing had opened up to me there, which would have been nice.

Rather, I looked over the six points I had and the spells I had available. If I put two points into Bolt, and Fireblast, I could finish them both off and have points left over if anything new came available.

Fire was about useless to me with Arden in the group, and Merlin was no wimp with it either, plus Fireblast was just a massive version of the spell that I couldn't hold onto. But with it being so close to complete and potentially turning into something new?

That was decided quickly. Two to Bolt and two to Fireblast, and I had notifications to read.

Congratulations on fully investing in a spell. Here is your fully upgraded new spell.

Bolt Havoc – For the cost of the spell, the caster can wreathe a limb or weapon to strike with empowered electricity, or throw a more powerful ball of lightning at a foe. 20 Mana.

That looked fun! I could also see that it was an upgraded version of the Bolt spell, so it was one out of eight points toward being another completed spell.

Congratulations on fully investing in a spell. Here is your fully upgraded new spell.

Inferno Haze – Choose a point within sixty feet to create a detonation point for a thirty-foot blast of

flames that then slowly dissipates and creates an area of effect that lasts ten seconds. 100 Mana.

That was insane! An AoE attack? That could be supremely useful, and this one looked like it was upgradable as well, up to twelve times!

Level 12
Stats
Brawn: 17
Dexterity: 15
Physique: 17
Mana: 30
Charisma: 21
Points to spend: 0
Spell Points to spend: 2
Spells Known
Wisp 2/6
Physical Buff 1/6
Bolt Havoc 1/8
Mana Blade*
Embodiment*
Inferno Haze 1/12
Hoarfrost*
Arcane Infusion
Icy Forge

That would be good enough for now, just in case anything else opened up later.

I looked up, only to realize that at some point during my speculations into personal growth, the others had finished eating and passed out where they were, peacefully strapped into their various seats. Including Cassia, even though she really didn't need to sleep like the rest of us, so she stayed with Amabala and kept her company as the smaller woman watched the skies with a soft shiver.

I kicked back on the couch and decided to try to catch a nap myself. Who knew what we might be getting into when we landed?

CHAPTER EIGHT

"My friends!" Hadish's voice filtered through the speakers overhead, chipper like it had been before. "We have arrived in Cairo at Her Majesty's compound. If you would please be seated in an upright position, we will be landing in ten minutes."

I sat up and looked around the cabin, the others looked to be in various stages of coming to, Cassia still snoring peacefully. Amabala crawled over to me on all fours, her human form back in place. I chuckled to myself and reached down to pull her up so that she sat next to me.

"You okay?" She looked around uncertainly and I patted her shoulder. "Hey, I'm right here with you, alright? All you have to do is just make it through the landing and you'll be fine."

She turned and stared up at me with her newly-hazel-colored eyes and muttered sullenly, "You promise?" I nodded and she just grasped my arm and held on.

"You know, you did really well in that fight." I kept my voice soft as I spoke to her so I wouldn't embarrass her. She just looked at me like she wasn't sure if I was serious or not. "I mean it. It takes real courage to pull someone out of danger the way you did."

"But you yelled at me." She frowned, her eyebrows knitting in confusion.

I nodded, conceding that my voice had been raised pretty harshly. "Yeah, I had an order to give you and I didn't want you to hesitate. You didn't and, because you were so brave, Cassia made it. We all did." She screwed up her face a little more and I finally snorted. "What's wrong?"

She shrugged and finally responded as we were descending from the sky. "No one has ever called me that before." She sniffed, tears forming in her eyes. "I was always the runt of the litter. No one wanted me, and I was constantly bad at everything. I was a nuisance."

This was such a flip from the woman we had met under the tree in Grestal shortly after running from the Wardens here on Earth. But then again, we all had our baggage, didn't we?

I offered her a small smile. "We all fuck up, but what you did was good. Remember that."

I gripped her shoulder and she leaned into mine until the bumping of us landing startled her and she jumped onto my lap to hold onto me.

I laughed and moved her back to the seat of the couch with only minor difficulty just before Cassia sat up with bleary eyes and a grimace. "Whassat?"

"We've landed, big, red, and horny," Arden teased the larger woman who took her human form, this time her hair neon green with a sloping emo cut that left the left side of her face covered until she moved it out of her vision.

"You have the red hair around here, fire crotch," Cassia shot back with a grin that almost sent the two of them into a fist fight until Merlin stood up and both of them were forced to look at him.

He stared at both of them in consternation until finally, he muttered, "You're both hot."

They blinked at him, then each other and back at him

before I lost my mind and started laughing hard enough that the gremlins almost bum rushed me to see if I was alright.

Merlin hollered, "I meant to say hot *headed*, can I do it again?" Which caused me to laugh even harder, making me hiccup and snort at the same time.

We continued to laugh and tease the young mage all the way down the tarmac and into the hangar where we stopped and the plane began to shut down.

Hadish joined us and smiled, obviously uncertain as to why we were laughing. "My friends, if you will follow me, we will exit the plane and make our way to the Cairo branch of the High Table. Please, follow me."

We all stood, Arden and Cassia eyeing Merlin teasingly as they winked at him lasciviously, Arden going so far as to whisper, "I got all the hot stuff, boy," as she passed him.

He just rolled his eyes and looked like he wanted to bury his head in the sand as we all passed him to follow our chauffeur out to a large bus-like van that would seat all of us with plenty of room for our luggage.

The gremlins efficiently grabbed our luggage, and carried each of the items to the destination in the back of the van as a single unit. They even managed to get the ammo safely in there, which truly impressed me.

He got into the vehicle after we all piled in. Amabala sat in the front of the vehicle in the passenger seat, Cassia with me after them, while Arden and Merlin brought up the rear of the vehicle. The midday sun over the buildings and sand was so bright. It was lovely.

Hadish turned around in his seat and smiled. "Normal traffic here in Cairo is as some of my American friends would call, 'bonkers', but with this vehicle, we will have no problems at all. I ask that you please keep your hands inside the vehicle at all times, thank you."

With that warning issued, he turned around and whistled a shrill piercing note that started the engine of the vehicle. It then lurched forward and began to move in a sort of jerking bound.

Like that of an animal beginning to build toward a full out sprint with you on its back.

Clawed appendages reached out and grasped the buildings but left no gouges where they met the stone and wood. Windows were perfectly fine though we should have shattered them as we passed by.

"What the hell is this thing?" I bellowed, grasping the seat in front of me.

Hadish turned around and grinned at me. "Modern-day magic carpet, my friend!" He smiled and shook his head. "We used to cruise the skies, but there were too many reasons not to until your battle earlier today. My queen made this to avoid any potential problems that a normal flying carpet might encounter along with what it might attract! Isn't it wonderful?"

"How are the humans not seeing this?" Amabala screamed, then cried out again as the bus leaped the distance over a large branch of the Nile.

"Flying carpets have a way of bending light around them to make themselves invisible—even the most sensitive Touched cannot find them in the best circumstances." Hadish patted the dash affectionately. "My family has tended flying carpets and our queen for generations untold."

"Who is your queen exactly, and what or who does she rule?" I tried to watch his face and he just shrugged and smiled. "Can you not tell us?"

"It isn't his place," Arden called over Amabala's fearful shrieks.

I looked back at her and she gave me that look someone gives someone as a warning they were treading dangerous waters socially.

I gave her a nod and apologized, Hadish just waving it away. "Do not worry yourself, my friend! All you need know is that you are welcome guests!"

We sat in relative silence after that, Merlin having cast a silencing spell on Amabala so that her shrieking screams wouldn't leave all of us deaf, for the ten-minute ride to what looked and sounded like a water treatment plant.

"Is this the right place?" Hadish nodded at me and the others just shrugged.

I can sense hundreds of people and beings inside there. Be on your best behavior, Galaxy warned us as she stepped out of my body in her human form.

A large metal door opened up to admit us inside, the view changing from a very rural area to that of a bazaar of sorts. There were silk scarves and lengths of colorful fabric hung and interwoven overhead, the ceiling painted bright like the day time but the room was cool and comfortable. The sound of soft speaking, music and water running nearby was enough to provide some noise, not the sound of machinery that one might expect at all.

There was food out all around us on tables, and I realized that the room was less a bazaar and more a themed receiving hall.

"Welcome, all of you!" A voice reached out to us as the soft, lilting music died down. The people that I had thought were real dissipated in smoke, and left us staring at one person seated on a pile of cushions as fans made of feathers spread widely in some kind of leather wrapping moved on their own. "Please, come. Join me."

Hadish bowed so low I thought his head would hit the floor, but he simply stood fully up and moved back toward the door with a serene mask on his face.

The woman on the cushions was larger, robustly built, and *tall.* Taller than Cassia was in oni form and she looked pleased to see all of us.

All of us blinked at one another, but I guessed that she finally gathered our combined curious confusion and chuckled softly to herself before stating, "My other half is coming. She's simply in a meeting. Please, sit."

We glanced at each other out of the corners of our eyes and did as she bid us. Server gremlins, dressed smartly in all black with little white frills and frocks milled about us with refreshments like water and tea. One even went so far as to bring out a small metal cup and a container of sand that had heat rising from it to make coffee of some type. It was very elaborate.

"I trust that your flight went well?" The queen smiled at us brightly, all of us just falling into an awkward silence, suddenly uncertain as to who should speak.

Galaxy spoke up. "Aside from the pirate harpies, our flight was wonderful." As the queen's eyes bulged and she looked like she was about to screech, Galaxy smiled and admitted, "They're all dead now. I do love the decor of your aircraft. Very sleek."

The queen visibly deflated, but she threw a look toward Hadish behind us. "I trust they are not covering for your negligence?"

"Your trust would not be misplaced, my Queen," Hadish replied simply without making too much a fuss over himself like I suddenly felt like doing.

What the hell is going on with me?

She has magic that makes those who feel guilt squirm. What do you have to feel guilty over, Marcus? None of that was your fault.

I continued to squirm as she turned her gaze on me. I blinked and the feeling was gone and a look of consternation replaced her intense glare. She blinked at me and I felt better.

She blinked a few more times, then turned her attention back to all of us. "I am glad you all made it here safely. Here we are."

Serpath walked from the side of the room off to our right with a solemn expression on her face. "There's been another attack."

The queen before us wailed hard enough to shake the room, the gremlin servants wailing with her until Serpath screamed, "Shut it, Umpta!"

The queen's lip quivered and she muttered, "But I am queen!"

"*We* are the queen, here, Umpta." Serpath sneered, then

shook her green head. "We are the same cursed person. Now quit your blubbering and dismiss our guests so that we might get some damn work done."

"No!" Queen Umpta growled, spittle and drool falling from her lips as she loomed over the other woman. "They're my guests and I will do as I please. It was my jet they flew on, my man who flew them, and my gremlins who oversaw their treatment. Mine!"

The two of them stared daggers at each other and for a moment, I thought they were going to get into a fist fight, so I spoke up.

"We are the Wild Hunt, here on a mission," I interjected, having decided I would rather be the fighter than the fought over. "If someone's just been found, then we need to be out there looking for the killer."

"You stay!" Umpta shrieked and the gremlins around her began to growl, their faces weren't any indicator that they were angry, but they all followed their master's lead.

Serpath put her hands on the larger woman and muttered something before the queen took a deep breath and nodded off to sleep. All of the gremlins around us instantly followed suit, some of them falling from a standing position with glasses of water and other items that clattered to the floor noisily.

Serpath just shook her head and nodded to the side of the room where she had joined us from. We all got up and followed her as the massive queen snored laboriously behind us.

Out the door in front of us and to the right lay a set of stairs that she led us up. The flight of the stairs was surprisingly bare for what we had just witnessed, though as I thought about that, we reached the landing and walked down the hall into a room that looked much like the room that I had seen her in while I was meeting with her in a dream.

Once we all filed in, she turned and motioned for the door to shut. Once it was, she took a deep breath and started in. "Sorry about that. She has a nasty habit of butting into things, especially when I order something specific. I knew you were coming, I just didn't think she was bored enough to do what she did."

"I am so lost," Arden whispered more to herself than anyone else. I had to admit, I was too.

"We've been a bit off lately since I can't be with her as much as either of us needs, and it's beginning to take a toll on her mind." She smoothed her small hands over her head and ears before looking at us all and sighing, "Yes?"

"What in the hell is... *all* of this?" Cassia spouted and then growled. "And what are you two?"

Serpath stared up at her until the larger of the two women began to look a little cowed by the staring, then she spoke. "Umpta and I are one and the same person, however our personalities were split due to a curse." She held up her hand to stop Cassia from interrupting. "I don't know who or what cursed us, but we are split and opposite. While she retained more of our former humanity, I took a more gremlinesque appearance. I retained all of our cognitive and intellectual processes, while she remained the more charismatic and emotional-minded one. While she maintains control of the kingdom, I tend to the High Table branch within it. It was a tenuous way of doing things at best, but it was manageable."

She clicked her fingernails together and a vision of the scene some kind of murder erupted around us as she muttered, "Until lately."

The woman that she portrayed to us could have been in the room with us, the table that she had in the center of the beige room. The body was intact, but the eyes and tongue were gone. Blood was all around it. "This isn't it, right?"

She blinked at me after I spoke. "What?" She pointed to the magical rendition of the corpse and said, "How can you say that? It's right there for you to see."

"As I recall, the others had been torn limb from limb, their eyes and tongues stolen and their blood gone." I motioned to the body with my chin. "This one only has the eyes and tongue gone. It's not connected."

She opened her mouth and blinked, then shook her head. "I don't know why it has changed, but it has."

"We need to see the body itself, not just your magical photographs." Cassia grunted and crossed her arms as if to say she would accept no other alternative.

"You cannot go there because it has already been cleaned up." Serpath sighed, snapping her fingers and changing the room around us to give us even more detail. "This is the best I can do. The corpse was found out in the open."

"Wait, where the public could have found it?" My eyebrows shot up as I regarded the room around us. It looked like a crowded street where the people around us were frozen in horror while they stared at the body.

"We had to have the local chapter of the Wardens mind wipe every witness in the area, and more than a few governmental officials' palms have been greased to advise on a soft curfew for residents surrounding the High Table." Serpath held the bridge of her nose for a moment longer and finally opened her eyes to look at us.

She was tired. Her green skin was dark and sagged beneath her eyes and there was a slowly dulling gleam to it. Even her clothes seemed dull. "I don't know what to do anymore."

"Get your shit together," I grunted and she turned to me and glared, some of the dull glaze clearing from her eyes, replaced by anger. "That's more like it. These people, things— whatever they are—are hunting in *your* backyard. Whatever this thing is, this group, I don't know, is disrespecting you and making your life harder. You need to fight back. That's why we're here."

I pointed to the scene as she watched me. "This scene is different from the rest. Before it was just so that other supernatural creatures would see the corpse and freak out. Now, it's civilians and Normies. What's different? What's changed?"

"Did you go to school for something like this?" Cassia muttered to me in confused awe. I shook my head and she just stared in newfound respect. "How do you know what to do about any of this?"

"The Mantle is feeding his instincts." Galaxy smiled widely and added, "He has experience from watching terrorist cells at work and getting to know their routines and schedules. This is just one of the growing benefits."

I shifted uncomfortably. I thought it had been all me and my own deductive reasoning. Serpath waved her hand and a top-down view of the map for Cairo and the land surrounding it hovered over the table for us to view. Another wave of her hand revealed the locations of the other attacks. All of them surrounded the marker for the High Table, with the last being damn near on its doorstep.

"How far apart have the killings been so far?" Arden asked as she regarded the map with interest.

"They started about a month ago." Serpath pointed to the outermost marker, on the other side of the Nile to the west. "Here first, then moving around the city on the opposite side, again closer a little south of here and then north. Finally closing in on the High Table."

"Do you think that they're actually targeting the High Table?" Merlin spoke up and frowned as he stared at the magical map. "It's almost like they're searching for something."

"What do you mean?" He blinked up at me and pushed his hand out, finger flowing from one marker to the next in a circle around the city that slowly worked its way inward. "I see. That does make it seem like whatever it is that's killing people is hunting."

It just wasn't making sense to me, though. Maybe it wouldn't for a while, or ever. What would something—that could kill these creatures without making a commotion until *after* they were dead—be doing searching for something in Cairo? If it was this capable, why not go directly for the High Table?

"Thank you for the introduction to the situation, Councilwoman Serpath." Arden bowed her head and looked up at all of us. "Where should we begin hunting?"

"Likely learning when and where to look." Amabala spoke up for the first time since we had arrived here. We all turned and stared at her expectantly. She cleared her throat and motioned to the map. "We know where it seems to be heading, at least for now. But this last kill is different, right?"

Serpath nodded as we listened and she continued. "So we could lay a trap. If there's something out there following in the original killer's footsteps, they'll be interested in killing again. How long between the kills now?"

"A few days, I think." Serpath blinked and shook her head. "They've been increasing in frequency, so you might have another couple of days."

Amabala grinned. "We can set a trap for it."

Galaxy spoke for her, completing her thought in all of our minds except our host's. *And that gives us time to make sure that there's nothing going on at this temple you spoke about first in the meantime.*

I gave her an appraising look before I grinned. "Good idea." I turned to Serpath. "We'll need time to prepare and everything, but we'll be around. You have our numbers and a way to get ahold of us."

"About your payment?" She tested the waters and we all stilled. "I trust you would like to be paid after this?"

"We ain't doing it for the exposure." Cassia grunted and grinned sardonically at the councilwoman.

"I mean to pay you, and for lodging and meals. I just ask for your discretion and that you not destroy the city."

"Do we look like the type to destroy cities?" Merlin asked, surprising us all.

Serpath answered without hesitation, "Yes."

CHAPTER NINE

"Pretty insulting that she thinks we would wreck the city," Cassia grumbled as we crowded into the lobby of the hotel after about a three-minute carpet ride from the water facility that Serpath and her other half inhabited.

The room was lush, more so than I would have expected for how dilapidated the outside had looked, but she had said that this was a place meant for supernatural creatures and I believed her. The owner of the establishment was a rather nice-looking fellow with a large mustache and eyes that gleamed in the light. His tongue was forked like a snake and, as he watched us, he couldn't help but stare at Galaxy and Amabala. Almost like he was hungry, and cat was what he wanted.

"He is a Salamander," Arden whispered as we walked by. "They're kind of like dragons, but not dragons or drakes? They're more elementally charged, and in tune with their element. I'd say he was a fire-aspected one due to being in the desert, but with us being near the Nile, he could be water-aspected. Either way, don't be in your cat form around him, Galaxy."

"I'll be the one eating him, if he's foolish enough to try

anything, but I appreciate your concern." Galaxy smiled like the hungry cat who found a canary and it was enough to make me laugh on the way up to our rooms.

The bellhop who was with us expertly held his tongue and pushed the button to take us up to the fortieth floor, saying, "This is your floor, ladies and gentlemen."

"Oh, awesome." I smiled at him and asked, "Which room is ours?"

"All of them," he answered seriously and my brain ground to a halt. "The hotel is specifically modeled to best suit the customer, and for a group brought here by the Half-Queen Councilwoman Serpath? Your floor is the finest. It will suit all of your needs and if it does not, please allow us to assist you in reshaping it to your desires."

I stared at the man until the doors opened. The hallway was brightly lit with gold and black like the plane had been. The short hall led to a large, open concept common area in the same color scheme, but it had a fully stocked bar and three refrigerators and a massive kitchen to one side.

Our bellhop bowed low at the waist as we turned toward him, saying, "We are all available at your pleasure to assist how we can. Should you need more food or drink, there is an intercom on the left side of the final fridge so that you can reach us. There is also a phone in each room that will go directly to one of our hotel phones so we are available to you at any time."

We all blinked at him and he stood with his fist over his heart and his eyes closed before muttering, "Far may the Hunt ride." He bowed once more and left us to gawp at him.

"What the hell was that?" Arden hissed and stared at me like I had any damn clue.

I shrugged and she asked, "Do you not know?"

"According to Manny's memories, that was a phrase that those loyal to the Hunt would say to show their faith in the work that the Hunt did." Galaxy frowned, then shrugged, adding, "I was unaware that there would be anyone who knew the old ways, but it seems that the rebirth of the Huntsman has awakened the fealty of the followers."

"Well, this is going to be interesting then." Cassia snorted and flinched as her pocket vibrated. She answered the phone, "Moshi Moshi."

I frowned at her and she continued to speak in fluent Japanese for a time before hanging up and swearing, "Fuck." She looked at the rest of us and said, "Kenshi just let me know that Serpath has made a formal request that we be loaned to her branch."

"Meaning?" Amabala asked as she came back from one of the fridges with an energy drink with clawed M on it. She popped the cap and before I could warn her about it, took a deep gulp. Her eyes widened and she stopped drinking but swallowed what was in her mouth and cried, "What is this? Did humans learn how to contain lightning?"

"It's an energy drink!" I started over to her and she tipped it into her mouth again and guzzled it down before I could get there to take it away.

Her wide eyes widened a little more and her pupils dilated until her eyes were back to their cheetah form, her body almost humming with the caffeine that no doubt screamed through her veins.

"Amabala, you're going to need to go for a run now, okay?" Arden came to stand next to us and took the woman by the shoulder. "You need to get that out of your system or it's going to make you sick."

"I feel great!" The cheetah woman said as her human form began to fail faster all over her body, leaving her tall, lanky body standing lithe in her too-big clothes. "But running sounds great. You wanna race?"

"Sure!" Arden said and threw a glance back toward us as she mouthed, *What the fuuuuuck?* "On the count of three, we will race to your room, I think it's the one with a cheetah on it. One..."

"*Three!*" Amabala roared and took off at a dead sprint as Arden tried to keep up.

We watched them round the corner into Amabala's room before I turned back to Cassia. "I take it that means we need to actually *work* at her location? It gives us an excuse to be there, but it definitely ties us here for at least a shift or so."

"It also means that I will be expected to work for the security there and they don't have any other oni here. Just the scorpion and jackal shifters. I think their head of security is actually a mummy."

I snickered. "You can't seriously know all that, right?" She frowned at me. "Are you serious?"

"I take my job very seriously, Marcus." Cassia stood taller and squared her shoulders. "The heads of security meet bi-annually to discuss matters of safety and potential threats to our branches. The only reason I'm not sure who it could be presently is because Dier retired a month or two ago, and seeing her go was probably pretty damn hard after two centuries of hard work."

I held my hands up. "Sorry, I meant no disrespect. I suppose that's about as close to 'small Marine Corps' as it gets."

"Small what?" Merlin asked politely.

"Small Marine Corps," I repeated, then elaborated, "Everyone knows everyone or someone who knows someone else. Basically, we will all eventually hear of someone else or develop weird networks. It can be useful at times. But this is just crazy. In a good way, Cass."

She just rolled her eyes and sighed and pulled out her phone, tapping away on it before she muttered, "Sent. Now we wait."

I pulled my own device out and found that I was roaming, and it would cost me an arm and a leg to do anything like texting. Which wasn't terrible, I guessed, since I had plenty of money, but it was still annoying to deal with if I didn't have to. Then there was the lack of service in some places as well that made travel with a phone a nuisance. "Do you have an international plan or something?"

She blinked at me. "No?" She frowned and took my phone. "Did Arden not get you set up with the phone gnomes?"

"The phone what?" I raised an eyebrow at her and she just laughed.

"Oh man, I'm gonna tease her so much for that, the jerk." Cassia continued to laugh, then caught a look at Merlin and stopped.

Merlin stared at both of us and muttered, "I don't even have a phone."

Both of us turned to him and I said, "You serious? She got you kitted out to play video games but no cell phone?"

"The Wardens use sheets of paper to communicate so we don't really need to use them if there's nothing tying us to the mortal realm." He shrugged. "I suppose I should get one?"

Cassia nodded and handed me my phone before pulling hers out and whispering, "Phone gnome, gnome phone, phonic friction fucking foam."

"What the hell was that?" I grunted and Merlin just looked at her in shock.

"That's basically how you call them. Shut up a second." She put the phone to her ear and a ringing began to sound on the other end. "Hey! Kazmeer! What's going on, girl?"

She listened and laughed. "Aren't they all? Hey, my boyfriend and another friend are having a little phone trouble. Think you could send someone?" She widened her eyes and laughed again. "Yeah, girl, me! I finally found one who could take a beating. Yup. Uh huh. Pie? You got it."

She listened intently for a moment then said, "Yeah, it'll be one phone line existing and the other one doesn't have one at all."

I heard a shrill, "*What?!*" on the other end and flinched with Merlin.

"Trust me, I know." Cassia clicked her tongue and turned a teasing, scornful glare at Merlin. "Yeah, that one will be on me. Gonna need the best you got on short notice, and it needs to be strong because he's a gamer who owes me a few games now."

Cassia turned around and walked over to the intercom and pressed the button. "Hi guys, anyone there?"

"Yes, madame, how might we assist you?" a deep voice answered from the box.

"I'm going to need six pies of varying flavor to our rooms as soon as you can." She paused and then added, "They're for a phone gnome."

The voice came back after a second. "Of course, madame. We have sent our best man to find the very best for you, as well as a... bib."

Cassia snorted and a cackling laughter echoed over the phone as she said, "Thank you."

"So when can we expect someone, dear?" Cassia raised an eyebrow and nodded. "Okay. See him soon, and you better come by the Table some time so we can get a drink. I shouldn't be in Cairo for too long if things work well."

She hung up and grinned. "Kazmeer said congratulations on landing me, and that she's going to send her best guy."

"What's with the pies?" I asked incredulously.

"Oh, she said that her man likes pie." Cassia shrugged and turned around to walk away to find her room.

I was about to stop her when Merlin grabbed my shoulder and cleared his throat. "Gnomes don't care about money. They will work for their favorite food. It can be any number of things, but having the highest quality food available to them when they arrive or before they finish their work is the best course of action."

"Did you know about the phone gnomes?" He shook his head at my question and I just grunted in reply after that. "Well, go make sure your room is everything you want it to be."

He grinned and ran off down the hall to the room with a staff on the front placard.

Galaxy and I joined him a moment later, though she pressured me to stop and look into the drink fridge so she could get a pop. The fiend.

The placards for the rooms were all indicative of who the room belonged to. There was even one for Galaxy, her placard having a star. Hers was large, and brightly lit with stars pasted all over the ceiling, but they reminded me of the stars you would see infomercials about when I was a kid. There was a bed that was massive, bigger than an Alaskan king, and there were coolers inside that surrounded the wall and at least seven big-screen TVs that had a different game system on each and even a computer near the bed.

"Oh, this is heaven, isn't it?" Galaxy muttered to herself as she looked around, then she turned back to me. "Want to go investigate your room together?"

"In a minute." I sat on the bed and patted it for her to come and join me. She just mimed that I should wait a moment, then pulled out a Mountain Dew and gave it to me. I just shook my head and said, "You just found out that you were the first god in existence a little while ago, and I wanted to make sure that you were alright."

She blinked at me, took a sip of the Pepsi that she had made me get her a moment before coming into the room and managed, "It's weird."

"Yes?"

She sighed and just shook her head. "I should be the most powerful being in and outside all of creation, but here I am. Weakened to the point that I need a vessel just to exist."

"Do you still need me even after all of the harpies you consumed?"

"Especially now." She belched and sighed, eyeing me strangely before grinning. "Do you have any idea how much heartburn I have from all those feathers?"

I rolled my eyes and she laughed before setting a hand on my leg. "I'll be okay, Marcus. I just want to figure out what happened to me is all. I think that there could be a clue or something at that temple you found me in." She looked around the room. "This feels so homey, you know? Maybe we should do this to your room at the High Table?"

I laughed. "Uncle Yen would likely kill me." But that made me pause. "You know, you, me, Cass, and even now Merlin and Arden all rely on each other. And with Amabala added into the mix now too, we're pretty spread out. What if we all went in on a house together?"

"A house?"

She cocked her head to the side and I nodded. "Think about it. The Hunt can work beside the Table, but we're a separate entity, and our being there can be a source of contention and confusion for them and for us, right?"

She frowned and thought about it for a moment. "I could see that being true. But what about those who would benefit most from being there faster, like Cassia?"

"What if we made a portal with Amabala's help?" Her eyes widened and then she frowned. "I know, it could provide an easy entrance into the High Table, or from there to us, but what if we found a way to make it so that only the Hunt could use it?"

She closed her eyes and frowned again. "We could do that, but it would take time and resources. Someone who could make the portal and then someone who could give it permanence."

I grinned. "Amabala and Merlin. Hell, Uncle Yen could too probably."

"How do you feel about leaving him there alone?" she asked suddenly, then added, "And about how he's more than he chooses to appear to everyone."

"You've noticed that too?" She remained quiet and just tapped her head then gave me a droll *duh* eye roll and I sighed, "Of course you have. Sorry."

"Don't be sorry. It's confusing." She paused and thought for a time before saying, "He chooses to appear the age he portrays, and he plays that role well. I think it's why people defer to him the way that they do. The reason I ask if you are okay leaving him is because I know that he cares for you, and you for him. Having that familial tie can be of benefit to you, I think. Is it okay to leave that?"

"I mean, he has the option to hide whatever he wants to. It's his life, his form. Whatever. I'm just glad to be around him." I grunted to myself and shrugged. "He seems to genuinely care about me, even after all the shit that went down with his family. It'll suck not being there with him, but it's not like I'm leaving for good, right?"

She nodded. "It was a rough life for him, I am certain, but he left for good reason." Now it was my turn to nod and go quiet. "I like the idea, and that you would remain close to Yen. I like him, though he does not trust me. When do you want to broach it to the others?"

"Sooner rather than later, but maybe after all this investigation stuff?"

She nodded and shrugged.

A knock at the door drew our attention and Cassia poked her head in. "He's here."

I nodded to Galaxy and she smiled. "I'll be in here researching."

I snorted and Cassia laughed as we both left her to choose a gaming system she wanted to use.

In the common area, a small man stood with a toolbox next to his left leg. He had a long beard and an impressive mustache that was slicked out to form small handlebars, a pair of goggles over his hair which was tied back in a neat ponytail.

He waddled closer to me and offered me a hand, speaking in a deep southern Texan twang. "Howdy, name's Cornelius. Kaz said you had you a li'l perdicament with your service."

I blinked at him and he raised thick eyebrows at me in response. "Uh, yeah. I was hoping you could give me a hand with it? Uh, Merlin too."

"What's your name, son?"

"I'm Marcus."

"Nice to meet you, Marcus." He smiled, white teeth flashing at me as I just noticed the slight whistle when he said the s in my name. "Reckon I could, let's see it."

I produced my phone and he just rolled his eyes. "Newer models are so needlessly easy to break 'em and put 'em on our network." He grinned up at me and winked. "Thought you were gonna be a troublesome bugger, but hey, there we go."

He took the phone and picked his tool box up before waddling over to the closest table and cushion. He set the phone on the table then put his toolbox next to it.

I cleared my throat, remembering what Merlin had said. "Sorry that your pies aren't here yet, but can I offer you anything to drink before you get started?"

He flinched and looked up at me, stricken and surprised. "Y'all got any sweet tea? None of that fancy stuff—I like my sugar with tea, thank you."

I checked the fridge and there was a small section of it on the side that had pitchers of juices and other liquids in it that were marked with labels and one of them said 'Sweet Tea, Southern.'

I blinked at the scary convenience and resolved to leave a sizable tip for the staff if we could.

I poured a glass for him, then another for myself to see what all the fuss was about. "Cassia?"

"Please?" She looked excited for it, and it was hard not to smile at her.

I poured another glass and brought theirs back before I doubled back for mine.

When I came back, he raised his glass and took a sip of it, pinky carefully held out before a thrill ran through him and he grinned. "Now that's good tea, boy."

I smiled and took a sip of mine, fighting not to spit it out. I worried if I did, the sugar would separate from the liquid and litter the black and gold carpet. Instead, I chewed it and swallowed, grunting, "Uh huh."

He chortled and opened his tool box, laying out a cloth and

putting the phone on it screen down, then pulled out a hammer that looked like a sledge in his hands. "Step on back, folks."

We did as he said, then he swung the hammer down on the back of my phone with a huge *wham!* I stared at the scene in fascinated horror, expecting the device to have been shattered to pieces even with how small he was, but it was perfectly fine.

Rather than having been smashed, the sides began to glow with a bright blue light that formed a ring, which rose out of it and tilted up toward him. He grimaced and sighed to himself. "Gonna be a minute for you. They threw in a surprise that's going to force me to actually get into the phone itself."

He flipped the device over then dug into his toolbox for a small package that held tools in it that he tapped. One of them looked like a guitar pick and he picked it up, sliding it expertly around the outside of the phone along the screen before it dipped into the device and he slid it a little more before the device opened and the screen tilted up.

"Ain't gonna be so stubborn for long, is you." He chuckled to himself as a chiming rang through the room. He glanced up at us and took a deep breath through his nose, a grin forming. "That'll be my payment."

Cassia went to get the pies for us and he continued to work. He pulled a section of the phone away with a small pick and growled, "That scaled bastard! I ought to skin him my damn self!"

He slammed his fist on to the table in frustration and pulled out a Bluetooth device that he shoved into his right ear and tapped it twice. He waited for a moment, then stood up and began to pace the room before he growled, "Put me through to my wife before I kick your ass!"

It was a heartbeat before his surly demeanor became lax. "Hey, Kaz-baby, how're you and little Georgie?" He waited and grinned widely. "Good, just checking in. Oh, he didn't get to go on his walk before I left, so he could be a mean little cuss later."

He stilled and nodded. "Yes, ma'am, they been real proper. Cassia was as nice as you said she'd be, and her man seems a nice sort, but the phone he's got is the reason I'm calling." He walked back over to the table and stared down at the source of his frustration. "I'm gonna put you on speaker."

He tapped his ear twice and then I could hear a feminine voice. "What's going on, Corn?"

Cornelius snarled, "That scaled sumbitch's gone and added runic interference to his devices again."

"No." Kazmeer seethed and raised her voice. "George, you put that dang chicken down right now!"

Cornelius chuckled and said, "I told you he was gonna be mean."

I had to ask. "Do you guys have a kid?"

I heard a screech on the other side of the Bluetooth that made me frown and Cornelius just chortled. "No sir, we got a honey badger."

A clipped cry from a chicken screamed into the room and his eyes widened and he hollered, "You get into your damn crate, you silly shit, go on. Get!"

A commotion on the other end of the line and a flustered sigh made him relax. "Clucky okay?"

"She's pissed, but alive." Kazmeer grunted then I heard pages flipping. "I really hope someone skins that bastard for this. He knows damn well what he's doing to us with this, and what it means for us to have to break these things."

"If you can't do it, that's fine," I offered politely, but Cornelius hit me with a withering glare that damn near made me gulp, and I was the *fucking Huntsman*.

"It ain't that we can't, it's just that doing it is going to be harder than what it would normally be." He grumbled, then sighed. "And here I said I wanted something difficult."

"You idjit," Kazmeer groaned. "It's like you like looking the fates in the eyes and wiggling that honkey-tonk donk of yours to see if they'll smack it for you."

Cassia's eyebrows shot up at the same time mine did and she was far and away less able to keep herself from laughing than I was. He blushed a little and grumbled again. "I'll call again if I need help, dear."

"No, you silly man, this is gonna take both of us." Crackling on the other end and the sound of something being unscrewed made me think of a thermos before she sighed softly. "So let's get her done."

He chuckled and walked back over to the phone as his missus and he went through the troubleshooting process and finally he hollered, "Got you, you damn varmint!"

"Did you leave any residue?" Kazmeer asked and Cornelius snapped his fingers and pulled out a monocle, stared at it, then clicked his tongue off the roof of his mouth. "Make sure you scrape it all away or the call could be dropped or sent somewhere else."

"Yes, ma'am." He hissed as he grabbed the small razor by the wrong end and shoved his thumb in his mouth.

Cassia reached out and flicked him and he shot her a confused glare before she explained, "I healed it for you."

He scowled at her and said, "No, you just Major Payne'd me into forgetting it hurt. See?" He held up his thumb and the blood was gone. "Well, I'll be damned! How'd you do that?"

"Focus on the job at hand, Corn!" Kazmeer grumped over the headset and he hopped back to what he had been doing. "Thank you, Cass."

"You're welcome." Cassia grinned and he just continued to scrape away whatever he had to. He gave it a closer inspection, then looked at the rest of the device and decided that it was good.

"Okay, we can get on with it now." He tapped the headset again and said, "Tell 'em bye, dear. I'm gonna need to squirrel you away to myself so we can get this on the network and fool his current one."

"Bye, y'all!" Kazmeer called over the headset and then added quickly, "I look forward to meeting you, Marcus; y'all be safe now!"

I grinned and said, "Yes, ma'am."

Cassia waved and said, "You better come and get some drinks with me, or I'm coming looking!"

Cornelius chuckled. "You come to the farm anytime, we could use a healer like you when the goats get ornery." He turned the speaker off and started to work with his wife on my phone. Then he looked up at me. "You want unlimited data?"

I frowned and replied, "Do I not already have it?"

He raised an eyebrow and said, "Not like this." I laughed and he just said, "Say no more, friend," as he shook his head and relayed the message to his partner.

Another ten minutes and he had the phone put back together, and wiped it off with an alcohol pad, then put on a screen protector and a thick case. "Life proof, and since it's of gnomish make—combat proof." He tapped it with his finger and grinned. "You break the case or the phone, and I'll eat my damn goggles after I get you a new one of both, eh?"

He looked up at Cassia. "That's three pies worth right there. I understand we have another one we need to get a phone for?"

Merlin came out of his room with Arden behind him chattering about the games they were going to be playing if they had the time or when they were off, and it was hilarious watching her be mid-sentence then shout—"You!"

Cornelius roared and hopped onto the table. "Me!" He beat his chest twice and put his hands on the side of his head like they were horns and huffed, "What're you doin' here, girl?"

Arden was across the room and had the smaller man lifted and into her arms in a hug so fast it was dizzying. So much so, in fact, that the gnome actually retched and she dropped him with him crying out, "Woah, Nelly!"

"What the hell is going on?" Cassia grumbled to me and I just shook my head.

Arden grinned. "Cornie worked on my phone, and when he found out that I was a girl who liked gaming, well, he decided that he had to check my credentials. We game together on the weekends occasionally."

"More like she drags me kicking and screaming into

dungeons to heal her a bit." He harrumphed but grinned all the same. He pointed at Merlin. "This one yours?"

She laughed and shook her head. "Nah, more like an adopted little brother." Merlin just blushed furiously and looked away. "My shy, adopted little brother."

"Ain't nothin' wrong with that, son. Keep that in mind." The gnome winked at Merlin and I snorted. "Now, I got the top of the line for you here, we just need to get you set up on a plan with the Normies so that you can get service basically anywhere."

Arden grinned. "I'll take care of that." She pulled out her phone and dialed someone and waited, pressing numbers. "Ugh, the cue."

"Press five, six, seven, seven, four, three," Cornelius offered and she did it. Shocked, she listened to the dull tone pick up a ringing. "That'll be Franklin, he's one o' ours."

"Hi, Franklin?" Arden grinned and began to go through the process of adding another line with Merlin on her phone plan. It took another fifteen minutes but it was well worth the wait.

"Now you're all taken care of, and I can get home to make sure that my beloved hasn't decided to saddle little George and run him into the dirt for bein' ornery." He grinned at us and looked at the six pies that he had around him. "Pleasure doing business with y'all. And Cassia, I'll make sure that Kaz comes out for drinks with you when you get back, hear me?"

The oni grinned at the man in return. "See that you do. Be safe, and thank you for all your hard work."

"Yes, thank you." I reached out and shook his hand and he winked at me before he wiggled his nose and faded from view with all his gear and rewards. "Can all gnomes do that?"

Arden nodded. "They make excellent thieves because of it too." She grinned. "Damn near no one can keep a curious gnome out if they want in somewhere badly enough. Not magically or otherwise. You'd have to prepare for that, and most people not only don't, but don't know *how*."

"I wouldn't say that to one of them though," Cassia added

quickly. "If they aren't already one, they'll ban you from their services for life. Also, don't ask how to keep them out. It's bad form."

"Well, what do we do now that we have phones here?" I asked and she looked at me like I was dumb.

"Get Merlin's number, then make any calls we need to?" Arden grinned. "We also need to see if the request to borrow us was approved or not."

"I say we let them approve it," Merlin said, surprising us all. When all of us stared at him, he said, "What better way to infiltrate their branch without raising too much suspicion? Who would look at new workers and think that we're a threat?"

"Anyone with half a brain?" Cassia retorted and rolled her eyes.

"Anyone with half a brain who wasn't there to relax in the first place," Merlin shot back readily. "These people are scared and they don't know who is killing their friends. It's likely they may be cautious, but when they find out that all of you are just employees from another branch, they'll see it as beefing up security and then leave you alone."

"Okay, smarty pants." Arden frowned. "What will you be doing while the three of us are working?"

"Researching with Amabala in the city's branch of the Warden's Heart Library." He grinned. "I can see if there has ever been anything like this in the area before, and then from there, we can at least be a little more informed than we were beforehand."

"Damn." I grunted and opened my phone. "I'll text Uncle Yen and let him know it's cool."

"I'll go get Amabala." Arden sighed. "That girl is *fast*. Do we know when we're going to go and check out the scenes that we can get to?"

"Soon as dusk falls." I grunted and pressed send. "We should have until tomorrow morning, at least, before anyone is expected to work or do anything, and it should be a couple days before the next murder—hopefully."

I glanced around the room. "Get some rest, all of you. We'll need to be sharp for tonight."

The doorbell rang and made me flinch. Cassia went and answered the door, all of our luggage in the doorway making me smile. "And we can cart the guns to my room."

CHAPTER TEN

My room was simple, really. It reminded me more of a squad bay than a room, and at the end of the room itself stood human shaped and sized targets, as well as some that were in the shape of monstrous targets. At the firing line was a weapons table about eight feet long, then it had individual podiums spaced every five feet apart.

How the hell do they make these rooms like this? I looked around for any kind of video recorders or cameras, anything that could tell me there was some sort of nefarious intent to all of this. I lifted the bed, opened the curtains, checked around the targets, and even looked under anything with a big enough gap to hide things in.

I found nothing.

I put my bag on my bed—it was a king size, which I was grateful for—and walked around the room and to the windows. The view outside was of the city and it was beautiful. It was still a few hours from when the sun would fully set and then we would be able to move around safely without worry and examine the murder scenes and how they were left.

Aside from the bodies that had been found.

Looking to the sand in the distance, I found myself thinking of the temple once more. When would it be safest to go there and get my brothers and sisters' corpses?

I grit my teeth and decided that I needed to do something. I couldn't sleep with this on my mind, and called down to the front desk with the phone beside my desk.

"Hello?"

"Yes, uh, this is Bola in the guest room for Serpath?" They were quiet so I added, "I was just wondering if my room is soundproof? I see that there's a range in here of sorts, and wanted to get some shooting in. If I start firing weapons in here, would it disturb the other guests?"

"Oh!" the woman on the other end gasped. "Yes, that room is soundproof and the walls are lined with Kevlar, so you needn't worry about any stray shots. Just ensure that your door and windows are closed before you start if you don't want any noise pollution to reach anyone else. Thank you for being so considerate, sir!"

"Of course, thank you." I hung up the phone awkwardly and just stared at it for a second before getting back to what I had on the brain.

First, I grabbed my weapons bag and then made my way to the larger table. I pulled out my Fae Frame, then the Silvaero, stripped them and built the Frame back up and loaded a magazine. Racked it back at the podium furthest to the left of the room and sighted in on the nearest monstrous target. The first round hit its neck and pinged aside, so I fired another round.

Thank god for the super healing I have, otherwise my hearing would be fucked. I grunted and fired again.

I emptied the magazine into the thing before I realized that I wasn't alone in the room.

"I take it that you've been thinking about things again?" Galaxy asked rhetorically. She knew.

I nodded once as I fed another magazine into the Fae Frame, but left the slide locked back as I set it down. I glanced at her where she stood near the door, then turned my attention to the Silvaero still on the larger table. "Yeah."

"We will find them, Marcus," she said quietly.

"I know we will. Though, what happens when we find the things that killed them all?" I finished assembling the weapon and slammed a magazine home and paced to the podium to the right of the Fae Frame before I released the slide and fired on the monstrous creature further away. My aim was off slightly as I shot low twice.

Small hands raised my elbows slightly as Galaxy pressed herself against my back and my aim improved greatly. I continued to fire until the slide locked back again, then set the weapon down and turned around.

She was careful to keep her face blank, but I could feel her concern. "I just can't escape the sands of my head when I think about that place and what happened." I stared at the monstrous targets as I fought to try to remember the creature that had butchered my people and just *couldn't*. It spiked my fury to the point that I picked the pistol back up, ejected the mag, and fed another in before growling, "And every time I try to remember anything about it, all I feel is fear!"

Round after round banged against the target, the pinging of the metal on metal making Galaxy flinch where she was. Once the weapon was empty, I set it down and screamed.

I screamed until I couldn't breathe and had to take air in again. It was one thing to have the thoughts of failing and be thousands of miles away, but I was here. Right here. So close that we could fly there right now and get them all back. Take the fight to this creature. But I couldn't do that. I had a different duty now. One to the living. And there were more bodies stacking up all around us, and there was something I could do about these ones.

She nodded. "I know." This time, she lifted the weapon and pressed a magazine into it, leaving it where it had been. "I take it that the rifle is next?"

I nodded. And she walked over to the table to get it, careful not to flag me with it when she loaded the larger magazine into it and racked the charging handle back with ease, like she had done it before. She winked at me. "Your memories make it easy, but I've never fired one. Want to help me?"

I found myself smiling weakly. "Sure."

I had her sighting down the barrel and was explaining how sight alignment and sight picture worked when a knock on the door drew our attention.

"Come in!" I hollered and the door opened with Cassia carrying some food in her hands. "Hey!"

"Am I interrupting?" she asked softly as she lifted the food. It looked like sushi from where I stood.

"Not at all, do you want to shoot with us?" Galaxy asked with a grin, then sniffed the air. "That's fresh sushi!"

Cassia grinned. "I love sushi, and being here, we're near enough to the ocean that I can make it well. You want some?"

"You bet your ass I do!" Galaxy clicked the safety on before shoving the rifle into my chest and proceeded to stalk closer to the oni. "It smells so good."

"I hope it does." Cassia laughed and held the plate out to her. "This is for you; I wasn't sure what Marcus would like so I made some salmon patties as well?"

"I'm down for that, thank you, Cass." I smiled at her, my mind a little more at ease with both of them here and a rifle in hand. I sauntered over and gave her a kiss on the forehead. "You alright?"

"Better with sushi." She smiled back and motioned to the larger table. "What's wrong?"

"He was thinking about what happened without us around and it's eating at him." Galaxy stuffed another slice of tuna roll into her mouth. "These would go *great* with Mountain Dew!"

Cassia actually growled. "You go anywhere near pop while eating my sushi, I will *fight* you."

I held a finger up. "I know what she meant that time."

Galaxy swallowed. "Same. Sorry." Cassia reached out and pinched Galaxy's cheek playfully as the former stuck out her tongue. "I'll go have some of this at the table. Would you like to play with Marcus' guns?"

"Always." Cassia turned her intense gaze on me and I found my mouth dry for a moment, then realized that I had a rifle in my hands.

I offered it to her playfully and asked, "Rifle?"

She grinned and took it, flicking the safety off and lowering the muzzle in one fluid motion. "What's my target?"

"Anything you want down range," I said and followed along behind her.

As she lifted the rifle and sighted in, I saw something flash at the end of the room and put a hand on her shoulder. *Galaxy, tell her to aim where I'm looking.*

Between the two humanoid targets, about shoulder height? I nodded and Cassia squeezed the trigger a couple times, firing in three-round bursts. She moved forward the same time as I cast Wisp at the end of the room.

The room lit up and there was a small silvery coin dangling from a string between the two targets in the center of the line that was completely unfazed by the rounds that had whizzed by it. Both of us continued forward until we were within ten feet of the item.

It was completely untouched and though the heat of my spell had warmed the string, it was completely cold. As soon as my skin touched it, I hissed and flinched away from it.

Damn silver allergy. I sucked on my index finger and Galaxy appeared next to me. *I checked this room, Galaxy. There was nothing here.*

She reached out and sniffed it, then closed her eyes and began to radiate dark energy. *This is a listening device. They've tapped the rooms.*

Cassia scowled as Galaxy spoke for her. *What do we do?*

We leave them as they are and leave this place. If they can come in and tap the room while I'm fucking in it—we aren't safe here. I closed my eyes and pulled on the bonds that bound me to everyone else and used them to get their attention, not summon them. *Pass this on, Galaxy.*

Already have been, but the bond thing was a damn fine start. She grinned at me as she let the coin fall and dangle as it had been.

We need to gather what we can that won't seem amiss, then leave and go home. This place isn't safe for us, which means we will all need to have a discussion that I was wanting to have later, sooner than I wanted, but shit happens. I smiled at Cassia and her confusion. *Amabala, can you get us back to the Table?*

Yes, Marcus, she answered readily. *Though it will take all of my mana, and I won't be able to bring us back for an hour instead of a half an hour due to the distance.*

That should be fine. I sighed and motioned to the door with the girls. "Well, it's time to eat dinner, right?"

"Sure is." Cassia smiled and turned with the rifle in hand. "I got some more out in the common room. We should go and get some."

"This tuna is amazing." Galaxy played along a little stiffly.

We made our way to the firing line and I went to my other weapons, pulling them to myself and slipping them into my inventory. It was easiest to put them there. I left the majority of my ammunition there in the suitcases that we had them in, but I made sure that I grabbed my bag of clothes and slung it over my shoulder. "I wanted to make sure that you see this outfit I have planned for the trip, guys. You mind?"

The girls gave their assent, looking uncomfortable as we left the room and sighed when they thought it was safe. *Galaxy, can you hunt through the room and find them all? I can almost promise there will be at least four.*

She nodded and took another piece of sushi and ate it before putting the plate on the table and closing her eyes. She tilted her head back and sniffed for a second before she shifted into her cat form and padded silently over to one of the cushions on the floor that Cornelius had used to work on.

She pulled it out of the cushion with her teeth and placed it on the table, then went to the opposite side of the room. She paced the room and found seven more in total.

Overkill, two of them are strong enough to listen to the whole room. She growled and shifted back. *Merlin recognizes them from his training, this is something that the Wardens use to spy on people of interest.*

More Warden bullshit? I sighed and ground the heel of my hand against my forehead and found that the others were in the room. *Let's go, Amabala.*

She closed her eyes and focused, then threw her hands forward and grimaced as her claws tore through the air and sliced through the fabric of reality and pulled it apart wide enough for us to go through single file.

On the other side of the portal, we came out of the wall of the gym in the basement. This was the room that had been where Amabala had been staying while we prepared to go to Cairo and though it was sparsely decorated, it was homey.

"What was it that you wanted to talk to us about?" Arden raised a brow curiously as Amabala stepped through, sweat beading her brow.

"I was thinking it was time for us to leave the High Table," I said. Both Arden and Cassia looked shocked. "Shit, that sounded worse than I meant."

"Marcus..." Cassia started, I held up a hand and she stopped, pursing her lips.

"I meant as far as living in it is concerned." Both of them looked a little more relieved, Merlin and Amabala relaxing a bit as well. "Our being here paints a target on this place just because of our presence. Living here means that the target is here constantly now, and I wanted to see if all of you thought getting a house of our own to live in would be a good idea."

Both Cassia and Arden seemed contemplative about it, but Amabala raised a concern. "Isn't this place a sanctuary of sorts? It's neutral ground. Our being here offers us a measure of safety, doesn't it?"

Cassia was the first to offer insight. "Yes, it does. But it also means that the reputation of the Table is put at stake too. We can work alongside them, even for them, but staying here does come with a level of debts that we may not want to pay. They could start to expect us to repay more than we should need to." She looked to me and sighed. "I think it's a sound idea, and it means that my people will be safe too. But it also means that there will be a lag in responsiveness should the Table come under attack while I am gone. I know that my second can handle herself, but I need to be able to get here quickly. That means that wherever it is needs to be close."

"We were thinking about that," Galaxy said, turning her gaze on both Merlin and Amabala. "And I think that both of you will be the key to making it viable."

Merlin frowned, then his eyes widened. "You want us to make a permanent portal from the house to the High Table?"

I told you that I had remade him well, Galaxy purred into my mind softly and it almost made me sigh. She had. "Yes, that was the thought."

"I don't know how to do that, but I could research it. The only problem would be that Marcus' uncle will know that we have been able to appear here." Merlin's statement confused me.

"Why is that?"

Footsteps in the hallway outside drew my attention to the door as four of the largest guards kicked the door aside like it was made of toothpicks and piled into the room.

Cassia snarled, "Stand down!" All of them came up short, their various stages of transforming stopped and then reverted.

Keith was one of them and he rolled his eyes and sighed in relief. "Damn, Cass. We thought we were being invaded when Yenny sent us down here to hunt. Shit, you could've called."

She looked back at me and said, "That's why. His tie to this place is more complete than anything, and he usually knows who is coming by portal or instant teleport at all times. Even when it's a surprise. He must not be able to sense who Amabala is and that would freak him out. Thus the security coming for us."

"So then we would need to open a line of comm between us or at the least post a guard down here for it." I growled and scratched my head. This was getting a lot messier by the minute.

"Well, if we need a place to crash before then, I live in Bexley," Arden offered and stepped closer. "It's pretty roomy for me, and it's just me and a few cats, so I can totally put you all up for a bit."

"A *few* cats?" Merlin perked up a bit. "You're the crazy cat lady who incinerates the cat poop so the house doesn't stink."

"Merlin, you've been welcome in my home for a little bit now, and you're eating into that welcome." Arden sniffed and glared at him angrily.

He threw up his hands and laughed nervously. "I'm just saying."

"It's a ten-minute drive if you know the streets and how to maneuver the way I do, and I have the room." Arden sighed. "It's not permanent, but at least it's something to get us out of here to keep our friends and families safe."

I shrugged, noncommittal. Uncle Yen did say that he knew a dragon who was an accountant. Maybe it was time to see if he knew anyone who was a realtor?

I like that idea more than being around a bunch of cats. Galaxy grumped and I looked at her incredulously. *I don't care if my first form was that of a cat, Marcus. They're petty and annoying when they don't know you.*

"I appreciate the offer, Arden. We'll see about taking you up on it if we can't find something more appropriate." She shrugged, not put out, but began to bicker with Merlin on his stance with her cats. "Hey Keith, how you doing?"

"Good, bubba, how 'bout you?" He gave me a fist bump and his normal grin. "Wish y'all would have called, I got my tail all in a twist for a fight. I been *itching* for a scrap."

Cassia snorted and rolled her eyes. "Me too."

I blushed and Keith gave her a funny look before catching

the meaning from me, his teeth flashing as he laughed. "Y'all are wild."

I grinned back and nodded. "Yup. You know where my uncle is?"

"He's in the bar waiting for—shit." He held the radio up to his mouth and radioed, "You can chill on the reinforcements, big guy, it's family. Kilo, India, Lima, Lima, Echo, Romeo."

"Why the hell did you just spell killer?" I frowned at him, confused.

"It's his call sign when he finishes radioing. Like a call and response." Cassia nodded to Keith then moved into the stairwell behind him, leading us all upstairs.

We found ourselves upstairs in the gym, then walked to the bar and found three massive security members waiting with Yen. Sabbath and his friends, all of whom looked relieved when we stepped through the doors.

"Glad to know that all of you are back." Sabbath groaned and leaned against the bar.

"Something wrong?" Cassia asked and took him aside and began to talk to him in hushed tones.

"Glad to see you back, but it seems a bit soon for the hunt to be complete." Uncle Yen growled at me and I nodded. "So what happened?"

"We found listening devices in our rooms where we were staying that popped up *after* we had looked for them." His eyebrows rose and he paused. "Yeah, that wasn't good. So we may be commuting for a little while back and forth with Amabala."

"Call ahead, then, dammit. I almost sent the host down on you, kiddo." He harrumphed and grabbed his drink from the bar, his hand shaking a bit.

"What's wrong?"

He took a gulp of his drink and shook his head. "We don't know." I just stared at him and he just shrugged. "Monsters have been dying here too. Not supernatural creatures like us, but *actual* monsters. Things from Grestal. It's like they're out and hunting for something. And then there are divine creatures out searching for something too, they fight with the creatures of Grestal on sight, and usually kill them easily but…"

"Divine wha?" Merlin gasped and pulled out his sheet of paper, gasping. "What the hell is going on?!"

He read from it: "All Wardens in the United States be advised: Someone has found and murdered the Roman God Janus, the Gatekeeper. Creatures from Grestal have begun to appear in small numbers and other Warden groups have been dispatched to curb the incidents that could arise as the Romans prepare a ritual to assign another Gatekeeper."

"Who the hell kills a god?" I snarled and turned around to look at my uncle. "Is that why the divine beasts are out?"

He frowned and nodded. "Could be." He sighed and nodded to Cassia. "They asked for your temporary transfer to the Cairo branch and if I hadn't already approved it, I would tell them to fuck themselves. We need you here. But there's nothing I can do about it now."

Cassia growled and seethed, then looked at Sabbath. "Security meeting in five. All of you will be prowling in shifts."

"House hunting will have to wait for now." I sighed and shook myself out. "What can we do?"

"Finish your job over there quickly and get back here so we can figure all this shit out." He shook his head and frowned. "I need to go talk to my friends and make sure all of them are okay. You mentioned something about house hunting?"

"We wanted to make sure that the High Table remains safe with us around, like we're close so we can work together, but far enough that should someone try to attack us, you're out of the crossfire." He looked to consider what he knew and nodded to himself. "You know someone?"

"I might." He sighed and ran his hand through his hair, grunting to himself then shaking his head. "Let me check on my friends first, then I can make some calls. No promises though."

"I'll send you a text with all the stuff we had in mind." He nodded again before walking up the stairs to his room. I pulled my phone out of my pocket and texted him the thoughts I'd had to see if he would approve of some. Then just said, "Thank you, Uncle Yen. I hope your friends are okay."

There was no response but at least he had gotten it. Amabala and Arden stood close by with the bartender seeing if they could figure anything out, Arden adding, "I've ordered us all some food for the trip home. I don't cook so there's never anything there other than snacks and stuff to consume for gaming."

"God, you really are the nerdiest person I have ever met." Merlin scowled at her playfully.

Arden glared at him, then replied, "No, *you* are the nerdiest person you've ever met. Nerds quest for knowledge."

"Then what does that make you?" he shot back, annoyed that he'd been slightly foiled.

"A geek." Arden grinned. "We quest for bitches and badass loot."

CHAPTER ELEVEN

The food was good, and when Cassia came back, we wolfed down more together, then were on our way to Arden's place in the SUV that Kenshi had collected from the airport for her.

"Can we stop and get pop?" Galaxy requested and Merlin perked up.

"Maybe a Monster as well?" Amabala asked politely.

"I don't have any of that at my place. I just subsist on junk food and booze." Arden grinned. "There's a corner store near my place, we can get gas for the guzzler and goodies to gobble before gaming for the night."

"Do we tell Serpath we aren't there?" Cassia asked suddenly.

"No. We can't tell if she was who orchestrated the bugging or not." I sighed and finally said, "The sun should be down there soon, so we should be getting ready to go back and investigate the places the corpses were found. What's your cooldown looking like, Amabala?"

"I still have about fifteen minutes before I can open another portal, but we should be able to get there and back within two hours." She smiled and pointed her fingertips together. "You know… if I had a Monster, I could be perkier. It might help me get through the cooldown sooner…"

I rolled my eyes. "Good gods, fine, we can stop at the corner store for snacks!"

Merlin, Amabala, and Galaxy hooted as Cassia and Arden snorted, Cassia taking the jinn's direction to the corner shop and gas station. The chain store looked to be a little deserted, considering the size of the lot and how busy the surrounding area had been. Behind it was one of those automated car washes under the shadow of a railway on a bridge above.

All of it was well kept, but the car wash place was hardly used or just not open right that moment.

Cassia pulled up to the pump and got out to begin fueling her SUV. Arden decided to go inside to get what the children wanted.

I resent that, Marcus. I am older than every Normie on this planet combined. I rolled my eyes at her as she swaggered away with the others in front of her. She stopped and turned back to look at me. *I know. I'll get something for your thirst as well.*

I sputtered and looked away to her laughing and found myself staring directly at a grinning Cassia. "Soon," was all she said and chuckled to herself as she pumped her gas.

I grunted and eyed the world around us, the afternoon light shining down on us.

A thick cloud bank drifted over the sun and the wind suddenly turned sour, whipping trash and debris across the lot. The breeze carried more than just the hint of how insane Ohio's weather could be, switching at the drop of a dime.

It carried the scent of blood.

"Cassia, you smell that?"

She nodded and put the pump handle back into the holder and began to look around. She locked her car and began to follow the scent behind the abandoned looking car wash behind the gas station.

We walked across the sliver of grass where the signs were

and poked our heads around the corner to find a massive dog feeding on something there.

The stench of blood and gore grew stronger and every bite the dog took came with the sickening wet sound of tearing flesh and noisy chewing.

The dog grew in my vision until it was easily my size and had hard-looking bony protrusions sticking out of its shoulders and spine.

"Demon dogs?" Cassia whispered. "They're tier eight when alone."

Two more heads poked around the corner of the car wash and I growled, gritting my teeth, and grunted, "And three of them?"

She whispered, "Tier six?"

I stood up and cracked my neck. "What is it with us and getting snacks that attracts assholes and things that would like to kill us?" The dogs turned, the one that had been eating much larger than the other two and his eyes a burning blue color. "Fuck me. Commence the Hunt!"

The mantle flared around me and suddenly the bonds of the others were pulled taut and I knew exactly where they were compared to me. Cassia's shadow surged up her body and covered her immediately as the dogs sprang toward us.

My Silvaero was out and pumping rounds into the smaller dog trying to jump at me and Cass had her massive maul out and batted the one harassing her into the wall of the bridge to our right.

It yelped once and shook itself out, preparing to attack again. A loud, baying bark sent a thrill of genuine fear down my spine as the dogs all lifted their heads and howled, the low rumble working to a high crescendo that made the hair on my neck and arms rise.

"Shit," Cassia's voice burbled next to me, sounding slightly less demonic than mine did with the Huntsman's Mantle affecting me. "They called for backup."

I yanked on the bonds a little tighter and growled, "So did I."

A long, low, and mournful cry came back from above us and suddenly there were another six of the things and the seventh looked like the large one we had seen at first and appeared as if it could have been just his bottom bitch.

They skidded down the side of the railway wall. As the presumable alpha landed, the dark-gray bone-like armor it had on its body shook with the impact under its weight. His— because I could finally determine he was definitely a male— head, shoulders, and back were covered in gently-spiked gray bone as thick as my fist and his teeth were so long and sharp he could have been a Sabertooth tiger for all I knew.

"Oh, that's not good." Cassia huffed and lifted her weapon. "We need to kill them, now."

"Anything to know?"

"Don't use fire, don't try to take them more than one on one and, for the love of god, don't get bitten by that thing." She took a few deep breaths and her shadow armor began to thicken and roil as her form grew bulkier and larger. As she looked at me, her eyes swam white. "Time to fight."

"Don't have to tell me twice!" I lifted my hand and summoned Mohawk's sword from the ring on it, then allowed the shadows to spring forth from my hands and catch it, forming my scythe.

The alpha snarled and boofed once, with almost all of the other dogs baying as they charged toward the beefy bodies before them. The last one hid behind the alpha and laid down panting to watch the fight, growling softly.

Arden suddenly stood in the path of one of the dogs as it flared with feral fire, fangs dripping with liquid flame as it tried to bite her. She took the bite on the arm and slid her fingers into its ear, making it yelp as its head went black.

She tossed it backward into the dog behind it and whipped her arms down to her sides, coiling whips of water spreading from her as she growled herself.

Merlin stepped out from around me on my left. "I'll funnel them as much as I can so that they can't get away, or gang up on us. You guys be ready."

Cassia slapped one of the dogs away from the boy mage with her massive club and grinned. "Get on it, then." She kicked another in the chest and snarled. "I got your back."

Merlin muttered a softly-spoken phrase that refused to stick in my mind before the earth on the other side of the alpha rose level with the roof of the building to our left, turned to stone I hoped was thick enough to hold them there.

The alpha snarled and all of the dogs turned to look at it before it lowered itself to the ground and took a deep breath in. The others followed suit and began to emanate a swiftly growing, ember-like glow from their chests that traveled up their throats.

"Arden, they're about to blow!" I roared and rushed between Cassia and Merlin so that I could help hold the line.

Arden's whips splashed to the ground as a wave of water crashed through the wall from the car wash and formed a wall before us. Not thinking, I put my free hand on the wall and cast Hoarfrost, willing the wall to solidify.

Hissing steam burned around us as the wall didn't immediately freeze completely solid, an eerie fog of warm, sulfurous-smelling water droplets filling the area and limiting our vision.

A shadow flitted across the ground to my right, my scythe swinging at it and catching a clawed paw before the demon dog slunk back into the fog.

"Wind to blow this away would be *really* helpful!" I growled as earthen walls began to rise in front of us.

A pair of massive paws battered the walls and crumbled them, then the alpha set on us with his dogs on his heels. My scythe bit into his armored hide a little, but there was nothing more than just the slight scratch that it had left, and then he battered me aside just by running toward Merlin.

A small creature, almost like a dog, surged between the boy's legs and lunged at the alpha, then shifted until it was this massive creature with black fur and white stripes the shape of a bear on steroids and growth hormones since it was born. The alpha slammed into the wall as the bear turned against the others and began to bat at them, its huge claws slicing into them and leaving them on the ground in tatters.

"What the fuck is that thing?" Arden shouted and turned to us.

"Don't know, but it's fighting the dogs," I muttered and waded into the fight scythe first, the damned thing actually cutting this time. The dogs who remained uninjured rallied around their slowly rising alpha, and growled menacingly as the beast towered over them.

The massive bear opened its jaws and roared so inhumanly loud and low that the ground beneath our feet began to shake. Lightning gathered around its claws as the demon dogs lunged forward to defend their alpha as one, the beast snarling and flicking one aside only to be bitten by three others.

Using Arcane Infusion, I wreathed the blade of the scythe in rime and frost, then cast Embodiment of Lightning.

Suddenly, I stood horizontally on the side of a mound of dirt and grass that led to the train tracks behind the alpha and swung my scythe for all I was worth as my bond with Cassia swelled.

Temporary boost to Brawn +3.

This time the scythe bit deeper into the huge demon dog's bone armor and it yelped loudly over the crackling of freezing air. I went the opposite direction of the swing, the blade stuck in the creature's hide. But its pain was enough to distract the rest of the pack and give the massive bear-like creature an opening to start crushing spines with impunity.

"Marcus, we need to know what to do about that thing!" Cassia called. "It could be a beast from the Fel!"

"It's killing the others!" I shouted back as I watched it killing and wiping the floor with the dogs. "If it makes a move on any of us, kill it."

"How?" Arden bellowed and I had to admit, I didn't know.

This creature feels familiar to me, Marcus, Galaxy said, finally. *Forgive me, I was busy trying to work the bonds so that you would be able to benefit from them like you did. You're welcome, by the way.*

I rolled my eyes and then allowed my body to do the same as one of the demon dog's claws raked my shoulder painfully. Fire seared across the wound and the dog slunk back away, staying low to the ground and trying to get to the alpha.

"No you don't," I snarled and pulled out my Silvaero once more. Shadows wreathed it and small portions of my mana began to wrap around the bullets as I fired three shots before the magazine ran dry. I reloaded with one of the magazines in my inventory, firing three more rounds before the demon dog fell to the ground in a heap and I was running low on mana. Trying to freeze that wall had taken a lot out of me.

All that stood now was the alpha demon dog, and it had locked claws in a frenzied battle against the beast, growling and snapping its fiery teeth at it, trying to gain purchase on the throat.

The beast shoved back hard and swiped a mean left paw at my sword, *slamming* it into the alpha's body and putting it on the ground in a whimpering heap. The beast rose up on back legs and cried out, long and low with enough base that a house DJ would have been envious of how it shook the ground. As it fell to all fours once more, both of its front paws landed on the alpha's head and crushed it like a watermelon.

Gore slapped against my shadowed armor as the beast looked at all of us and rumbled low. Something shimmered around it, then it was gone as if it had never been there. A low voice I didn't recognize said slowly and plainly, as if through clenched teeth, "I don't know what business the Wild Hunt has here, but if you're a threat to me and mine, I'll kill you. This is my territory now. Leave."

"I don't know who or what the hell you are, but we just wanted to keep this place safe from them," Merlin snarled, pointing at the area where the beast had been and muttering a simple phrase. The air shifted and a figure in a hoodie and shorts stood there with hands in the front pockets. "So you need to give it up, and tell us who you are and what it is you're doing here, right now!"

A sense of foreboding bloomed in my chest as a semi-familiar figure rose over the man standing there and loomed over him, transfixed on Merlin. The voice that came from the hood was the same, "I told you who I was. Now, I'll show you."

The figure in the man's aura reared up and seven tails spread out behind him in a fan. "Zeke, stop!" I reached out and the man's whole countenance shifted as the shadows in the area wreathed his body and sped for Merlin.

Even the shadows that were beneath me ebbed. A spear of pure ebon darkness stopped inches from Merlin's chest as the figure lifted his hands and pulled back the hood to reveal that it was him, but it wasn't. He was taller, broader through the chest and shoulder, and slimmer than before too. His whole body had shifted to this state along with his skin. His face and hands were like Galaxy's, covered in pinpricks of lights that swirled in different colors, but where some would be white on her, his were golden and lustrous.

I let the Mantle fall away and faced him as Marcus. "Zeke? That's who you are, right?"

He nodded once and the shadow armor fell away from the others as well. He turned and blinked at Merlin and waved a hand, the spear of shadow falling to the ground and splashing before all of the shadows flitted to their proper place.

Oh, what a plot twist... Galaxy whispered through my head as she stepped from me in her elven form.

His mouth opened and his eyes narrowed. "You do look just like her... your hair is all wrong, but..." He closed his eyes and shook his head. "I'm sorry, I can't... I..."

"It's okay, you can tell us everything." Galaxy spoke softly with a hand forward as the others, including Cassia, readied weapons and spells just in case. "Stand down, all of you."

I started to step forward with her, but as soon as I moved, his head snapped up and he growled, "You get a pass, for now, but I no longer need the High Table for protection. I'm awake now. I can protect me and mine."

He held up a hand and pointed at Merlin. "I know it's easy to sound tough when you're in a group, man, but don't talk shit to someone you don't know or can't kill. And especially not both at the same time. Can't tell you how many times it got me into a shit show that I had to yell about."

The man looked contemplatively at the ground and sighed. "I know that you have questions, Marcus, Galaxy." He looked up and smiled at us softly. "I do too. But I'll be okay. And I give you my word that I won't hurt anyone who works at the Table, or any of you if I don't have to. I swear it on my power as King."

A garbled mess of text flickered into view, then solidified and a weight of sorts pressed against my chest.

The King of the Unseelie Court, and member of Clan Mugfist has given you his word. Failing to keep his word exactly as stated will have extremely dire consequences. An oath of power such as this could result in much, but pay heed—to cross the oath is to show that it is null and void.

I frowned. "Meaning, if you think any of us are a threat to you, you'll kill them."

He just stared at me quietly, then dipped his chin enough to be noticeable without too much movement.

"That is a very broad stroke, King Zeke," Galaxy chided carefully. "Would your queen agree to such an oath?"

He turned his gaze to her and suddenly the air around us grew thick. The aura I had seen before reared up again and looked like it was crying out in agony with arms out wide.

The man before us snarled, "Don't you *dare* bring my wife up. Especially not after I just helped you and spared one of your own." He took a few calming breaths but it really just looked like his adrenaline was spiking and he was about to start a fight.

"Look, she didn't mean any disrespect," I offered and took another tentative step closer to him. "Honestly, we could use someone as strong as you on our side. We want to help you and protect this place. Hell, protect the world from creatures just like these ones. Someone's out there killing gods, man. We could use all the help we can get."

He frowned, then sighed and muttered, "I already protected this world once." His gaze rose and rested on Galaxy. "And it cost me everything."

I shook my head. He was hurting, and I would have to check with Galaxy to see if she could have gleaned why, but it was just beyond me how someone so strong could turn their backs on those in need. "If that's the case, why help us now?"

"I planned to kill all of you the way I did them," he replied simply. "But that was before I knew you were the Hunt. You ever... been to the Fae Realm, Marcus? How long has this been a thing?"

He frowned at me as I remained silent, then narrowed his gaze at us. "Not long then. That's why you were asking about them in my books?" He grinned viciously. "Then there's a way to strip the power from you?"

My stomach dropped and everyone took a step back as he laughed, shaking his head. "I didn't say that because I want it. Fuck the Hunt. But if someone is going to try to take it from you, let me know, and I'll come fuck them up with you."

That made me pause. "Why?"

He grinned. "Better the devil you know than the one you don't. I don't want anyone else out here screwing around in my territory that I don't know." He looked to be considering something, then rubbed his head. "Look, if you promise not to interfere with me doing what I have to so that I can protect what's mine, I won't be a threat to you unless you really fuck up. Deal?"

He genuinely looked hopeful at that. I was about to speak when Galaxy reached back and touched my arm. *Any promise we make to him right now will be binding, it doesn't matter if we swear or not. He's offered a deal which, to the Fae, is a contract that will bind us to our word unless we refuse. We need to counter it in such a way that leaves us a loophole so that if we need to... we can find a way to kill him.*

I considered what he said for a moment, then another, and the hope began to fade on his face, slowly to be replaced by consternation. "Stop trying to look for obvious loopholes, guys. I'm offering you a good deal, here." He shrugged, then crossed his arms over his chest. "But if you don't want to take it, and you would rather be at odds, I can take that. It would suck, but I've had to deal with a hell of a lot worse. Trust me."

I nodded once and countered, "We promise not to interfere in anything except what we find so wrong that we have to stop you. We would prefer to remain friendly and work together if we can, but we can't have you trying to take our power. My people and the Table are strictly off limits, and if this is to be your territory, you keep the people *and* supernatural creatures that aren't a direct threat to humanity safe."

He started to speak, but I stopped him and even Galaxy frowned at me as I added, "And you leave the Unseelie Princess and her family alone. Especially her son and husband."

He seemed genuinely surprised by that and spoke in a language that I didn't understand. What I did understand was that the shadows around him and the hill behind him opened up and dozens of elves and other creatures stepped out of them. "Figured that out?"

"I had a hunch when I saw the notification." I crossed my arms, then explained, "Her son is my son. His name is Connell. If you hurt him, or either of his Fae parents, I will hunt you down and kill you. I swear on all my power now, and all the power I will ever gain that I will do exactly as I said."

He flinched and whistled low, then strode closer to me and stared me in the eyes, his unflinching as mine shifted color of their own accord with my emotions. He held out his hand for me to shake. "I won't swear that if they come for me, I won't defend myself, but I'll make sure no one touches them without severe consequences if they're innocent." He tilted his head to the side before adding, "My queen would never allow a child to come to harm if she could avoid it, and neither will I."

I took his hand and grunted, unhappy in knowing that was the best I would likely get.

"We have an accord then, we both stay out of each other's ways, and help each other as we can." His gaze never left mine. "And all the other fun bits you've likely figured out too. Look, Marcus, you're a good man. I don't have any real beef with any of you. I'd still like to hang out sometime."

I stilled, chuckling to myself. "You could nuke us all, and you want to *hang out?*" He shrugged and his body began to morph until his skin was peach and he was a bit shorter than I was now. "I don't get you, Chris."

He shrugged again. "I don't either, sometimes. I can be a pretty simple dude. So long as my friends and family are safe, I'm a happy man. But I've been asleep for far too long to risk anything anymore. And I've been away for far, far too damn long to just sit idly by and allow myself to waste away when my family could be in danger."

He scratched his bald head and sighed. "Look, we just made a binding deal and it sucks that we had to do that, man. But now that we know where each other's lines in the sand are, we can still be friends. Or at least amicable. Like all the countries that have allies or armistices and shit?"

"How did you get to be so fucking powerful and still be so ignorant to how things work?" Arden asked as if to herself, but she looked genuinely mortified by the man.

He grinned and laughed softly before answering and looking back up at me. "Good friends and more than a little luck." He snickered. "'Cause it sure as shit wasn't my good looks."

I snorted and so did Cassia. He smiled good naturedly and offered me his hand. "We can still be friends, Marcus. All of you." He looked pointedly at Merlin. "Even you too, kid. One of my best friends is the biggest shit talker you'd never want to meet, I swear."

A notification popped up and he sighed. "Goddamn it. You go so long without Fae abilities and now that I have them back, I can't even use a fucking figure of speech."

That made all of us chuckle a little and I took his hand. "Okay. We can be friends." I thought for a moment, then added, "I'd hate to have to kill you."

He grinned wider. "Same."

"Think you could teach me how to control shadows like you?" I raised an eyebrow hopefully. If this was going to be a thing, I could hopefully learn something from him, which got a mental nod of approval from Galaxy.

He shrugged. "I don't see why not, though I have to warn you, I'm not as good a teacher as Maebe is. Though, she would likely have slaughtered all of you without a thought. God, I miss her." He sobered up for a moment and sighed, walking over to the alpha, and pulling out my sword. "Decent blade you have here. Seems like the metal is basically enchanted to keep it sharp from normal wear and tear."

"I didn't know that." He looked at it for a moment. "Something wrong?"

He lifted his head and smiled at me. "Nope. Just a show of good faith popping into my head. Want me to supe it up for you?"

"Say what now?"

He just grinned and shook his head, flicking a finger out and shapes began to hover over his fingers, Galaxy's eyes widening to the point that I thought that they would pop out of her head. "*Yes!*"

He laughed and sat on the ground as the Fae around him milled about, then faded into the background until they were well and truly gone.

CHAPTER TWELVE

"Are you sure that's what this thing will do?" I asked uncertainly as he carved into the blade with nothing more than pure mana.

Even distracted as I was watching him, I could feel the drool in Galaxy's mouth as she stared at the power in front of her covetously. *Can you blame me?*

No, I can't. I sighed mentally and added, *Could he have really killed us all?*

Marcus… Galaxy started and that was answer enough. *No, it's not. He would have wiped the floor with all of you, but if you had more access to the full power of your bonds, you would be able to siphon power from the others and stand a chance. A child's chance at taking down a gladiator, but it's still a chance.*

Good God… I watched as the man continued his work and chuckled to himself. "So what do you have planned for it again? And how do you do all this?"

"Well, back on Brindolla, shitty granny liked to have me take differing approaches to the same items. Which was useful, but annoying as hell when she would toss and destroy them." He sighed wistfully and grimaced. "Really wanted to kill her, but she was just too damn good at what she did to bother."

"You loved her too," Galaxy muttered and the enchanter laughed.

He shook his head and nodded. "Yeah. Yeah, I did. Hard to imagine what she might be doing now. Any of them, really. Especially Azlo and Nadir."

I frowned. "Who are they?"

He grunted, "My children." He tilted his head and admired his handiwork. It was a seven-tailed fox with the tails fanned out behind it. He grimaced. "This is going to be a little more ridiculous and kind of expensive. Anyone have any diamonds or other precious stones?"

Everyone shook their heads and he just grunted and shrugged. "No worries." He tilted his head to the side and whistled once sharply. A massive white tiger burst into existence beside him, making him flinch. "Goddamnit, Eve. Go and get me some of the elemental cores we've been farming and diamond dust."

The tiger huffed and disappeared again. He cracked his neck and stared at the sword some more and sighed. "Not gonna be enough for this. Needs to be adapted a bit more." He glanced up. "I can't have you all back at my place, my fiancée would flip the fuck out. Anywhere we could go?"

"My place is just down the road," Arden muttered sheepishly. Galaxy had been thorough in explaining to *everyone* how fucked we would've been if he had decided we had to die. I shook my head at that and walked away.

"That works, if you don't mind the company?" He looked over at Merlin. "I'll even upgrade that staff for you."

I hadn't seen Merlin pull out his old staff, and he frowned. "You can do that?"

Chris chuckled. "Yeah." He winked. "Think of it as an... I'm-sorry-for-almost-killing-you gift."

Merlin nodded and turned to Arden, but didn't speak out loud, instead through Galaxy. *Merlin says he doesn't know if we can truly trust him. I agree, but for now, we have a powerful almost ally and we cannot refuse at least some help without knowing who or what we are up against in Cairo.*

I agree, begrudgingly. Cassia spoke up and startled us all as she spoke aloud. "Chris, we can't trust you fully. I'm the head of Security for the Columbus High Table, and I worry that you may not know what it is that we offer, and that is safe haven and neutrality. Is there any way I have of knowing that you may or may not be a threat to my people, or our mission?"

"Just that as long as no one gets in my way, or is a threat to the people I hold dear, I'm kosher." He frowned, then smiled. "I am salty and fat though, so I guess I could be considered pork? Whatever. I'm not going to attack anyone at your bar unprovoked and I'm assuming your security would see to it that the aggressor regrets it? I'm good, Cassia. So good on that. Though the booze there is nice, so I might start dropping in a little more often, if that's cool?"

"Your word that you won't attack anyone in the High Table," Cassia insisted and crossed her arms in front of her stubbornly.

"Cass, he just gave his word to us," I started, but he was already standing and stepping closer to the woman as his body shifted to that of the king.

"Cassia, I will not hurt anyone in the High Table so long as no one offers me a reason to think that they are a threat to me, my loved ones, people, or friends." He held out his hand and offered it to her. "I swear it on my power. I swear, I swear."

The ground around us shook and everyone stumbled a bit. Her eyes widened and she nodded, taking his hand. "Very well. You'll be welcome at the Table, as king and as human. They'll likely treat you like a Touched."

He blinked at her. "Look, I know that I used to joke about my characters talking to me, but that was my soul straining at the bonds it was under." He shook his head slowly and spoke softly, "I'm not crazy."

She snorted and guffawed as Arden rolled her eyes and

explained, "Magically adept and powerful humans are referred to as 'Touched,' man."

He made an O with his mouth and shrugged. "Well, let's get it then, I'll just do enchantments all around as a show of good faith, yeah?" He looked to all of us and then to Arden. "Are we still taking this to your house? Because I'm not kidding about my fiancée. She will murder me. And king or not, she will rip my fucking throat out if I bring another woman she doesn't know to our house without her there. Even if she knew them—even then, that's pushing it."

I frowned. "Isn't it weird that your relationship with her is based on a lie?" He frowned at me and I just pointed to his left hand, the aural copy of the ring he wore still visible. "You're still wearing your band."

"It's soul bound," he said simply. "Like my connection to Mae. But even then, she was the one who encouraged me to find someone I trusted and to live 'my life' here. She knew that this could have been an eventuality, or at least would have thought of it."

"How can you be sure?" Galaxy asked softly.

He shrugged and smiled. "Faith. I still love her and Vrawn like crazy, and there's a lot that I would do to see them again. But I don't think either of them would want the normal, weird human me to be alone either. Just like I wouldn't want that for either of them. I guess I'll know when Servant returns from telling my beloved wife everything."

I couldn't help but shake my head in disbelief. "You know people are going to look at your relationship and scoff, right? It'll freak them out, or just drive them away from you?"

They will do the same of ours, Galaxy muttered through my head, and I saw Cassia stiffen with a similar look on her face to Galaxy's.

"They will." He smiled and looked me straight in the eyes as he said, "And I don't fucking care." He shrugged happily enough and added, "Besides, until they have a Fae Queen for a wife, an orcish badass for a girlfriend who your wife also loves, and a human fiancée who just indulges that you might be slowly losing your mind to what she calls a hobby, they can just be happy doing what makes them happy."

Merlin chose then to laugh, and it was not a chuckle, but a burbling of noise I had never heard before. He wiped his eyes and held his stomach as all of us watched him in confused shock, then he heaved, "She thinks he's going crazy because he's a writer." He snorted and laughed again, "How classic is that?"

Chris blinked and turned to look at me. "You sure I can't kill him? He reminds me too much of my friend Nick. Which reminds me, I owe him a call."

"Let's just go and get this shit over with." Arden heaved a sigh and rolled her eyes before motioning to Galaxy and Merlin. "Did you guys ever grab the stuff that you wanted?"

Merlin froze and said, "No." He looked to Galaxy and muttered, "You want to clean up here and I'll get us some stuff?"

Chris chimed in excitedly, "You guys getting snacks?" Merlin nodded as Galaxy began to walk toward the corpses of the demon dogs. "Can I throw in an order too? Ever since I came home, I've been a fucking pop fiend and it's driving me nuts. Good faith is good and all, but can I get a drink? Mana manipulation is terribly thirst building…"

He looked hopefully at the boy mage, who just snorted. "Sure."

Chris pumped his fist and grinned at me. "Y'all are so nice to me."

"Do we have a choice?" I shot back halfheartedly.

He stilled and suddenly looked very serious. "Always, Marcus. Choices are the stuff of mercurial destiny. Choice defines us. Choices define the world—the galaxy."

"Someone want me?" Galaxy raised her voice, making me laugh and cutting through the sudden tension.

Chris sniffed the air, then blinked and turned toward the

demon dogs that Galaxy was nearing and growled, "Wait." He turned toward her fully and said, "Do you smell that?"

She sniffed and said, "Sulfur?"

He shook his head. "Life."

Both of us looked at him as if his fiancée was right, but he came to the one demon dog that had been hiding the majority of the fight and growled low in his chest as he knelt next to it. "Barely there. No wonder she had been hiding. Damnit."

He flicked his index finger forward and a long, thick claw that shimmered in the light burst from his nail bed. "Who has an affinity for fire among you?" He blinked and barked, "Arden, right? I need you to come here."

"I'm not your servant." Arden crossed her arms and he just cast a baleful glare over his shoulder.

Cassia just rolled her eyes and stepped over to him. "I don't have an affinity for fire, but I'm not exactly flammable."

He shrugged, grunting, "That works, I guess."

He slid the claw along the dead demon dog's stomach and grumbled, "So messy." He rolled up his sleeve before reaching inside the corpse and rooting around until he pulled out a small object that wasn't moving. His hand glimmered with green energy and then he handed it to Cassia. "Try to get the fluid off it and then get it into a fire or something with heavy demonic energy."

"Is that a puppy?" Arden asked as she stood on the balls of her feet, trying to see over the two figures.

"Yup, and it's dying," he just said back as if she hadn't been a dick to him first.

She rushed forward and lit her palms up in a heartbeat. "Gimme gimme."

Cassia just shook her head knowingly and gave the puppy to Arden to tend. The amniotic fluid burned away and the puppies' fur began to bristle and burn the way that the other demon dogs' had.

"Good. Let's see how many we can save." Chris spoke softly

and pulled another out without thought and the same green light filtered from him into the puppy.

It took another five minutes, but he was able to save three of the four puppies that the dog had been carrying. The fourth had unfortunately been a victim of something in the womb. But the other three were fine, so far as the Druid could tell.

CHAPTER THIRTEEN

Cassia had taken the puppies back to the High Table so that they could be taken care of by Kenshi for now, one of the security staff having come to collect her in a van. He wasn't one for animals from what she said, but having three demon dogs growing on the streets of Columbus would be an absolute nightmare.

Arden's house was simple on the outside for a house surrounded by damn near modern-day mansions in a city this size.

"Are you fucking serious, Arden?" I grumbled as we pulled up in the SUV and parked in her roundabout driveway.

The white paint on the walls of her home was so bright it could have been bleached bone against the green of her yard. There were people currently caring for the property that looked like some kind of service and she muttered, "Of course I am. A lady needs to keep up appearances. Also, I'll let you in momentarily. If I come home while they're all here, I have to tip and feed them. It's my persona."

She stepped out of the vehicle, and the workers—all twelve of them—cheered, "Ms. Arden!"

She giggled and tossed her hair over her shoulder. "You caught me, boys." She fluttered her eyes at them. "You've always taken such good care of me and my mom's house. You know the rules—dinner's on me tonight! What are we feeling?"

"Tacos!" one of them shouted and Arden giggled again, pointing to him as he bellowed, "Yes!"

"Regis, you taco fiend!" one of the others snarled at him playfully and the other man just laughed and went back to watering the plants and bushes by the house.

"Don't worry, I have something extra for all of you as well, so if tacos won't do, you can order something. 'Kay?"

Is anyone else perturbed by this bubbly side of her? This is never even in her head when I rummage through. Galaxy watched with us in shock as the woman came back to the SUV and motioned that we come along.

We exited the vehicle and the workers waved at us politely with smiles and grins as Arden unlocked the door and motioned us inside.

The smell of cat wafted toward me, but it wasn't the typical smell one might associate with cats. Like litter and pee.

No, this was mustier. Older. "What types of cats do you have?"

Arden smiled as a rumbling sound reverberated through the entrance hallway. A massive striped tiger with deep orange eyes strode into the hall and arched its back languorously before trotting over to the jinn for a loving scratch on its big chin. "Tabbies. And some others."

"That's a goddamn tiger, woman!" Chris roared and the tiger regarded him as if offended. "Believe me when I say, I love your house now."

Arden laughed as the shorter man rushed forward to try to pet the beast. Her eyes widened as the tiger shot forward and stood up on hind legs to throw its paws forward. "Raja, no!"

Chris tackled the tiger and the two of them began to roll on the floor, the tiger and man playing, much to Arden's shock and our surprise.

"Okay, seriously, you can stop being overpowered and adorable all at the same time now," I muttered to myself as he cackled and smacked the tiger playfully.

Don't be jealous, Galaxy chided me playfully, then the man shifted shape into a massive panther the color of a starless night so that he and the tiger could play more and she said, *Be jealous. What the hell is he?*

Arden moved us out of the hall and into a dining room twice the size of my room at the High Table. She picked up her house phone and pressed two numbers then held up a finger for us to wait. She smiled when someone spoke over the line. "*Guillermo? Hola, soy Arden. ¿Puedo comer ciento veinte tacos, por favor?*" She paused and grinned, "*Gracias, mi amigo. Buenos tardes.*"

"You speak Spanish?" I raised an eyebrow at her, only to have her do the same. "Sorry, I know. You're old as hell. Got it."

Arden turned and bellowed, "Can we get on with this instead of having a pissing match with my damn cats?"

The panther looked up from the cat he was busy hissing at and padded forward, then stood in the room once more as a man. "He's happy you've brought friends over to play instead of holing up in your room on the cube that you like to be on. He thinks you're lonely."

Arden's face reddened. "Raja, you traitor!" The tiger roared piteously as she swatted at him.

"Alright, let's see them items!" The Druid clapped his hands and spoke into them after that, summoning a woman with pale skin so white that it was a wonder she didn't glow. "Got the goods, Eve?"

She smiled. "And then some. I grabbed some extras for you just in case. I know how you like to deviate when inspired."

He grinned. "Thanks!" He scratched his head as she placed the bag of goodies on the table. "Could use Hubris as well."

I blinked and said, "Galaxy *is* a god, but I don't want to get a beating so I'm not going to talk shit about her."

He snorted and pointed at me. "Not the act of, just Hubris.

It was a scepter I had. Helped me channel mana a bit more intuitively."

Oh. "Sorry."

"Don't be, let's just have some fun and get messy with it, yeah?" He chuckled to himself and Cassia put a hand on his shoulder, her arrival surprising us all. "Yes?"

"Ms. Frizzle the shit out of this." She put her massive mace on the table and he laughed harder.

The others set the items they wished to have enchanted onto the table, Galaxy producing a ring for him to take, Merlin his staff, my sword, and Arden actually offered the man a chair, of all things.

"This is my favorite chair, but sitting in it makes my butt go numb sometimes." She shrugged as the man stared at her uncertainly. "If you're as good as you think you are, you'll be able to make it so that it doesn't do that, right?"

Chris stared at her for a moment before looking at all of us and saying, "I don't know if I should be insulted or happy that she literally just asked me that."

He closed his eyes and shook his head and began to work on the items in front of him as all of us watched. It was easy to see why we would want someone else to do this for us. Enchanting wasn't my thing, that was for sure. The level of control it looked to be taking from him was immense as he worked on my sword. Eve stood over his shoulder, watching all of us casually like a bodyguard.

Eventually, we grew bored of him working on just that and decided to go look around Arden's house.

The place would fit all of us easily if the various kinds of tigers would control themselves and sleep in a room or two, but I had to ask, "Is that a fucking liger?"

"Muffs? Yeah, he's a liger." The gigantic cat huffed and stared at us as it lounged on an equally gigantic box in a room that could well have been a ball room.

"How is the house this big?" I asked eventually, Arden having shown us four floors and the stairs never seeming to end.

"Spatial magic," she answered. "Yearly, I get one wish without being bottled, and three or four years ago when I bought this house, I wished that it was larger."

"Then why don't you wish for your family back?" I asked and Cassia hissed at me as if it were a sore subject and I regretted it immediately.

"Bottling makes them inaccessible by magic other than locating them, and even then, it'll be vague." She sighed. "Usually, I just wish for something that will help me now, or future me. Like people to forget what my former identity looked like, or for them to believe that they had died and left me everything. On paper, it all looks good, but people's memories and emotions are so much weirder and can interfere at times. It's happened before."

"So, if we bought a small house and used spatial magic to have it be larger on the inside, that would work well for the Hunt." I frowned and thought some more, then turned to Merlin. "Is that something you can do?"

He shrugged. "The magic I know makes me a formidable battle mage, not an every-day wizard, man." He snorted and rolled his eyes. "Is this why you keep me around? Magic stuff?"

"Dude, it's so up your alley, you have no idea." I pointed to myself. "Me crayon eater. Nose-picking, spider and snake teasing Marine rifleman. You smart man. Egg head with magic and no robots."

He closed his eyes and growled, "I swear to Galaxy, if you just made a Sonic the Hedgehog joke about my liking magical research, I will fucking *deck* you."

I grinned. "Bring it. You and Tails can both give me a go." I ran my thumb over the side of my nose and took a fighting stance playfully.

A wall of force so thick that I couldn't ignore it blasted me into the hallway wall behind me hard enough that the wall shattered and I pushed into brick painfully.

"Okay, fuckheads, let's *not* wreak havoc in Arden's house if you'll be staying here for *any* amount of time." She pressed between the two of us and sighed before looking at me. "Didn't Yen give you a whole spell book to read? Maybe there's something in there?"

I frowned, then looked at Galaxy. "Yeah, but I thought you were going to read it and relate the spells to me."

She blinked, eyes widening. "Did I say that?" I shrugged. "You think I did?"

"I thought so? I mean, it made the most sense." I opened my inventory and looked around for it. "I don't even have it, do you?"

She frowned and closed her eyes. "Oh. I do." She frowned. "I can look through it and see if there is anything we or Merlin can use."

She smiled at the boy and he just harrumphed and crossed his arms.

"Arden, would you mind showing me to the rooms you'll let Marcus, Cassia, and I use? I would like to study a bit before we go back." Galaxy smiled at her and Arden acquiesced with a nod before throwing a dirty look toward me and Merlin as Galaxy said, "Try not to destroy anything, boys."

I grinned sheepishly and Merlin nodded solemnly. As soon as they were gone, Cassia announced, "That was dumb, you two. Also, you should have just decked him like you said. The physical pain would be good."

"Magic is my thing, kind of like he said." Merlin sniffed, then winked at me, the cheeky thing. "Sorry, I just want to be able to do so much more and this bit of bother with Cairo and being back here so soon is just... irritating. I should have been able to sense those bugs. I don't know why I couldn't."

"They were well enough made and dropped in such a way that they should have just blended in," Cassia suggested and shrugged. "There was just no way for us to. And the distractions of all the goodies too? It was our own personal dreams."

"We should go and study too, think over what we know and

plan. It would be a good idea to try to know what we're up against and rest while we can. We have a lot of work ahead of us."

Merlin nodded at me as I spoke and Cassia agreed with a grunt as we turned and headed down the hall toward the stairs Arden had taken Galaxy toward.

———

The tacos were delicious, and as we ate outside in the evening air, it was hard not to wonder if that nap earlier had been worth it with how run down I felt.

Not physically; I felt tip top. But mentally. Galaxy had so much more going on than just translating spells for our ease of use, and yet here I was making her do the legwork when I should have been.

Her mind brushed against mine and I could see that she was lying in the room above with tacos rolled on a plate and at least a twenty-four pack of coke beside her. *I approve of your thoughts, but I should have just done this sooner. So far, there is nothing that you truly need, or would find useful. Especially not with where we mean to go. You would likely be better off trying to tap into the bonds of those around you and working on that.*

Thank you, I replied lamely and she blew me a kiss before turning the page and breaking contact.

"What could be killing them, do you think?" Merlin asked as he lifted his gaze from his book. "Nothing I could find in here pointed toward any sort of creature we know of, unless it's something new. Which isn't impossible if it's something from Grestal, but even then, Amabala would have been able to sense the tear, right?"

"I have trouble with them, remember?" She seemed a little more irritated than usual as well.

"You okay?" I asked and she shook her head. "What's wrong?"

"It feels like I'm hardly ever relevant here." She sighed and folded her legs up to her chest. "I'm transport, sure, but I'm not a magical powerhouse, I'm not a fighter."

"Transport is important too." I tried to offer her anything else, but I was blanking.

Cassia stood up and walked over to her. "What he means to say is that doing what you are good at and understanding your limitations isn't a bad thing."

She just groaned and sighed just before Cassia lifted her from her seat and self-pity. "Because usually that means you can work around them, or break through them. Knowing oneself and your weaknesses is the first step to true enlightenment for a warrior, sissy Amabala."

The cheetah woman sniffed. "You mean that?"

Cassia grinned. "Of course I do. I'm a warrior. I used to have a much worse temper a while ago. I worked through it, and look at me now."

"You use rage with the best of them," I offered, trying to be helpful.

She grinned. "Sure do. So, I know that you want to learn more about fighting. What if Marcus were to teach you how to shoot?"

I grinned and offered her an eyebrow raise. "What do you say? You wanna lay some hate the way I did with those feather-brained birds?"

She smiled. "I would like that." Cassia snorted and rolled her eyes, making Amabala frown. "What?"

Cassia shook her head and said, "I was hoping you would tell me you would rather fight with your fists."

We all laughed at that and an alarm went off on my phone. Time for us to make the trip back to Cairo and see if we could make heads or tails of some murder scenes.

Since we were just going for recon, we didn't need the weapons just yet, but we did make sure to tell Chris we were heading out.

"Oh, yeah sure, I'll finish up and leave things here before I fuck off." He waved and went back to his work while his guard stood next to him and watched us leave.

CHAPTER FOURTEEN

Amabala's portal deposited us in the room, the space feeling as alienating as it had been welcoming, and the only reason we stayed in it as long as we did was due to the fact that a certain cat had a hard on for all the soda in the fridge that had been provided.

She turned to glare at me as she sauntered back with her inventory full to bursting. *You're just jealous that I can handle more caffeine than you.*

I'm just jealous that your inventory seems bottomless in comparison to mine. My retort just made her snort and roll her eyes.

We can work on that, but for now, let us focus on the task ahead. Now it was my turn to roll my eyes. *I have plotted the sites of the attacks and murders; would you like to split up or take them as a team?*

I grunted, then paused. *Merlin, go with Amabala to the Heart of the City here and see what you can find out as a Warden. Keep Galaxy in mind as well.*

Galaxy passed my orders to him and he nodded, motioning that Amabala follow him. *And be careful! We don't know what this thing is so if you see something, run, I don't care if you leave the rest of us stranded for a bit.*

Galaxy told them both that and though Merlin seemed okay with it, Amabala looked like she wanted to say something about it. I shook my head, pointing to my ears and motioning to the room. She grimaced and put her human form on to go out into the world with Merlin.

She does not like the idea of leaving you all here. Galaxy's words bounced off my mind; I didn't care about that. She was our expedient ticket home and she was one of my people now. I couldn't have either of them in danger needlessly.

Suddenly Amabala stopped and glanced back over her shoulder, then grinned at me and flounced off with the young mage, seemingly in better spirits.

A mental nod from Galaxy let me know that she had passed the sentiment on and the gauge over her shoulder had gone from **Interested** to **Trusted.**

I blinked to myself. *When had she become interested?*

Shortly after you kept her safe during the landing is when she became interested, but it was during the fight with the demon dogs that her bond read as such.

I nodded to myself. It made sense and tracked for me. The rest of us would be okay on our own, but it would be easier to go and look at them in pairs as well.

Galaxy, can you pass along to Arden and Cassia that they should go and take one of the other sites themselves?

Both women looked at me and their eyes narrowed at me. I mouthed *outside* and they nodded once and turned to walk away and into the elevator.

The attendant took us in politely. "Where to?"

I grinned at him. "Lobby, please."

He pressed the button with the star on it that was lowest on the wall and smiled pleasantly at the wall opposite him past us. It kept us in his peripheral vision, but made it less like he was ignoring us and like he was just waiting.

The bubbly music above from the speaker was just loud enough that it would inhibit whispered conversation, so we just waited awkwardly until the doors opened once more and deposited us into the main lobby. He nodded and said, "Good day," tilting his hat to us as we stepped off the elevator into utter chaos.

People were calling for rooms in a massive crowd at the front desk and it was a miracle we could make it out unmolested. I checked to make sure my wallet was still in my pocket on instinct and found that it was, a sigh leaving my mouth unbidden.

"Sorry about that. Tourist season." The doorman on the inside of the doors spoke apologetically, but remained composed. "Everyone's heard that the Wild Hunt has returned and that there are deaths in the city. Everyone wants one of the safest rooms that we can muster and we're one of few hotels in the area who provide that level of security."

I nodded to him and offered a fake smile. "We're glad we got here ahead of the rush, and into safe rooms then. You be safe out there."

He nodded back pleasantly and opened the door so we could push past the newest gaggle of arrivals.

"That was a madhouse," Cassia grumbled as we began to walk northerly. Once we were well enough away, she lowered her voice a bit more. "Why is it you want to split from us?"

"I think we can cover more ground that way, but we should travel in pairs, that way we're safer." I looked around then added, "I have Galaxy and Mako, and I know that if anything were to happen, you and Arden can take care of each other. At least with Merlin and Amabala, he can defend her long enough for her to get a portal open."

"We would be safer together, en force." Cassia growled and stared at me as if I couldn't refute her logic.

"We would. But that also means that there are more sites that could have clues degrading in them the longer it takes us to get there," Arden pointed out, though her arms were crossed as she spoke. "I don't like it either, but the reasonable thing to do would be to cover as much ground as possible swiftly, then meet up and discuss it before going home."

Cassia looked at Arden as if in shock, then hissed, "I would think out of anyone, *you* would be the one to see reason in sticking together."

"I do, but I also know that I don't want to be here for more than a few hours tonight with all these other supernatural creatures who fear us in the area." She glanced around us at some of the people in the area and I noted some of them had auras but nothing that would make me think they were anything too powerful. "We need to be discreet, and we need to be faster than we have been so far. That means splitting up the gang and letting Shaggy over here go with Scooby while we do the hard work."

I blinked at her and narrowed my gaze. "Hey!" She hit me with a droll look that just begged me to say something to tell her she was wrong. "Do I seriously give off Shaggy vibes?"

"You and Mako eat anything you possibly can, and so does Galaxy." She grinned and laughed at my frown. "You guys are the perfect comparison to those two characters. Daphne and I are going to go check things out at one of the other scenes, while our version of Velma and one of the Hex Girls research what they can."

I blinked at her and grimaced. "How long have you been thinking about this?"

She frowned. "Twenty minutes or about as soon as we learned about being sent here?" Arden shrugged and cocked her head to the side. "Not like it matters now, so Scooby snack up and let's get this machine on the ground."

She turned to Cassia and winked before she walked off to the east of where we stood and the oni woman just sighed and trudged off after her in mock defeat.

I just went through all your memories for those references, and if it hadn't been for the fact that I like those characters, I would have slapped her with a debuff so hard her hair would have fallen out. Galaxy's hiss through my mind surprised me and I had to laugh at the absurdity of the reference, but admitted it was probably accurate. It didn't help that Galaxy mentally cleared her throat and added, *Mako heard snack and is hungry now.*

––––––

Darkness clouded overhead as Mako soared above the clouds and banked left to dive toward our destination. Drakes were flightless, but the Huntsman didn't give a shit about the laws of physics or supernatural ability.

Getting a little full of ourselves?

Nah, just antsy. And now that I can feel the rumbling of his stomach, I know why they called us what they did. She watched me from within my mind. "I don't want to say it."

R'uh r'oh, Galaxy teased and I rolled my eyes. The site we closed on stuck out to me as an odd spot to attack. It was off the main roadway, sure, but it was also in a place that was between two well-maintained and lived-on streets. So it wasn't the *most* obvious spot to lay an ambush, but it was also well enough traveled that someone would spot the corpse of whatever victim had been here.

As soon as we landed, we made sure that we stuck to the shadows and that Mako was on high alert while on me. I couldn't risk him being off my person without someone seeing me, and I didn't know for sure yet if the mantle would keep me obscured from Normies.

You sound like one of the fold, now, Galaxy stated, but this time, I didn't rise to her provocation.

My eyes wandered the area looking for anything that might have been left behind, and when I found nothing, I growled to myself quietly and sighed.

Stand still, Marcus, I want to try something. She had me close my eyes then added, *Focus on your bond to Merlin and feed it some mana.*

I frowned in consternation and concentration before collecting my will and cooperating with her command. My bond to the young mage opened wider and images began to flood my mind.

This is not a spell, but his excellent memory at work here. Open your eyes.

I blinked and suddenly there were still images in front of me that I could see clear as the hand in front of my face. Images of the scene of the murder that were just *there*, rendered as if in three dimensions.

"Is this what he got from those magical renderings?" She nodded in my mind and I had to fight the urge to let out a low whistle of appreciation. "I need to buy him a gun and see if there's any kind of trick he can teach me to remember things this well."

You have me. She purred and I snorted and let it go.

The body was pinned to a wall by something, like it was stone. It was some kind of naga-like creature, half snake and half man. His hooded neck was broken, but there were slashes on his body—what was left of it at least—and as with the others, his eyes and tongue were gone.

I stepped closer and stared up at the image of the dead creature. The arms had been *pulled* off, strips of the muscle and meat of the shoulders and chest having gone with them, the hole in the arm clean, almost pristine. Whatever had done this was stronger than almost any creature I had ever met or heard of.

A lycanthrope could do this, but it wouldn't be so clinical looking around the wound and there would be some kind of telltale that they had been here. A scent, or a claw mark on this body. Bite marks. Something *to denote that they had been here.* She paused and then offered, *Mako also says that he could have done this himself, but he wouldn't waste such a fine meal.*

The shadowy tattoo on my flesh moved and I could feel a whine building from him. He really was hungry.

Looking at the overlay of the area with Merlin's memories, it was hard to tell if there was anything that was out of place. The street had been especially dusty that day, I guessed, because there were footprints all over the place. Human, animals like dogs and cats, and children. But there were other markings too.

But any time I tried to focus on them, they bled away and disappeared.

They didn't appear to take any kind of real space either. So they were all over the place.

Galaxy, are you seeing this too?

I am. It makes no sense. She paused and my map fizzled before opening up and zooming in to where we stood. *This is where all of the markings are.*

I watched as a pathway cut through the scene and it looked like the lines of a fucking brawl.

Looking back at the creature, I noted some small marks along the torso and neck that didn't line up with the slashes.

Do you think these could have been from something else? I growled to myself and closed my eyes. *Let the girls know what we found, Merlin too. We need to look for something that can hide its passage from others and that travels in groups perhaps?*

Galaxy stepped out of me and stared around the area for a moment, then nodded. *It's done. They will be looking for things that don't make sense already, but this has added another thing to look for. Merlin is complaining that the whole traveling without a trace thing will be like finding a needle in a needle stack.*

I rolled my eyes and ignored it. *We need to check the next place. Where we heading, Galaxy? Also, can we stop somewhere and get something for this guy? He's starting to wear on my nerves.*

Mako growled at me as he stepped from me and stared down hungrily at me, then the image of the snake person.

"I get it, big guy, let's get you some shawarma or something."

CHAPTER FIFTEEN

Mako sang me the song of his people over the site of the third attack site we visited that night, his noisy snapping and eating having driven me to the brink of what I could take.

"You noisy shit!" I growled at him affectionately.

At each of the scenes after that, we had found that the fights didn't add up. The strength was there, the clean attacks with a blade or talon there, as well as the untraceable steps. It was like whatever attacked these creatures was doing more than absolutely necessary to kill them and then take them apart, but it was all so contradictory.

This time we were closer to the desert itself, Galaxy standing about twenty feet from me, as I puzzled my way through everything, then growled and snarled, "It just doesn't fucking make sense!"

She turned and blinked at me, motioning with her hand that I continue, so I did. "Like, they pull the limbs off in an obvious show of strength and machismo, right? But the limbs are *gone.* They're nowhere to be found. Not even as bones. And that's possible, sure. Killers keep trophies, right? I mean, shit, I carry the sword of a former enemy I killed."

That gave me pause, but I just shook my head, carrying on. "But the fact that the blood is gone and the eyes and tongue? Who the fuck takes those too? Is it symbolism? Is it some other thing?"

I pointed to the stone-like flesh of the creature that had been one of the first victims and noted the same sort of slash marks in almost the *exact fucking place*. "And this shit!" I ran my hands through my hair and growled again. "This is overkill! What the hell is it even for? The damn thing was probably dead already!"

I glanced back up at Galaxy and found her staring back out over the sand, silently like a stoic sentry standing guard over her post.

"Thinking about the temple?" She turned back to me, caught by surprise. "It's okay to be thinking about it, Galaxy. We need to go there anyway."

"But when?" she asked quietly.

"We can try it tomorrow after work." I opened my phone, looking at the text that Uncle Yen had sent me. It looked like Arden and I would only be working four-hour shifts, which was okay, but we would be under heavy scrutiny by the regulars, so we had to do well. "We just need to make it through that, then we can go and see if the temple is connected somehow."

"And to see if there is anything that I can recall." She lifted her head a little and sighed aloud. "I worry, Marcus."

"We all do." I grabbed her and pulled her close, hugging her from behind. "But I can imagine not knowing what is going on is driving you insane."

"I could never be driven insane." She huffed and leaned back against my chest, a soft click of her tongue in disgust making me frown. "I'm the first true god in the cosmos and here I am, weak as a kitten and dependent on a vessel for sustenance with no idea what happened to my powers and how I got like this. I feel like I keep saying this, but it's not any less true."

A wry chuckle escaped my mouth.

"What, you think that funny?"

I shook my head. "Not in the slightest. More like a kick in the balls."

She went the kind of still that only she could pull off, then muttered, "Sorry if that sounded more rude than I meant it."

"I'm not mad about it." I shrugged and hugged her tight once before I let her go and turned her around so I could talk to her directly. Looking into her eyes was always disarming, but this was a time to be serious. "You've been through a lot. In that time, you've come to learn about all of us, and protected us. Given us so much. It's only right and fair that we do the same for you. Besides, being an all-powerful god isn't all it's cracked up to be if someone is capable of killing one, right?"

She took my hand and pressed my palm against her cheek, leaning against it for comfort. "That's true, but it still leaves so many more questions than answers. Who could have stripped me of my power but not killed me? Why would they do that?"

"We'll find out," I offered softly, kissing her forehead and pulling her head to mine. "Or a lot of creatures are going to die until we do."

She snorted. "You act like finding out wouldn't take a lot of the latter."

"It likely will." I grinned grimly. "How are the others doing?"

"They've finished and are on their way to the hotel to return." She paused, then sighed, and said, "They've come to much the same conclusion as we have and things don't add up. Let's go."

I nodded and we mounted Mako and took off for the hotel, hoping to get home and get some decent sleeping in.

It took us about ten minutes flying to arrive and then another half an hour of keeping constant tabs on the others to ensure they made it to us safely before Amabala took all of us back to Arden's home where the door was locked and there was a note on the door.

Yo!

Finished up before you got back and played with the kitties for a little while before I left like I said I would. You should really give Cringles a bath. That boy smells like dookie. All of your items are on the table. Marcus and Galaxy have my phone number so be sure to get it if you need me!

- *C*

"How the hell did he lock my door without a key?" Arden grumbled more to herself than anyone else.

"He formed a spear with literal shadows, do you honestly think locking a door is going to be an issue for him?" Merlin answered her shortly, his sour tone catching more than a little of Arden's attention.

Cassia spoke first. "What's wrong?"

"The Ventricle in charge of Cairo gave me a lot of crap for having Amabala with me, and made me jump through all these hoops for information." He rubbed his head. "He's ancient and the fact that I'm a chimera made him even angrier for me being there."

"Is that something you should talk to Theodorous about?" I raised a brow at him and he grimaced. "I mean, he *did* offer to help. He's your age and a Ventricle himself."

Merlin scowled at the wall as the door swung open and finally said, "I guess it wouldn't hurt to try him out. It just sucks that I can't move the way I thought I would be able to within the organization."

I nodded. "I thought it would be that way for me when I picked up sergeant in the Marines. Turned out I had power in its most weakened form. I was basically just a grunt for the people pulling the strings. They call us the backbone of the Marine Corps, and we get a lot of shit done, but it was few and far between where true movement among the ranks was some-thing we could actually achieve."

"What did you do?" Cassia asked, curious.

I shrugged. "Made friends in high places where I could, and where I couldn't, I learned the lay of the land as well as I possibly could so that I could navigate it better than some of the people who were there so I could circumvent them." That made me grin. "Couldn't tell you how pissed they got, but they couldn't touch me and that made the hard work on the front end worth it."

Merlin frowned to himself, then nodded before walking away, muttering, "I have a call to make, then."

I smiled at him as he left and found that Cassia and Galaxy were watching me, both uncertain.

"What?"

"Did you truly do all that?" Galaxy asked, despite knowing that she could just read my memories. I nodded and she added, "Why?"

"When you have good Marines, you want to keep them and keep them safe. It means that you need to be able to maneuver people who are a danger to that sometimes." I scratched my neck, "NCOs and Staff NCOs who are out of touch, officers who don't care about their troops—stuff that runs rampant in all the services—are a jeopardy to troop welfare and the mission as a whole. It took me having to save one of my Marines' lives while I was on duty to really understand how removed I was by my rank and what I could have been."

Cassia frowned, but my mood had soured a bit, then the memories of that night came to me unbidden, as if Galaxy was at the helm but this time, I could see her rustling through my mind like a hipster shuffling through vinyls in a music store.

The scared private screaming for help three barracks down, my heart racing as I sprinted to him so fast my cover flew off my head. Another private pounding on the door, screaming Aguillar's name as I came into the commons.

My booted foot crashing into the door just under the lock four times before the others joined me and we could kick the door in to find the young Marine's pale body on the ground with a bottle of pills next to him and a bottle of Jack spilled on the bed. Another on the floor and another bottle of something I didn't recognize opened and spilled just under the bed.

Barking orders to call medics and get assistance to us, I took him and began to try to at least get him breathing with CPR. I yelled something at him. I had seen him just that morning at PT. He'd been kicking ass and taking names, running faster than the other privates that had come to the unit just a couple months before. He was on track to pick up first class in a week, and then could go to the boards for meritorious Lance Corporal. What had happened?

Sirens in the distance fed me hope but he still wasn't breathing, I had to do something to try to get him to throw it up, right? I pressed on his stomach and it didn't feel right to me. But as soon as I touched him there, his body flinched and he tried to inhale. A retching noise and a whimper came from him and I moved to the side just in time to avoid a face full of vomit.

"Put him on his side!" one of the privates ordered his friend from the door and I helped move him. A stretcher came in and two medics flooded into the room with a purpose I couldn't have been more grateful for in my life. They got him the help he needed, and I ended up having to write reports all night as to what I had found.

The next day when I went to check on him, I found out that his leadership had been beating him to ensure that the cocky little private knew his place. It was a decidedly 'old Corps' method to keeping troops in place, and when I worked my way through his chain of command looking for the culprit, I almost got attacked myself.

But I knew enough to find the bastards who did it, and on whose orders. The surly staff sergeant who did it ended up being medically retired after a fall, and after that, I dedicated my life to making sure that no one I knew of in my unit ended up like Aguillar.

The flow of memories stopped and I found myself blinking and catching Cassia, Amabala, Arden, and Galaxy staring at me. Amabala had tears streaking down her face, Arden and Cass both comforting her. "We saw."

I turned to Galaxy. "You showed them that?" She nodded and I didn't know how to feel.

"You were brave," Cassia insisted but I just shook my head. "Do you not think so?"

"If I were brave, I would have done more than just see to a simple 'fall' during a run that tore a ligament in his leg. I would have done what he was trying to do and succeeded." The guilt and remorse returned after years of neglecting to sort through them, and I did what I could to breathe through it. "All I did was what I could."

I found myself angry, for some reason. No one else should have had to experience that, not unbidden. Not without my permission. It felt like an invasion of privacy on my part, and one on theirs. To have to live with my thoughts and emotions in a way that was more personal than probably anything they could have ever found out through conversation.

Galaxy touched my arm and I shook my head. "No." I shook my head again and stalked off to be alone and make sure that what I was feeling and thinking was justified or not. I didn't want to overreact, and I sure as hell didn't want to blow up on someone who wasn't thinking straight. "I'll be in my room."

They nodded, the girls parting so that I could move past them and walk away.

Some of the large cats that inhabited the home seemed curious about me, their eyes following me, but any time they stood to move toward me, I was already away from them.

Eventually I found the room with vivid pink walls that I was sure Arden had teasingly allowed me to use, but it was a room with a bed.

I sat on the bed and leaned back against the wall, my head bowed. Aguillar had been one of the Marines that went into the temple with us. He should have been medically separated but when what was going on with his leadership came to light, he was allowed to stay in when he was passed by the wizard. I didn't remember if he had been one of the Marines to have made it out of there or not.

But I was almost morbidly glad that I hadn't seen his face among the dead. Would I find his body rotting in that temple? Would he have been picked clean by the bugs or animals out there? Whatever had been attacking us?

I fell into myself, dwelling and obsessing over what I found to be my own failings when a knock on the door drew my attention. I rolled my eyes and just grunted, "Yeah?"

The door opened and Amabala came in, her normal cheetah visage staring at me inquisitively. "I wanted to talk."

I blinked at her. "Uh, sure?" I patted the bed and leaned back once more as she moved into the room and closed the door behind her.

As she sat on the bed, her tail began to twitch, until after a moment, I thought she was going to run off. "You know my family used to treat me poorly."

I raised a brow and muttered, "Seems an understatement to me, but I get it."

"You all aren't the first ones to try to get me away from that though." She frowned, her whiskers rising as she spoke on. "There was a boy. Grell. He was strong, smart, and kind. He was the only non-litter Keeper we had in the city, and he was so nice. Strong. Confident."

"You said strong twice." I offered and she just smiled, so I quieted. "Sorry."

"The point was this: he saw how my family treated me and he acted, just as you did." She sobered a bit, then put her hands in her lap and began to wring her wrists nervously. "My mother killed him for it. From then on out, I was so afraid to defy her that I could never even begin to think about leaving the city or her control. Until all of you came along."

I frowned. "I get that that's pretty terrible, and I really regret not killing her, but I'm not sure how to take that for you." I grimaced at myself. She was trying to open up.

"I'm saying that you were brave then, helping that Marine, and I think you were brave helping me too." She sighed and took a deep breath. "I know that my primary purpose for now is to provide instant transport over large distances, but Galaxy and Cassia—even Arden and Merlin, have let me know that the possibilities for me can be endless."

I stayed quiet and watched here for a moment, then nodded. "They can be. And I want that for you if you want it."

"I do," she stated quickly and firmly. Resolutely, even. "I cannot allow my mother to control me anymore, like you couldn't let the villain of your story stay in charge. Someday, I will return home and usurp my mother and her authority and free myself fully." She glanced back at me. "Until then, I could use your support and guidance."

I blinked at her, surprised. "Uh, yeah. You have it."

She smiled and nodded. "Thank you." She frowned to herself and said, "I think it is okay for you to be upset with Galaxy. What she did was unexpected and out of your control. But she thought it easier to show us what you meant, and I do not blame her for that. If anything, that memory has allowed me the insight I needed to trust you more."

She smiled at me and moved off the bed, unconsciously brushing herself off as she said, "I know you have a right to be upset, and I think you should feel that. But don't take offense for the others. Well, at least not me."

I frowned, then nodded once at her before she walked out of the room.

I thought about it; she was right. Of course she was right. I was being a sulky baby.

I forgive you. Galaxy purred and stepped out of my shadow.

I stilled and hit her with a narrow-eyed glare. "Do you now?"

She blinked up at me with her huge eyes and muttered, "Uh oh."

CHAPTER SIXTEEN

I grinned for the umpteenth time as I nodded and let Galaxy translate for me at the High Table in Cairo.

Surprisingly, it was in a facility right down the road from the water treatment plant and looked almost suspiciously like the High Table in Columbus, only this one had hookah lounges a little further back from the front of the bar that the main bartenders took orders to with Arden helping.

The folks here had auras that all seemed to be tied to the heat, or the local mythological scene, though there was one woman who claimed to be the first woman, Eve.

Cassia threw her a series of ill-hidden glares as the woman once again lifted her shirt to show me her rib cage where there was an extra rib.

"You're cut off, Eve." The barkeeper, Osiris, growled and the woman pouted and sulked away from the seat she had occupied. It was closing in on the end of my shift and he was tired already. "Sorry about her, Marcus. She's usually a little more relaxed around the rest of us, but as soon as a human man is in sight, she can't shut up."

He'd been helping me out the entire shift, letting me know

when people were trying to get to the new guy, or just being their normal selves. He was pretty cool.

I smiled and just grinned at him. "Thanks. I could have handled her, but it might not have been pretty after a while if Cassia had gotten involved."

He shot a glance at her with his night-sky-colored eyes. "The oni? She that dangerous?"

"Protective," I corrected and he chuckled and shook his bald, dark-skinned, head. More comfortable with him, I decided to ask, "What's it like around here? I mean, before all the killings."

He raised an eyebrow. "Before it all? It was great." He smiled. "Booze flowed, people would dance, and the only issue we had to truly worry about was the queen making an appearance with her Gremlins in tow to make a nuisance of herself. Ever since she was banned by Serpath, she's kept her head down and we haven't seen much of her."

"She banned her own other half?" That struck me as odd, but then again, life was weird for them, I guessed. "Why?"

"She used to come in and tell people to leave so she could spend time with herself." He shook his head. "Serpath put a stop to that—could've done it a lot sooner if you ask me, but I'm just a bartender who talks in her ear when she needs it. Tells her when she's being too lenient, like a spotter."

"It happen a lot?"

He frowned and seemed to think on it for a while before answering, "Once a century or so, I think? But here recently, it had gotten a lot more frequent." He went back to wiping his glass dry when he glanced up my way and asked, "You finding anything? Need help?"

It took me a moment to realize he wasn't talking about the setup of the bar, and even then, after I did get it, I remained quiet. Everyone was a suspect. Finally, I offered a lame, "Some leads, but other than that, nothing concrete yet."

He'd been great all night, but nicer people could kill me and feel as little remorse as stepping on a bug or having to put down a rabid animal.

Osiris nodded. "I see. Well, good luck out there. Lost a few friends to whatever it is, and I can't stand the idea of losing more."

He lifted his chin and nodded to the other side of the bar before turning away and leaving me to it. A gentleman had come in and smiled wearily, so I gave him a friendly smile and asked, "What can I get you, friend?"

He smiled and winked at me. "It's what I can do for you, really."

I raised a brow and nodded. "Oh?"

He grinned wickedly. "Yup. See, your uncle sent me, Marcus. I'm here to talk to you about a house." I blinked at him and he held up a hand. "No deals at the High Table. I just couldn't wait to meet you any longer, so I flew here on my own. How about something Cairo-themed for me to drink, huh? Flying is such a parching business and I haven't been here since before Jesus was born."

I frowned at him and took a closer look. He wore a business suit, but the light gray jacket hung on the back of the chair behind him and the collar of the crimson button-up shirt he had on was unbuttoned a couple times. His tie was likely else-where. He had an easy look about him, but it was like his pores were larger than they should have been.

He caught me eyeing him as he glanced up from his phone. "You admiring my scales too?" He held his phone up so the light would hit his jawline a bit more and the light looked like it shined on metal. "Gold dragons have a harder time passing for white or black folk, so we typically just go middle-eastern for our human form. The scales are a little harder to hide, you know?"

"You're a gold dragon?" I asked incredulously, then stared at him as he nodded. I couldn't see his aura at all.

"You'll have to trust me." He smiled again and this time his teeth looked a little sharper. "Now, about that drink?"

I nodded, surprised I had forgotten myself like that and decided that I would make him two, just in case. Into my shaker, I poured an ounce of bourbon, dry gin, a teaspoon of lime juice, a small splash of Angostura Bitters and shook it to hell and back for about twenty seconds on ice.

Cracking the shaker like an egg on the side of the bar for show, I poured the concoction into a tall glass before stirring in four ounces of chilled ginger beer and broke a small mint leaf into it for garnish.

I smiled at him and presented, "A Suffering Bastard for a guy who just got off work."

He smiled and winked at me before taking a sip while I got started on cleaning my shaker using the cup cleaner behind the bar. Into it went ice, then two ounces of bourbon, a quarter-ounce of a delicious smelling red wine, another dash of Angostura Bitters and shook it for fifteen second before pouring the drink into a shallow cocktail glass and garnished it with three cherries.

He took this one and sipped it before a glint filled his eyes and he plucked a cherry from the drink, asking, "And this one?"

I smiled once more and said, "The Drunken Pharaoh." He nodded, but I added, "I could have gone a more traditional route with some Egyptian Moonshine, but that would have been a little rough for some, and I don't know if they have it here."

He chuckled. "I don't doubt that they would." He nodded to his drinks. "These are delicious. And I do believe that is the end of your shift." I looked up at the clock and, sure enough, it was. He nodded toward one of the booths across the room. "Come and join me once you're fully off the clock. Oh, and do bring yourself a drink, won't you?"

I frowned and nodded before checking in with Osiris. "You good?"

He nodded, then asked, "Could you run trash to the kitchen? The gremlins will take it from there."

I nodded and gathered the bags behind the counter and then the one in the center of the room before taking them to the kitchen. I no sooner made it to the doorway for the kitchen before a horde of gremlins shot out and screeched excitedly about the garbage, snatching it from my hand surprisingly roughly.

A spill poured from one bag and the gremlins stilled before one of them cleaned it up so thoroughly that the rest of the floor just looked dirtier for it, even though the floor was pretty clean.

Blinking after them, I watched three of them team-carry a bag and any spills that happened after were just gone as two more followed along.

"They hate messes." Osiris smiled as I returned to the bar to make my own Drunken Pharaoh, but I made mine a double. I was certain the taste would come through still, but just doubled all the ingredients to be safe.

Once I was poured and content with my drink, I ordered food for the two of us and went to the booth. "Hope you don't mind a burger?"

He snorted. "Marcus—I'm a dragon. Meat and bread are my meat and potatoes." He frowned, then blinked to himself and raised a hand. "Did you order fries as well? Because potatoes are *very* good."

I nodded and he sighed as if a worry was gone from his mind. "My name is Bilastrian. But you can call me Billy." He held his hand out and I took it tensely. "What's the matter?"

"I thought that the majority of the dragons were… gone."

He nodded. "They are." Billy took a sip of his drink and hissed. I thought something was wrong but he just grinned and shivered. "Alcohol is so good. I can't get drunk, but the flavor and burn are just so… lovely." He cleared his throat, then lowered his voice. "We slowly rebuild our numbers, but I will be honest with you, there are some who *would* seek you out in a misguided attempt at retaliation for your assumed mantle. The memories of dragons are long and notoriously fraught with perceived slights, truthful or misinterpreted."

"Okay. And you said my uncle sent you?"

He chuckled and nodded. "Yenasi and I go back a way, and he helped me find my second hoard, so I owe him a great deal indeed." Billy sipped his drink and sighed. "I came here to let you know that I would like to represent you in your search for a home."

"You just told me that the dragons would like to try to kill me just because it might tickle their fancy, and you want me to trust you to find a house for the Hunt?" It was hard to keep the doubt trickling into my voice contained but he just shrugged at me. "That can't possibly be it."

"It is." He blinked at me and put his hand on the table under the dim light of a flaming lamp above us and the skin shifted until the hand was covered in golden scales and his nails had become claws. "This is to show you that I truly am a gold dragon, and any supernatural creature and the majority of the Touched who know anything of dragons will tell you that if I had meant to attack you, I would have—Table or not. There would be nowhere for you to run, nowhere to hide, and even fewer options to defend yourself from me."

He leaned back as his hand became the same hand that had held his glass before. "We golds are rare monarchs among dragon kind, and our word is our bond. If I say I will do something, give my word, or make my intent known, I am bound to it by my honor and the very core of my being. I told your uncle that I would assist you if you allowed me to do so as a favor to him. Are you saying you don't need my help?"

I frowned. *What is it that has so many supernatural creatures bound by their word and ideals?*

Many of them came from a time before magic was as it is now, and humanity was more honorable, Galaxy interjected. *The gods felt the same way. If a magic user was to lie, it could weaken their ties to magic and ability to use it. Something about a lie changing who you were, or what you stood for.*

Blinking, I took a deep breath and held out a hand for him to shake. "Pleasure to work with you then, Billy. I think we might have some things in mind so far as to what we would like to have, but it would be a matter of us trying to see what it would take for the others to be comfortable."

He took a deep breath with his eyes half lidded and opened them with a flutter, muttering, "A jinn, oni, half jinn Warden, a golem?" He grimaced and took another whiff of me, leaning forward slightly. "A cheetah woman, a goddess, and a drake."

He chuckled at the last bit. "I take it that the drake serves as your mount?" I nodded and he raised his eyebrows in surprise. "Powerful. They're only second to the great wyverns in power and intelligence. Not quite so powerful as my kind though."

"Thanks?" He nodded once and our food came to the table and he tipped the server with a single gold coin the size of a drink coaster. The server smiled and returned a moment later with water and hot sauces, Billy smiling all the while.

"Thank you for the meal, Marcus." He bit into the burger and groaned, savoring the bite. "So tender and tasty. Needs hot sauce though."

He poured a good amount on his food, the fries as well, and offered me some. I just shook my head and said, "Not for me, man."

Billy munched happily as I did and finally said, "I can take all of their personalities into consideration when I search for something. My assumption is that you would like something nearest to the High Table, but far enough to remain aloof and a primary target on your own, should someone attack?"

I frowned. "Uncle Yen tell you that?" He nodded once and took a sip of his drink, then glanced at the bottle of hot sauce and back at the drink. I almost rolled my eyes. "You won't hurt my feelings if you want to try it."

He grinned. "Am I so easily read?" I nodded once in return and he laughed. It was a boisterous thing, and honestly made me want to laugh as well. "Once I get a taste for something spicy, I obsess. Forgive me."

I waved the idea away and he continued. "He told me what you plan for the Table as well, as far as travel, and there are a few places that I could show you that are on ley lines, but the issue will be managing the magical power and they are costly to do business on in our world." He frowned, wiping his lip and sighing. "I've seen your funds and working here is nothing to sneeze at, though I can imagine you'll be receiving recompense for your... mission here."

I nodded and he grinned. "Combined, all of you could cover it easily, but the thing becomes a matter of repayment and getting a loan."

"You said that I had a good amount of money and I do." He nodded and I continued. "I could just do it by myself if I needed to."

Hey grimaced and said, "No. No, you couldn't." Which surprised me. "We're talking ley lines here, Marcus. If you want to live on, or near one, your home will need to be reinforced to take in mana from it, and then convert it for your use and travel. Then, if you wanted it to be made of higher tier materials that could take an enchantment the likes you'll need to defend yourselves, and any other magical means, you're looking at a home that would cost you tens of millions of dollars."

"You're serious?"

His teeth flashed. "As death."

I frowned deeper. "How does that make sense? Humans have been living all over the city and world forever; there's no cost to them to live on a ley line, is there?"

He shook his head. "But they can't use them the way we can." He held up a hand. "I know, but that just means it's harder trying to find a home there. They're coveted spots, for certain. And I know that the argument for how they can be allowed to live along them, on them, or near them is much the same. Think of it like people without children living near an excellent park. Sure, it's nice to look at, and they benefit by having better housing prices if they decide to resell even if they have no need of it, but they get the home anyway and it's purely cosmetic to them."

That didn't mean much to me, but I guessed that it was the case. "So what, we talk about a loan?"

He grinned again. "I know someone. Someone discreet and someone who doesn't ask questions and who doesn't care who he loans to so long as he gets his return investment."

I thought about that for a moment then groaned. "Is it the dragon accountant that my uncle knows?"

Billy looked surprised. "You know Phil?"

———

I shook my head as I stood outside the entrance to the Table with Cassia and Arden. "You sure they said they were going to meet us here?"

I nodded and Arden sighed forlornly. "Don't forget, we were supposed to look for my family out here too."

I nodded. "I know. And we will." I pulled the map out of my inventory and looked at it. It hadn't changed. And while Galaxy might be able to pinpoint it on my mini-map, it was still a ways away. I turned to Arden and said, "I always try to be there for my family, okay?"

She took a deep, steadying breath and nodded, not saying anything else, but she relaxed considerably.

Cassia reached out and took my hand, squeezing it lightly once. "And you're sure that you want to look into the local areas for all of this?"

"Yup." I took a steadying breath myself. "We can go to Galaxy's temple soon, but today I want to take a look around and see if there's anything out of the norm in the city."

They both nodded at the same time that Amabala, Merlin, and Galaxy walked around the corner and down the street toward us. "'Bout time!" Cassia growled playfully. "What took you so long?"

"Convinced the Ventricle here that stopping me was impeding the safe conduct of Wardens in the city and that I was here to assist." Merlin grinned broadly. "Theo may have helped a little."

I raised an eyebrow. "Calling him by his given name now?"

Merlin almost blushed. "He's smart enough and powerful enough that he got us the pull to get in with the Ventricle here in the first place."

Arden snickered, then said, "Nice deflection, cap."

Merlin rolled his eyes.

It was hard not to laugh at that, so I coughed and growled, "Focus." All eyes swung toward me and I nodded to the roof of the High Table. "Let's go."

They nodded and we stepped into the side alley and climbed the fire escape onto the roof with ease, pulling the ladder up behind us and securing it.

As we all stood in the surprisingly clean area, free of any dust and debris, I blinked at the ground and wondered why this seemed familiar.

"What's the plan?" Merlin asked after a moment and I glanced up. "Sorry, I just know that we're on a time crunch here before the sun starts going down."

I nodded and pulled myself together. "We're going to need to pair up again to patrol the city like last time. Galaxy?"

She stepped forward and my mini map expanded in my vision until the whole city was visible. I was certain she did it for everyone, but I checked with her and waited for her sign that she was done. She winked at me and I began, "If we all split the city into sectors and patrol them for a couple hours, we should be able to get a good general idea of what's going on."

"How high are we flying?" Cassia frowned at the map.

"We'll be under cover of the Hunt, so we should be able to fly low enough to look for the auras of any supernatural creatures." I muttered, "Commence the Hunt."

The blackened armor of the hunt pooled around our feet and slid up over our bodies like a secondary skin. As I looked over the rest of the Hunt, it was hard to see anything other than demons. They all looked the same to me, but as I looked at them, I could tell exactly who was who thanks to my bonds to them.

"Cover your zones and remain in constant communication."

I glanced over at Galaxy. "You'll be flying too so you'll have to be extra careful. What are you going to be doing with Rocky, Merlin?"

"He's already underground searching the city for areas of interest." Merlin nodded to me and I called Mako out of my body and onto the ground. "Alright then. Let's ride."

CHAPTER SEVENTEEN

Dusk bent the light of the world around me, the wind whistling past my ears as I stared at the city below. The populace had quite a few Touched with softer, lingering auras, but the supernatural creatures with enough strength to be visible to us were careful to remain well hidden. And those that had been in the streets earlier in the evening were gone now.

As if with the waning light, they got the hint that they should be somewhere safe and off the street.

Something is wrong near Cassia's side of the city, Galaxy dispatched to us, Mako banking and running on the air as fast as his legs would take him. His breath huffed out in wheezes as the distance seemed to drag on and all hell broke loose in the distance.

Fire rained from the sky as Arden reached the area before me, Merlin alighting after her and a ring of blue burst into a bubble around the area.

Mako dove.

We crashed onto the street in the middle of a busy intersection with car horns blaring and people staring slack-jawed into the bubble of blue light.

Merlin grunted and fell to a knee. "Can't hold this much longer!" He gnashed his teeth, gasping for breath and tossing his head toward this left shoulder. "Get the body out of here."

I blinked at him and turned to find the others standing around a dark-skinned man with the tell-tale signs of having been mutilated and all the blood was gone. But this time, it couldn't possibly make sense.

We don't have time for it to make sense, open the bonds between you and Arden, then Merlin, and funnel him mana while Amabala gets us the hell out of here with that corpse.

Galaxy's snarled order broke me out of the curious stupor I had fallen into and I did as she said.

Every time I touched the bonds between all of us, they felt so much easier to manipulate. Funneling mana from Arden as she spread flames around us was easy enough, but I was careful not to take too much from her, and added some of my own to the mix as well.

Cassia has it, and Amabala is about to break through with the portal. We need to go now. Galaxy's voice was urgent. *Merlin can't move; he's about to drop the spell. You'll have to make the suggestion to all of the people here and make it convincing.*

I stepped forward and grabbed Merlin from behind, shouting in my best carrying voice, "What you witnessed here was a catastrophic gas-main rupture and explosion caused by a spark from a muffler dragging on the ground, igniting the gas in the air. Rescue the injured, and all of you closest to the fire are heroes."

I turned and sprinted, Mako slithering onto my forearm as the rest of us entered the portal and popped out into Arden's house around her dining room table.

There was a thud and a curse so vehement it made me perk up and look over to find Osiris's corpse on the wood with the same sort of treatment that the other corpses had received. But this time it looked a little more savage to me somehow.

"Is it because we *just* saw him today that this seems so much more... I don't know—personal?" Cassia asked out loud, making me pause.

"How do you mean?" Arden raised a brow, then stared at her. "And really? Dead guy on my fucking table?"

"We can get you another." Cassia rolled her eyes. Then mimed Arden shouting, *It's an antique!*

"Oh, I will burn you to a crisp for that, Cassia." Arden snarled and stepped forward.

"Stop it!" Amabala bellowed, surprising us all. We looked at her and found that she was pointing to the corpse. "There's no blood to ruin the table, and you two *don't* fight like this!"

Cassia and Arden blinked at each other, then shrugged and said in unison, "Sure we do. All the time."

"You don't nearly act on it like that. Not that I've seen." Galaxy spoke softly, then blinked around the room. "There is a residue of sorts on this body that looks to be affecting all of you in some way. All of you get out. I will look it over."

I stayed behind and she turned to me. "You are not immune, no matter how close we are, Marcus. You need to step out and calm down. Look into yourself and how you're acting."

I blinked and looked down at myself, clenched fists, my jaw tight and my muscles tensing as well. When had I started clenching up and preparing for a fight?

She put a hand on my shoulder and shoved me toward the door. "Go."

It took me a moment to get my feet under me and to get going, but as soon as I was out of proximity from the corpse, my body relaxed and I could look around at the others.

Cassia and Arden spoke in hushed tones and Merlin patted Amabala on the back. He grimaced and sighed. "We left Rocky in Cairo."

I frowned. "Shit, he going to be okay?" He nodded and I sighed. "Let's go chat, then. We need to touch base and see if we can't get this solved. Otherwise, an attack at the High Table could be imminent."

"What makes you think that?" Arden asked with concern and suspicion. "What have you found?"

"I don't know if it really makes sense yet, but I wanted to talk to all of you about it." Arden led us into her den as I spoke, the majority of the tigers and her liger lounging on the sofas without a care.

Arden snapped her fingers and all of them fled the room except the liger, who stood and stretched languorously before sitting next to the couch where she sat. She scratched his massive head and he chuffed happily as she watched me explain everything to the others.

"But it's weird that there's some kind of emotional residue now." Merlin scratched his head and waved a hand, Muffs the liger hissing violently as the mage summoned a white board from nothing and began to write on it with a marker he pulled from his pocket.

The white board had notes and scribbles with photos of the crime scenes on one side pinned to it, then little red strings tied from them to a pin on a map at the point they had been found. The newest death hadn't been pinned yet but as he did so, the cycle of moving inward stopped and broke.

The killer had broken the pattern.

"Cassia, what happened?" Merlin asked as he turned to her with a notebook appearing in his hand.

She frowned at him, then blinked. "I was patrolling the area closely, for some reason. Felt like it was necessary to me, and there was a rather large population of both humans and creatures like us in the area too. But everyone with the ability to touch magic had stopped and started to stare at the middle of the intersection and traffic. I couldn't figure out why, until the body dropped into the street and that first car almost hit it."

She shook her head and paused, then said, "So, I rushed toward it, Galaxy having called you all already, and then Arden was firing flames to set up our alibi."

"That's not why I was doing that." Arden frowned, then

scratched her head. "I saw something on the ground near you and lit it up."

Cass snorted. "I checked all around me before I went in; there wasn't anything there."

"Yes, there was," Arden argued and stood up from where she had been sitting.

"Stop it!" I snarled and yanked on my bonds with both of them. Their attention snapped to me and their eyes were laser focused.

Galaxy put a hand on my shoulder and the tension released. "It seems I'm the only one who is immune to it then. I only opened that door for a moment."

"What the hell is going on with it?" I asked as the anger drained away. I turned my gaze to the girls and muttered, "Sorry."

They just shrugged it off as Galaxy reached out toward Arden, then stopped and pulled her arm back. "Before I make the same mistake—may I share your memory of what you saw?"

Arden nodded and Galaxy held up her arm as our bonds flared open and her memory played in front of me like I was there. Cassia looking around as she rode her shadow horse toward Osiris's body lying on the ground, still bouncing from the impact.

There, just as she was about to reach him, something that I could just barely make out, small and compact, almost touched her mount before a gout of flame slammed into it. Whatever it had been fried in an instant and turned to nothing but char.

I blinked and the memory was gone as the rest of us landed. "Galaxy, do you know what it was that she killed?"

"No, I just know that she killed something and she gained experience from it." She frowned and stared at me. "What is it, Marcus?"

I frowned. "I think I have a guess as to who it could be that is doing all this, but it doesn't make any sense to me."

"You think it could be the queen?" Galaxy asked and I nodded.

"Small creatures that hate messes—hence why all the blood is gone at the scene of the murders, and the area is always cleaner than what it should be. She is something with immense strength, she has a grudge—at least with Osiris from what he said—and over the last few months, she had been throwing wrenches into Serpath's running her branch by being a pain in the neck." I scratched my head and sat down on one of the couches, tiger hair flitting into the air. "I just can't understand *why*."

"Jealousy?" Cassia offered, making us look over at her. She tapped her ears and muttered, "I was listening in on your conversation and from what I understand, the queen is mad that her other half doesn't spend any time with her. She might be thinking of it like her branch of the High Table is an obstacle that needs to be eliminated in order to get to her goal."

I hung my head. "And the other victims must have been those she thought of as the ones trying to keep the two of them apart." Arden frowned at my revelation and I explained, "Osiris said that he was one of the people telling her to ban her other half for the good of the bar and the patrons. Somehow, she has to know about that."

"She has the gremlins spying for her." Merlin spoke excitedly, a book in his hand, finger pointing as he read, "'Though they might be meek in size and stature, gremlins are some of the most mischievous and stealthy creatures. Able to hide their comings and goings with ease because they despise a mess not of their making. They will typically devour the scraps of whatever their master does not consume.'"

"The limbs," Amabala gasped. "They've been eating the limbs."

"Okay, that explains the majority of it, but that doesn't explain the emotionally-radioactive corpse on my dining table." Arden pointed out and began to massage her temples. "If all of this happened, how did Serpath not figure it out?"

"I don't know if she's capable of figuring it out, because the killer is a part of her," Galaxy muttered, then sighed. "You saw the way she put the queen to sleep when she was about to be a nuisance to all of you and her getting us out of her chambers— what if the queen can do the same to her?"

"And the rage-inducing residue on Osiris?" Cassia asked.

"I don't know." Galaxy frowned and looked at me. "You said that for some reason unknown to anyone, she started to more frequently impose herself into Serpath's business?"

I nodded. "It went from once a century or so to monthly, from the way he made it sound." I scratched my head and shrugged. "Then she got banned a bit ago."

"That timeline is close to when the temple you found me in appeared, Marcus," Galaxy said with excitement in her eyes. "What if something from it is somehow able to force people to feel things like this?"

Arden sucked air in through her teeth softly. "Doesn't that seem like a bit of a stretch for this?"

Cassia shook her head. "No. If there was some kind of keeper there, it likely left in search of her or its food. I would be hunting for a way to find my charge if I were in its place; that is the next logical step."

"So I guess this means that we need to make sure we get to that temple sooner, rather than later." I grunted and stretched. "Question is, do we go in when it's dark, or do we go in during the day?"

"You got there in the morning and whatever it was that attacked you killed your men in broad daylight." Galaxy's state- ment was true, but it stung nonetheless.

"Galaxy," Cassia snarled, the goddess's attention training on her. "You know that wasn't the way to say that. Apologize."

Her head hung slightly. "I am sorry, Marcus. I just worry about all of you too." Her shoulders sagged. "I hate that all of you are willing to go into danger for me. I don't know if there *is* a best or safe time to go."

I put a hand on her shoulder and pulled her close so that I

could hug her. "Then we'll go when we're prepared. But in the meantime, we need to call Serpath and let her know what's going on."

"Are we sure that's a good idea?" Merlin posed and that made the rest of us pause in various states of readying to move on. I tilted my head at him and he continued, "She's essentially two halves of the same whole. What if they share some kind of link?"

Arden blinked, then her eyes widened. "You don't think she would go nuclear, do you?"

I growled, "We can't risk that." I began to tap my hip with my fingertips while I thought. "Okay, so we can't tell her yet. Business as usual and if anyone asks, we have some leads that we're looking into, but don't want to lean too heavily against."

"Seems fair." Cassia nodded, then leaned back. "So what did that gentleman at the bar want?"

"He was a friend of Uncle Yen's and wants to help us find a house on a ley line."

Merlin whistled and raised his brow. "That's going to take a dragon's hoard to secure. Did you say yes?"

I nodded. "If it means that we will have what we need, we can finance, I guess."

Arden rolled her eyes. "That means you'll be working with Phil, and he's a real peach, that one." I looked askance at her and the others just stared. "He comes in from time to time. Likes to drink schnapps and talk about the stock market like he didn't invent the damn thing. Do you know how mind numbing it is to listen to a miserly old dragon talk about a four-oh-one-kay?"

I stared at her and crossed my arms. "No. No, I don't. But it looks like you have a rapport with him, so I'll ask you to set that up for me."

She screamed, "You're *fucking joking*, right?!" When no one laughed and I didn't budge, she pointed a finger at me as her hair began to burn. "You owe me, Marcus. I swear to you. I will own you if he starts trying to talk me into fucking stocks. I will *kill you*."

"You don't have to do anything other than just get him to give us a loan and bring me the contract to sign." I held up a hand. "Or convince him to come talk to me. Billy said he would talk to him, but dragons are a little more bureaucratic when it comes to meetings and it could take a few months to get into his office."

She growled and huffed, but finally relented. "Fine." Then she pointed into my face again, "I'm warning you, Marcus Bola. He tries to get me into stocks, you'll rue the day you thought of this."

I chuckled as she shoved her way past me, shoulder checking me on her way through, then was gone. There were char marks on my shoulder and I had to wonder, was she really going to try to kill me if he did?

CHAPTER EIGHTEEN

My weapons were clean and freshly wiped down and I was working on ensuring that my blades were all clean and cared for when Cassia and Galaxy joined me in my room.

Cassia spoke first. "You okay?"

I frowned and nodded at her as I removed the punch knife from my belt to wipe down and oil it. "Yeah, what's up?"

"You're carrying a lot, Marcus." Galaxy spoke softly and stepped closer to me, then stopped and looked conflicted about joining me on the bed, but did so anyway. "You have all of the rest of the group to do things and you somehow end up shouldering most of the burden yourself."

"And I know that you're thinking about Connell as well." That made me pause and slide my finger across the blade of the small knife. Blood welled there and I grimaced, but just wiped it away as the wound quickly healed on its own.

I hadn't been. I was so focused on the mission that I hadn't really had the time to, and now that she had brought it up, I needed to check in on him. "Thanks for reminding me of him."

Cassia flinched and I looked up at them. "I'm serious, thank you. I had put that aside for now—what's going on with you both?"

"We've both said and done some things that you haven't liked and..." Galaxy paused searching for the words but I got the general idea.

"Look, ladies—"

I was about to go on but Cassia stepped forward and grabbed me by the front of my shirt, lifting me off the bed and into the air before pulling me close to her. "We worry that you don't want to fight us anymore. Are you that upset with us, Marcus?"

My eyebrows shot up and I had to bite my lip not to laugh out loud.

"What's so funny?"

I shook my head and gripped her shoulder. "I'm not mad at either of you." I frowned, then amended, "I was a bit because of some of the low blows, but I get where you're coming from. Honestly, I'm more worried about what we're going to find and protecting you both from whatever is going to be there."

Cassia put me down and raised her chin. "A warrior's nerves." She patted down the wrinkles on my shirt and grunted. "I wish to fight you."

I patted her cheek. "I love you too." She smiled at that and grabbed me again. "Woah now."

"I was serious." She insisted and pulled me close, her lips pressing against my shoulder. "I worry about you."

"I know." I held her cheek for a moment. "But you reminding me about Connell means I need to check in on him. Let me text Luca and see how he is, then I'll come back and we can cuddle."

I glanced back at Galaxy and added, "All of us."

Galaxy grinned and held her hand out to Cassia. "Come here, you." Cassia went to her and I pulled out my cell phone.

I tapped along on my keyboard so that they knew I was alive.

Hey Luca, just wanted to let you know that we're back and forth on the case. How is Connell doing?

I put my phone back into my pocket and turned around to find Galaxy and Cassia on my bed watching me curiously when my phone began to vibrate.

I pulled it out and it was a number that I didn't recognize, so I answered it. "Hello?"

"Do you know how irritating it is that you text my husband and not *me*, Marcus?" Aeslyn sounded a bit upset, but mainly tired.

"I can imagine it would be as irritating as finding out the woman you once thought the world of had run off with your son because she was planning to become Fae royalty." I *just* managed to keep the snark out of my tone with that.

There was a pause. "Will you ever forgive me for that?"

I frowned. "It's eight years of his life, Aeslyn. Eight years of mine. It may not seem like much in the grand scheme of things for you with your immortality, but it was forever to me. I missed everything. No matter how much I cared about you, I was never there for his first steps. His first smile. To watch him grow into the boy he is from any more than a few videos here and there from an email you likely checked once or twice a month. It hurts."

She remained quiet, so I broached the silence. "How is he?"

"He's fine," she answered mechanically. "He's learning to control the magic within him, but it's not like mine, or Luca's. It's more feral than we've seen. It's dangerous."

I frowned at her voice and said, "Is there anything we can do to help him? If you like, you can bring him to the Table; Uncle Yen can look at him and see what's going on."

"We are currently under lockdown and can't leave Court grounds." She sighed and spoke quickly, "We're on Earth, not Grestal, but the Unseelie have lost enough people that the Queen and King think we might be under attack."

I paused, Galaxy stating plainly, *If you tell them about Zeke, they'll attack him and he will kill them. You'll be putting Connell in harm's way. It may also be a roundabout way to say that we were interfering and put us on the chopping block as well.*

I nodded and took a deep breath. "If you send me an email or text with what's going on, I can have Uncle Yen do some research, or I will myself and we can try to help him. If nothing else will work, Galaxy and I will come to you ourselves and see what's going on."

"I will come as well." Cassia jutted her chin out again and stared at me as I blinked at her.

"Is that Cassia?" Aeslyn asked.

"Yup." Then added, "Cassia, Galaxy, and I will come to make sure that we can help him."

"Why would you bring them both?"

"Because they're important to me," I answered truthfully, but I felt like she was probing for more. "The three of us are dating."

She scoffed. "Really? You can't have a normal relationship, so you go off and start a harem with people you barely know?"

"A polyamorous relationship with the goddess who knows me better than anyone else in this world and Grestal, and an oni who happens to care about me very much, thank you," I growled back. "I tried for vanilla, and it turned out to be a limited time thing, so if you're done judging a relationship you have no right to judge—you know, after going off and marrying a prince *you* barely knew—we can make sure our son is taken care of."

"He is." She hung up and I seethed quietly for a moment, battling hard not to squeeze my phone so hard I would crush it in my grip.

"Don't let her try to get inside your head, Marcus." Galaxy spoke confidently from the bed as she and Cassia stood up to come and comfort me. "She's jealous, you know that."

"And using my son as a weapon against me for it." I sighed.

My phone vibrated again and it was the same number, I picked up and tiredly answered, "Yes?"

"Hey, dad?" I perked up at Cornell's voice.

"Yeah, buddy, it's me. How are you?" I had no luck hiding the surprise in my voice. "I heard your magic is rough, you okay?"

"I think so." He sounded uncertain. "Mom and everyone else don't know what to make of it, so they keep trying to get me to do normal Unseelie stuff, but it never turns out right."

"Hey, that's not your fault." I hoped I sounded encouraging. "What are they trying to have you do?"

"Turn invisible and stuff, like Luca, freeze things like you." He grunted and whispered, "Mom even tried to make me sing to a fern. A *fern*."

I laughed with him. "That does seem a bit out there." I took a breath. "Does your magic tell you what it wants to do?"

He made a sound like he was thinking. "I don't know, it tells me it's hungry. It wants to eat things and sometimes it does. Other times, what it eats it gives to me."

Galaxy's eyes widened. *Ask him if he sees or hears numbers, or if screens pop up in his field of vision.*

I asked and he paused. "Sometimes? It's like the magic knows what I want, but it can't do it, so it looks for something similar. Like, when I tried to turn invisible like one of the Flern Chameleons that mom keeps, the magic reached out to one and ate it. Then I could make my hand blend into the environment for a little bit."

My mouth fell open, was his power like Galaxy's? But. How? "I mean, that seems cool, right?"

"Yeah, I just wish I could leave here, you know?" He sighed. "There aren't any other kids here, and there's no one to play soccer with while Luca is gone at Court."

I smiled softly, I was really going to need to get over my jealousy of Luca someday. "Well, I know I'm not good at soccer at all, so you would beat me."

I could hear the grin in his voice as he said, "Yeah, I can take him too, but I let him win sometimes. Mom should be back soon, I think. She's supposed to be looking into my magic and sent an email to someone."

She hadn't even bothered to tell him it was to me? Damn it. "Well, that's good." I was quiet for a minute, then said, "You know, when I get done with the job I have, I would love to come and see you do the magic you can do. Maybe help you learn to harness it?"

"I would like that." He said something that was muffled enough that I couldn't hear it, then came back. "Hey, I gotta go. Thanks for talking to me!"

"Any time, buddy." He hung up before I got the chance to say anything else, and even despite not knowing how he ended up with power like Galaxy's, it was nearly impossible to keep the grin off my face.

———

The next morning, I sat on the edge of my bed polishing the sword that Zeke had enchanted for me. The engraving looked like little more than lines carved through in a simple pattern that I didn't recognize, but the different colored gem-like fillings corresponding to each of the elements were interesting and from what he had left on the note posted to it, any element that I channeled through it would receive a boost in power. Not to mention making the blade denser, more durable, and sharp enough that it would cut diamond like butter.

So I had to be careful with it, otherwise I would lose a finger.

"Is that what he did for your sword?" Cassia asked as she came out of the bathroom in a towel.

"Yeah, it's nice, right?"

She nodded and grinned. "Have you named it yet?"

My eyebrows knit at her. "I'm sorry, what?"

Galaxy snorted, walking out behind her. "He doesn't pay attention." She rolled her eyes, not even bothering to hide the fact that she was still nude and dripping water on the carpeted floor. We had gone to the High Table to speak to Uncle Yen about Connell, but he had been in a meeting so we were in my room. "You know named weapons in video games? It's common to name powerful weapons."

"How do we even know it's that powerful, though?" I asked in an offhand manner, not really believing it could be.

"Channel Bolt Havoc into it, then." Galaxy shrugged. "See if Cassia can touch it."

"Don't we need a control for that kind of thing?" I raised a brow at her and wreathed my hand in electricity with the spell.

"This is going to be fun!" Cassia grinned and reached out to touch my hand. The current passed into her and made her hair rise a bit, but the most she did was flinch and grimace. "I don't like that. The sword now."

I shrugged and focused the spell into the sword. Electricity crackled from it in a hair-raising display of azure and yellow that sent a chill down my spine. Cassia reached out and touched the blade, her body stiffening before she shot backward into the bathroom with a crash.

"Cass!" I bellowed and tossed the sword onto my bed to run after her. She lay sprawled out on the floor with the water from the shattered sink beginning to fountain out of the broken pipe and pool around her. "Cassia?"

Her hair stood on end and her skin was beginning to turn the telltale mottled red when she was close to taking her oni form. I reached down and touched the tips of my fingers to her neck, her pulse steady but she was definitely unconscious.

I reached over and shut the water off with a twist of the shutoff valve and used Wisp to start drying it all as Galaxy tried to get her to wake up with mental urging. I turned and noticed the weapon had slid through the mattress with an inch or so of the blade and the hilt sticking out. It was so sharp that it had gone through it all?

"What the fuck was that?" Cassia grumbled as she shook her head and started to come to, trying to stand. She blinked, then looked up at me. "Name that fucking thing."

I blinked and just pulled it from the bed. "I need a new bed now." I shook my head and sighed, "Could call you Pillow Cutter."

"I will punch you so hard," Cassia growled and her form began to shift.

"Okay!" I snickered and looked at the blade again. "I'll call you Reaper."

"Better." Cass grunted and limped into the room, trying to pat her smoking hair down as she fully shifted into her oni form. "Fuck, that hurt."

Reaper it is, I thought to myself. "You good?" She nodded and loosened up her neck as much as she could before I grinned. "Let's go visit the temple."

We made our way downstairs where Arden, Merlin, and Amabala ate breakfast at the bar with Xerxes smiling at us. "Anything to drink?"

"Nah, we're going to be heading out and I don't want anything in my stomach." I sighed and looked at the others as they turned to me. "You all ready?"

Amabala shook her head, but grinned. "Let's do it."

I raised an eyebrow at her and shook myself out before Amabala held out her hands and pulled the veil of the worlds apart and we rushed through into the alleyway beside the Cairo branch of the Table.

Ready to try to figure this all out? I asked Galaxy as she stepped through. She took her raven form and cawed loudly before taking off in the direction that the freshly-made green arrow pointed at on my mini map.

CHAPTER NINETEEN

The desert sky was brighter and harsher on us. Even with the cool shadows our armor from the Hunt provided us, it still beat down on us. The sand below us moving like the ocean waving toward the horizon as we proceeded toward it.

As we zoomed through the area, the map around us began to update and move past us as well, but the interesting thing was that if I focused on it, there was about a mile radius around us that was visible in it while the rest was grayed out still.

How far out are we, Galaxy?

She thought on it a moment. *Not too far now, I think.* She sensed my additional question and answered, *The temple seems to have… migrated closer to the city than it was before. I don't know if it's the shifting sands or something else, but it's closer. We might be looking at about another ten minutes or so.*

Then we should stop about a mile or so away from it and observe it from the outside if we can.

That could be a good idea. She flew on in her raven form in silence after that and we followed along.

Cassia called, "Something's on the horizon."

I blinked and focused, then saw it, a small point that swam closer to view. It was the temple.

"Back down the speed everyone, we have no way of knowing what's in there." They slowed down, and I could tell it took everything she had for Galaxy to pull back with us. Once we were a mile or so out, we stopped in the sky and watched the building. It was exactly as I remembered. With the power of my Mantle, it felt like I could see further than I had been able to before.

But the sights I was seeing were ones that would be engraved in my soul likely for the rest of my life.

The pyramid-like shape was odd, to me, made of darker stone material than what the pyramids were made of, and at the top of the building there was this flaring out of stone that looked like it could have been the start of another pyramid on top, but it was snapped off after a couple dozen feet or so.

The entrance to the temple looked to have been scrubbed clean of all the blood that had been left behind by the more injured and dying members of my platoon, the sand likely having claimed it and sifted it away.

The large pillars that stood on either side of the door were chipped, but stood as they had before, thick and imposing even from this distance. And like the last time I had seen it, the doors stood ajar, inviting us into the darkness within.

A chill ran down my spine and suddenly it was harder to breathe as the screams of my brothers and sisters-in-arms died around me in horrific ways. Something I couldn't see flitted around the temple in the shadows. Bright, cruel eyes watched from the void and chuckled at my inability to respond. To fight back.

To control the fear.

"Marcus!" The voice echoed and I could just make out someone shaking me as the shadows deepened and the creature stepped out of it.

Suddenly, the sun glared down on me and something cold

woke me with a shock that made me sit up and bluster, looking around wildly.

"What the hell was that?" Arden asked softly, her arms crossed as she stared at me.

"He was having a flashback." Cassia growled as she reached toward me, then stopped herself and spoke calmingly. "Marcus, you're safe. We're still a good distance from the temple and there's nothing here that can harm you."

It took a few breaths to collect myself, as embarrassing as it was, but I was able to get myself up onto my feet at least.

"Maybe you and Galaxy should stay out here for the moment while the rest of us make entry," Merlin suggested from where he patted the stone golem at his hip, comfortingly, like the boy mage or the animal were discomfited by the proximity as well. I shook my head and he said, "Marcus, it's okay. We're capable of defending ourselves."

I grunted. "So were we, and whatever was in there took us out like we were nothing more than mice and it was a mouser on a bender." He stared at me and I sighed. "Yeah. Magic. I know. I still don't want any of you in there without me. I couldn't live with myself if... if..."

Galaxy put a hand on my shoulder and said simply, "We know."

Cassia touched my leg and muttered, "Take a moment to get yourself together, then we can go in." She turned toward Merlin and his golem. "Or send Rocky in?"

Merlin gasped. "That's no way to treat him!"

I nodded and watched them walk far enough away that I could no longer hear them bickering about her wanting to send the golem into the lion's den. It was also far enough away that they couldn't hear me if I spoke out loud, I hoped. So I decided to say a prayer for strength, and if being this close nearly took me out, it would need to be a good one.

"Hail Thor, Son of Odin and Jord, he who awaits the coming of the serpent who would devour the world. Troll slayer, and Jotun bane. I ask that you grant me strength in the coming trial, that I might be worthy of the Mantle I wear. If my body might falter, I look to you for courage and vow to stand once more. Hail Thor."

"Spoken well," a deep voice said from my left. I turned to find a man in scrubs standing next to me, his beard closely cropped and his gaze intense despite the dark void in one of his eyes. "Well met, Marcus Bola."

Though my mouth hung open, he continued to watch me. "I am Odin." He smiled at me as I fell to my knees and lowered my head. "Stand, warrior. I am not here for that."

I stood but still didn't look at him. Out of all the creatures in the mythology of the world, the legends and tall tales that were out there—even having met Lucifer himself—I had never truly expected the All Father to come to me.

"I came for a reason, Marcus." He looked down at himself and I could hear a jovial lilt in his voice as he prodded my deference. "Even in work scrubs, you won't look at me?"

It was almost laughable. "What work could there be for you?"

"The same as there is for many others, but mine is the same as some others who could be considered heroes." He smiled and lifted his hand under my line of sight and motioned upward so I would look up to see his one-eyed gaze soften. "Many of my furies and Valkyrie work in the hospitals that your warrior brethren reside in. They tend to their ills, aches, pains, and wounds so that they can live, and when they fall, lift them to Valhalla should they be worthy. Many of them are. Many more are."

"There was a post online a few years ago that made me smile, about all of the 'warriors' you took into your hall whose songs you sung the loudest, over even some of the more fearsome men and women to raise a horn in toast." I dwelled on that for a moment before adding, "About abuse survivors, those who fought their own bodies to last another day. People who fought for others when they had given up on themselves."

He smiled, the first time I truly beheld him, and nodded.

"And so many more. I inspired those who wrote it. I wanted to seed hope into the world for others. Because we will need many hands for Ragnarok."

I stilled, my heart gripped by true fear. "Is it coming?"

He nodded. "Not for quite some time yet, but there is another end of sorts coming too." He paused and took a moment before saying, "I take it that you heard of Janus?"

I nodded and he said softly, "Someone killing a god is not normal, Marcus, and, as the Huntsman, it may fall to you to investigate this. I just wanted to check in with you to ensure that it wasn't actually *you* who did it."

"I wouldn't even know where to begin on killing a god." I tried to make it a joke, but he didn't laugh or even snort. "How would you know?"

He looked into the sky and muttered, "I would have been able to sense a Dominion in you."

I blinked at that, opening and closing my mouth before finally managing, "A what?"

"Dominion," he said, clarifying with a soft huff. "A Dominion is what a god has within them that allows them to maintain their divinity. It gives them strength and power above that of the Touched and other supernatural creatures from here and Grestal. Some Dominions are different and others stronger than the next, but a Dominion is still a Dominion."

That made me frown. "How close do you have to be to sense one?"

"Depends on the strength of it, but I can tell you don't have one." He closed his eyes and the world around him began to shimmer and warp in a way that reminded me of the heat rising off blacktop but it wasn't right. Then an immense pressure bore down on me from him that almost knocked me to my knees. "That should help to give you an idea of what it feels and looks like when you come across a Dominion."

He focused on something then shook his head. "It feels like there's one around here somewhere, but it's not right."

I nodded, not really knowing what to say and he reached

out and touched my shoulder. "Praying for strength is never a bad thing. For courage? The same." He tossed his chin in the direction my friends stood watching us curiously. "But never fail to trust your friends. My children had faith in one another to the point where they knew without a doubt that they would die killing all before them to recover those who belonged to them. It's part of why I adore your kind." He grinned and patted me on my shoulder before letting his hand fall away. "Never a brother or sister left behind if you can manage it. And you Marines typically do."

He took a step back and as he did, the scrubs became fur-lined armor of leather and hammered-steel plate, his smiley-face eyepatch becoming a dark-brown leather patch with runes carved into it. And the raven earring he wore took flight in front of me, obscuring my vision for only a heartbeat during which Odin disappeared. His final words echoed around me. "Fight well, and trust in those around you."

Recovered and rejuvenated, I joined the others as they silently eyed me. "Odin said that we need to be careful."

"We know that wasn't what he said." Arden crossed her arms and smiled softly.

I turned my head and glared at Galaxy, but Amabala cleared her throat and tapped her ears. "Sensitive hearing."

They all laughed at my disbelief, but I was well enough once more to journey forward with the others into the unknown of Galaxy's temple.

We rode forward over the sand on Mako and the horses of the Hunt, the sand displaced underfoot rising behind us and forming a cloudy trail until we arrived on scene at the front of the temple.

As I had suspected, it was pristine if only covered by the sands of the desert that it resided in. There was no blood on the ground or stone, no bones or remains visible to me, or the others that they let on.

"Anyone else feel like they could be starring in a poorly-writ-ten, straight-to-TV sci-fi film?" Arden asked cautiously and

Cassia snarled at her. "It's true! I mean, mysterious temple and all."

"What is it with you and shitting on our situation like this?" I stared at her for a moment. "Most people would be quiet in a moment like this with everything that could potentially go wrong in a place like this. My friends died here. How about a little decorum?"

"Decency," Merlin corrected, offhand, then added, "Well, I suppose that word works, but unlike most people, she was around when Jesus was alive, so…"

Arden nodded and pointed to him. "Why I keep him around. At least he gets me."

Merlin said, without missing a beat, "You're still a bit of a dick about it."

Cassia snorted and wiped her eyes theatrically. "He's learning."

Amabala perked up. "Oh, oh—that's all he does?" She looked around hopefully at our faces for a sign that she had done well in joining our impromptu, inappropriate roasting session.

My lips twitched, rising in a smirk that made me shake my head. "You did good." I sighed and rolled my eyes. "Heads on a swivel, eyes too. Let's get in there."

CHAPTER TWENTY

It took Cassia and I both pushing to get the door to open fully instead of just a bit like it had been before. It didn't close on my Marines and I last time, but we weren't sure about whether that would change with Galaxy being here or not.

Speaking of. *How are you doing now that we're here?*

She was quiet for a moment, then responded, *I feel called to this place, but I can't exactly tell why. It's like there are answers here, but I'm not asking the right questions.*

It sounded like the kind of problem someone in her condition might have, so I left it alone to focus on what was going on around us.

Everything was as it had been before, except all the corpses of the fallen weren't where I remembered them to be. Scientists and Marines—all of them—should have still been where they had been, right? What kind of creature moved its kills and kept house?

One who likes order? Galaxy offered and I just frowned again. The fight hadn't been ordered and thought out, it had been a downright massacre with guerilla tactics if I had ever seen them before.

The entrance led to a walkway that led to a path-like walk with small walls on the sides that then led to the walls of the pyramid and rooms around us. Once we made it to the center, it was hard to contain my concern.

"Are those…?" Merlin whispered softly and I just nodded.

All of the corpses had been moved down to the bottom of the pyramid at the base, where a monolith of sorts rose in the center of a dais pointing downward toward the floor.

Arden began softly, "Anyone else think that looks like…"

"A giant key?" Cassia finished. She glanced at the other woman. "Yeah, I'm betting we find some information there."

"There's nothing on the walls here either." Merlin huffed angrily as he glared around with his fingers over his eyes. "Mage sight is lit up all over the place though."

"Mage wh—never mind." I gathered from the gist of the name that I would need to either learn it, or make him use it often. "How this thing got us before was when we split up, so we're going to move together and have someone facing the rear so we can watch all angles."

"Rocky will watch my back, but just to be safe, Cassia?" Merlin turned to the oni woman who tilted her head to the side. "Would you like to carry me so I can cast if I see anything?"

She smiled down at him and picked him up like an adult lifting a toddler onto her hip. The boy mage pointed his newly-enchanted staff over her shoulder and kept a wary eye behind us as we moved forward with myself and Cassia bringing up the rear and Amabala in the middle.

The buttstock of my rifle floated just in front of my right shoulder as we walked slowly down the path along the right side of the pyramid in search of a way down.

"I don't understand why we don't just go down the center." Cassia grumbled and tapped the ground with her massive club like a cane of sorts.

"Leaves us vulnerable to whatever that monolith could contain, magical traps, attacks from mysterious monsters—you know, the usual." Merlin said it so casually that I didn't question it, but Cass raised a hand and swatted his rump, making the boy yelp and grumble, "Just saying."

She grinned, her teeth flashing widely. "I know."

The rooms we encountered were unusually clean for a place that could have been hidden for gods-knew-how long and anywhere we found any sort of marking of any sort, Merlin would stare at it unblinking for a time before letting us move on.

His memory is extensive, Galaxy commented offhand, then spoke softer. *Marcus, I'm scared.*

I don't blame you for being scared. My tone was gentle as I stared down the pathway we walked. One of the rooms didn't seem quite right. Like the doorway had bent outward just a bit before snapping backward. *Did you see that?*

One moment. She paused and rifled through my memory. *High alert! There's a mimic ahead.*

"Contact right!" I growled, my rifle lifting as I stepped around Arden on her left. "Light it up, Arden!"

Flames surrounded the mana-infused rounds I shot at the mimic that appeared to be a doorway. As soon as the rounds touched the other end of the wall and the flames licked the doorway, the creature screamed horrendously and the 'door' slammed closed as it shifted shape.

"Stay on it!" Cassia bellowed as she jumped over the two of us and sprinted off down the walk after it while it fled.

"Cass, don't run off!" I shouted but something dropped from the ceiling that made the hair on the back of my neck stand on end immediately.

The pale-white creature stood hunched over at six feet tall, with long arms that were thin and wiry with muscle which just didn't make any sense, and a beak-like mouth that opened wide and screeched so loudly that my sight began to wane and darken.

Shoot it! My trigger finger moved of its own accord as the screaming bird-thing advanced with its shrill cry grew louder. The retort of my rifle was muffled to the point of near silence and the only reason I didn't fall forward was for the fact that the recoil pushed against me.

It scuttled back with the round hitting it, and suddenly Merlin stood in front of it with his hands weaving back and forth and his sword slashing this way and that.

Even Amabala skittered forward to begin slashing at it with abandon, snarling, "Fucking bird!" Her tail thrashed behind her as she hissed and drove one of her blades into the creature's neck.

These aren't the creatures that were here, Marcus. These are different—strong still, but different.

"We kill them anyway." I grit my teeth and used Embodiment to step around the bird-like creature, using Mana Blade to stab it in the back as I went, killing it as effectively as Merlin's sword slicing through its exposed neck. "We need to get to Cassia."

Galaxy stepped out of me in cat form and began to swallow the creature as fast as she could, but I issued orders as I strode away. "Merlin, Arden, protect her. Amabala, come with me."

The cheetah woman caught me easily as we sprinted down the walkway after Cassia, something screaming ahead spurring us on faster. My gun raised and the amorphous blob trying to wrap itself around the oni in front of us took each round like it was nothing.

Into the ring it went and out came Reaper. "Incoming!"

I wreathed the weapon in Bolt Havoc as Cassia stepped back and slammed her mace into the ground, walls of stone shooting up to block whatever it was that was trying to kill her. My sword pierced it and the electricity spiked through it just before I leveled Hoarfrost on the area, the air cooling to the point where my breath became visible. The blob gurgled and tried to shrink away, but anywhere it moved, the ice was already setting in as the spell on my sword forced it to still.

"Now, Cass!" I hopped backward as the woman brought her mace down right next to my ear near my shoulder onto the icy blob.

A huge crashing shatter made me flinch as a large portion of the creature crumbled to shards, but there was enough of it left that it tried to reform and become something else, but all it did was bleed mercurial blood onto the floor which began to burn and stink as it created a cloud of noxious fumes.

I had more than enough mana to freeze the fumes but instead we just backed away and as soon as my leg touched the side of the pyramid, part of the wall folded inward behind me.

Galaxy and the others joined us and the former immediately went to work devouring the… "Hey, was that the mimic?" Cassia nodded and I frowned. "God, those things fucking suck. Acid blood?"

"Yeah, among other things." Arden heaved a sigh and poked the doorway that had folded in behind me. "This looks promising."

"Yeah, it's trapped as hell," Merlin muttered, looking between her legs at something on the floor. "That looks like some sort of activation rune?"

"Can Galaxy siphon the magic from it?" Cassia looked hopeful, but Merlin just frowned as he shook his head. "Why can't it be easy?"

The boy didn't look back as he explained sarcastically, "This was her *prison*, Cassia. This place was designed to make her magic fail, or to be so enticing to her it would make her useless and easy enough to put back into whatever kind of stasis they had her in."

Galaxy finished her meal and as soon as she looked toward him, she tilted her head and walked toward the doorway that he knelt in front of. "That looks so tasty."

"Get back into Marcus, Galaxy," Cassia muttered and put a hand on the smaller woman's chest. "We need to make sure it's safe."

"It's not active," Galaxy whispered, a green glint taking over her eyes. "It's just sitting there with all that mana coursing through it."

I looked at the others, then sighed, regretting what I was going to say immediately.

"Get in me, Galaxy."

It took us more than ten minutes to convince the goddess to take her place inside me so that we could at least try to experiment with the stairs.

Every time I took a step too close, Galaxy would try to spring out of me for a snack. Finally, Cassia had had enough and persuaded her to take a nap with a sleeper hold that made me proud.

"She's going to be mad at you when she wakes up." Arden crossed her arms and watched her drag the woman to me and I pulled her into myself with an immense effort of will.

Once I grew close enough, a sense of dread ran through me so strong that I stopped moving completely. I took a deeper breath and stepped forward and the sensation was gone so suddenly it was jarring and I had to stop again. "What the fuck is going on?"

Merlin frowned and scratched his head, looking to Arden. "Do you have any ideas? Because I'm stumped, and I haven't had the time to try to decode everything I've memorized since we got in here."

"I'd say something about her magic draws her to the trap, and something about his nullifies it and makes him want to stay away." Arden gestured to the rune that now glowed slightly in a shade of burgundy against the stone floor.

"Fuck this." Cassia snarled and turned to walk away, jumping over the side of the walkway toward the monolith.

"No!" I bellowed and started to follow her over, but Merlin and Amabala stopped me as Arden soared over the small wall like an Olympic diver plummeting toward water.

As they dropped, we watched in horror, but nothing happened. Finally, Cassia landed on the ground below with a crashing thud, then she stood up as if she hadn't just fallen for more than a hundred feet.

A gout of flame burst from Arden's feet as she completed

her flip thirty feet from the ground, slowing her to the point that the fall didn't do anything to her.

"See anything?" Amabala called curiously.

"Just more murals of sorts, symbols that make no sense and the corpses of the victims." Cassia bellowed back. "I think it's safe!"

I glanced at the others. "What do you think?"

Amabala just grabbed Merlin and asked, "Help a lady down?"

He snorted and jumped, his feet emitting a barrier of sorts that softened his landing as he carried her down to the bottom with him. I stood on top of the wall and looked down, ready to cast Embodiment of Lightning to just step onto the floor with them, but something grabbed me by my right ankle and whipped me into the air and toward the monolith.

CHAPTER TWENTY-ONE

Pain exploded across my back as I hit the stone.

"Marcus!"

It's here, Marcus. That's it! The panic rising in Galaxy's voice made the pain all that much more real and threw me into the place I went to kill people so fast that I should have had whiplash.

Or that could have been the contact with the obelisk. *Obelisk?*

The difference isn't fucking important, Marcus—it's coming!

"Commence the Hunt!" I roared, the shadows around us screaming to our bodies as Mako roared from beneath me as we hit the pillar behind us. Stone cracked and groaned as the massive drake pushed against the stone I'd hit with all his might and launched us toward the hulking creature that I assumed had thrown me.

It was massive, bone white, and almost blended in with the stone behind it, but the aura around it dripped red with hatred. I shouted to the others, "The rage radiation came from it!"

"We can see it too!" Merlin snarled and raised his staff at the beast, a bolt of blue zipping from it toward the creature.

It raised a hand and the bolt stopped, and so did Mako. Everything paused and started to run so slowly it looked like time had paused, or everything moved through molasses.

It looked directly at me and smiled, sharp teeth flashing in the dull light of the temple around us. "The traitor is here."

I realized that Mako was no longer moving forward at the same time and I just rolled my eyes. "I don't know who or what you are, but we're about to kick your ass, so let's just skip the bullshit."

The creature's smile widened to the point that it could have opened its mouth and shown less teeth. "You don't know what you are despite us trying to teach you? Very well. You will learn if you survive."

I stared for a second, taking it in. It could have been a damn killer croc knock off for all I cared, but the skin was smooth and not scaled. There was a tail, but there were no ridges on top, but there appeared to be something at the tip that flicked weirdly. The eyes were a sightless black that I could see, but it appeared to be looking at me fine.

"Then let's start the lesson, sister."

She blinked at me, frowning. "How could you tell?"

I blinked back and time returned to normal, the bolt shattering against her outstretched palm into a mixture of light and texture that fell away like glitter. Arden shot flames at her, then a rain of boiling water too, but when the stream was gone, so was the creature.

The voice echoed around the chamber. "So many champions, Garellia—you've been busy." Her growl after that was mainly to trip us up as we eyed the area for her, but found nothing. "Maybe I should take the fight somewhere where the playing field is more even? There's a whole city just a small flight away. I wonder how many of them have to die before I can coax you back into your *cage*."

"It crumbled." Galaxy stepped from my shadow in her elven form and stared at the black stone in the center of the temple. "Just like this is about to."

"No!" The creature appeared in the same spot that it had been in and dropped toward us as Galaxy punched the obelisk with all of her might and hissed as her skin smacked the stone without effect.

"Now!" Galaxy bellowed as Merlin and Cassia appeared next to her.

Merlin reached out with both hands and *slapped* them together as hard as he could while holding them, while Cassia swung her mace at the obelisk like a baseball bat.

The stone cracked and Mako surged from beneath me at the creature as Arden snatched me off his shoulders. The creature stopped her plummet with a pair of leathery wings that burst from her back, but didn't look to be able to fully extend them.

As the obelisk splintered loudly and began to fall, the creature's eyes narrowed and the world around her became distorted for just a fraction of a heartbeat, then she was no longer there, but to the left just far enough that the falling stone missed her entirely and her wings could spread fully.

"I had thought you still weakened. Apparently, I was wrong—I will not make this mistake a second time." She stared at us all, then her smile returned. "See you at the party."

I blinked and she was gone and suddenly I could breathe again. *When did I stop breathing?*

"About the same time she started to use *my* Dominion." Galaxy growled.

"He's what?" Arden asked as if she was confused.

She is. Dominions aren't common knowledge. Galaxy cleared her throat and blinked before turning back to the obelisk. The stone on the ground began to quiver and move toward larger pieces before it returned to the same shape that it had been and moved as if in reverse to stand as it had. "That thing has a part of my power in it. I want it."

"How do we get to it?" I asked and reached out to touch it. The second I did, it felt like my hand had come into contact with a live wire. I tried to pull my hand back but I was stuck to it.

Galaxy reached out and touched it and the pain ramped up to the point that it tore a single, long, ragged scream from my throat as the stone warmed to the point of burning now.

Hands on my back grasped and gripped, tugging and tearing to try to get me away from the mass of stone, but I wouldn't budge. I tried to use my mana to cool my hand but as soon as I tried to, it siphoned from me into the stone and runes burst into life along it in formations that made no sense to me.

Searing pain exploded in my palm that threatened to force me to cut the damned thing off at the wrist when whatever held me suddenly stopped and I flew backward into Arden, Cassia, Merlin, and Amabala, all of us landing in a heap.

"What the *fuck* was that?" I snarled and held my hand at the wrist. I turned it around and into my palm there was a section of flesh removed in a stylized pattern that resembled an X but there was something off about it. It wasn't *quite* one, it just looked like it. There was something else about it that I couldn't quite place. Other than that, my lycanthropic healing wasn't touching it, I wasn't sure what to make of it. "Cass, can you try to heal this?"

She reached up from beneath me and grasped my wrist, warm magic soothing the ache, but it didn't heal the mark.

Because that was what it looked like—a marking of sorts.

"Ha!" Galaxy's voice startled me. I looked up to find her standing near the obelisk with a massive grin on her face. "This was what kept me here, and I know that they have more of it now."

"More of what?" Merlin grunted. "Little help here? Marcus, you're heavy."

Arden growled, "And he's the only one who is, *right?*"

I heard the boy grunt and gasp as I shifted before he yelped, "Yup!"

I stood with Galaxy's help, and the others clambered up on their own as Galaxy sighed and looked at all of us. "They're using *my* power to make themselves stronger. They're using *my* Dominion to keep me contained."

"We haven't established what that is yet." Amabala lifted a finger then paused. "Wait, that's what gives gods their power?"

Galaxy nodded and the others did the same, as if she had just impressed all the information into their brains. *I did. We don't have time to waste on explanations. She's flying toward Cairo as we speak, and it's not going to be good.*

"So we can just teleport to Cairo, right?" Cassia scratched her neck and shifted uncomfortably. "And if she has your Dominion, how is it that you plan for us to fight her?"

"She has a part of it. There are bits of it scattered all over the world, and even some on other planets, and in Grestal." Galaxy's nose wrinkled in disgust. "They *stole it from me* and used it as the key to my prison cell."

I blinked and held up my aching hand. "And what is this?"

She stepped forward and frowned. "Familiar." She shook her head. "It makes my head hurt to stare at it too much. We can fight her now, because I stole part of my Dominion back. I'll be able to keep her in check with it while the rest of you keep Cairo safe."

"This got so much more complicated," Arden whispered to herself softly before shaking her head and grimacing as she set her shoulders and clenched her fists at her sides. "I swore I was all in, and after this, we can look for my family. Let's go kill this bitch."

We all looked to Amabala as she smiled. "Keep your hands and feet inside the ride at all times. One portal to Cairo, coming right up."

"We really need to make sure that we curtail your TV time," Cassia grumped at her playfully.

Amabala, confused, said, "But you were watching it too."

"It was a joke!" Cassia snorted as the cheetah woman grinned and shoved her through the portal with a war cry.

"What the hell is even going on anymore?" I rolled my eyes and stepped through after her.

To absolute chaos in the city.

Gremlins tore at the walls of the building we appeared next to, their high-pitched shrieking and wailing slamming into my eardrums as if it were a physical fist.

I guess it was a bad idea not to tell Serpath ahead of time. What the fuck is going on?

"It's an uprising," Arden whispered to herself just before the gremlins took note of us and shrieked together and lunged toward us.

CHAPTER TWENTY-TWO

The gremlins were on us in seconds, their furious cries of mindless rage keeping our attempts to get through to them by word at bay.

Their little fingers stung at our skin and their teeth bit at us as we fought to keep them away from us without hurting them.

"Just fucking kill them!" Cassia roared before grabbing one of the little creatures and shaking it violently, her breathing growing more ragged and her eyes glowing dangerously.

Cassia lunged at the gremlins and began to try to swat them like the flies they were acting like until Galaxy stepped through the portal with Amabala and touched her, clearing the oni of the red haze that I now noticed had swallowed the gremlins.

"She's controlling the queen and Serpath now, and they're using the gremlins to infect the supernatural creatures and humans of the city with the rage that she's filled her with." She looked at all of us. "I can make you immune to it, but you'll need to feed me quite a bit if you want this put to rights and for me to nullify her stolen Dominion."

"So we basically need to go on a rampage and kill anything

that comes at us." Merlin grimaced. "Doesn't that negate what we were sent here to do in the first place?"

"Only if we fail." I shook my head as all of our bonds opened wide and Galaxy's influence ran through them, clearing my head instantly. "The High Table here is already under siege. We need to stop the gremlins from tearing it apart, and stop the two halves from spreading their rage."

I looked at Galaxy. "If we can get you to them, do you think you can clear them of the rage?"

"I can try." She was noncommittal about it, but there was something else there that I was concerned about. I could feel her hunger. She was ravenous and it was eating at all of us. She turned her eyes to mine and the hunger was gone as suddenly as I had placed it. "I have a gift for you with me reclaiming some of my Dominion."

I frowned. "What's that?"

She stepped into my shadow and merged with me once more and suddenly I could see the health of the gremlins around us as well as something similar to a health bar for the rest of the Hunt.

That's not all, Marcus. Something about what happened to you when you touched my Dominion has resonated with you and now you can sense the bonds of those around you like this.

I blinked and my vision sharpened—now floating above the shoulder of the gremlins attacking Cassia and the others who helped fend them off was a small gauge similar to what the others had. Only these ones said **Mindless Hatred**.

The bond was tenuous at best, but with my higher charisma, I could actually interact with it. Touching it, I was presented with a notification.

Ability Unlocked:

Bond Thief – Using the bonds you have with others, friend or foe, will allow you to steal one ability, spell, or stat point from one given person at a time that you could not otherwise gain through your bond.

The stronger the bond, positive or negative, the better the bounty.

And it also had the ability to level up, up to ten times! Holy shit!

"There's no mana cooldown." I frowned and would have looked at it again to see if there was something I missed, but Arden yelling grabbed my attention.

"Maybe our fearless leader could quit powering up for sixty episodes and give us a fucking hand here?" Her voice grew loudest on the last three words as her hands spewed flames at the gremlins that tried to bowl her over, cutting them down only to be replaced by more.

"How many are there?" I bellowed over the screeches as I waded forward to assist them. "Galaxy, find the queen and her sister!"

They're inside the High Table, but the building is surrounded by magic, it will be impossible to get in.

"Can't you eat the magic?" Amabala called as she gored a gremlin on her claws and danced around the six that tried to jump down onto her.

This is High Table magic—if I try to eat it, there's no telling what will happen or how the Council will perceive it. She glowered at the magic and turned back to me. "Kill all of these creatures so that we can focus."

It wasn't necessarily an order, but a suggestion from the way she had said it, but the hunger had returned once more.

Merlin's arm raised with his staff in his right hand and the weapon came down and crashed into the ground next to his feet as his magical sword appeared in hand. Waves of rippling earthen energy whipped around him as the gremlins tried to press forward and found themselves stuck in the stone at their feet like it was quicksand.

Arden, Cassia, and I then immediately began a deadly round of whack-a-gremlin that Galaxy found delightful based on her throaty chuckles. I blinked and suddenly I knew what was going on.

Your hunger is driving us to kill like this. That's the portion of the Dominion you have. She blinked and stared at me for a second before looking down at herself. *You have to know that it's true.*

I... I think I do. Her lip quivered at the bottom, then she looked up at me. "Why am I so ashamed of that? My Dominion is a part of me."

"It's a facet, Galaxy." I stepped over a severed gremlin head to get to her and she choked back a sob. "You're learning something about yourself with this, and it's okay to be confused."

"We just need to bottle it up and use it for later," Cassia added, her bulky form sidling closer to us so that she could hold our girlfriend.

Galaxy looked up at me. "You mean it?" I nodded and Cassia grinned. "Bottle that shit up and shake it like a coke, baby. I know just whose face it should spray on."

"Phrasing!" Arden barked and I came back to myself as she peered around us. "This is messy enough, guys. We don't need your relationship coming in here and stealing into this just now. We have a couple of assholes we need to go rescue from rage and can't get in without a shit show of epic proportions, remember?"

I frowned. "Stealing?"

"Common phrase, Marcus." She raised a brow at me then threw her hands up. "There's a fight for a city going on right now—do *not* make me get the crayons!"

I rolled my eyes and pointed at her and Cassia before snarling, "I just figured out how to get inside the High Table, you flaming asshole. Call Kaz and Cornelius. I want to make them a deal."

———

Cassia, Arden, and Merlin had gone off together as a group to round up as many of the gremlins as they could for Galaxy to munch on, and keep as many civilians as they could safe from the internal invasion as possible, while I spoke to Kazmeer and her husband Cornelius.

"You serious about this, now, Marcus?" Cornelius raised an eyebrow at me while he stared at Galaxy. "Y'all want me, a certified Phone Gnome Technician, to turn coat and sneak into the High Table right here behind me? And for what? 'Cause, that's a contract I ain't fixin' to fuck up for my friends, ya hear?"

"It's not to do anything other than just open the doors for us, Corn." I scratched my head and pointed at the magical barrier. "Arden and Cassia swear there's nearly nowhere that you can't get into, and the city is about to get a whole new asshole if we don't get in there and stop what's going on."

He seemed even more reticent than before at that, but Kazmeer spoke up over the phone. "People are gonna die, baby. This ain't no shameful thing to be doin' for the good of a bunch o' folk, you know that near as I do."

He nodded. "I know, I know. It's just the sort of slippery slope that slops schlups right on into the shitter, hon."

"You're alliterating again, Corny," she chided him softly and he blushed angrily. "Since you won't ask for it, I will—Marcus, if we do this for you, we want into the Hunt. Exclusive rights to your needs for tech as far as we can muster, and a whole *shit ton* of pie and spaghetti. If you can promise us that, Cornelius will get into the High Table for you. We have a deal?"

I hadn't considered how far I would need to go for this at all, but how bad of a deal could it be if both Cassia and Arden were friends with them? "You want to be a part of the Hunt?"

My question was asked with a deeper tone than I meant it to and the small man just shrugged. "We don't have to be card-carryin' or nothin', now. Just let us help out. We believe in what the Hunt can do, and if good people like y'all seem to be are out here helping our folk, we want to be part of it. Even if it means unsavory deals and sneakin'."

Kaz added, "Yeah, that."

I grinned. "I can live with that. Welcome to the Hunt." I reached out and shook Cornelius' hand and the gnome grinned widely. "Don't put yourself in danger. Just get in, open the door and poof the hell out of there."

He nodded and closed his eyes as he reached out toward the barrier and the door through the magic, his hand gliding through as a ring I hadn't noticed on his hand sparkled and *shoved* the barrier aside.

"What's that ring doing?" Galaxy tilted her head as she held my phone.

"That's runic interference." Kaz sounded proud over the phone as she spoke. "Made it myself for occasions like this. We were going to use it to mess with old scaley ass himself, but this will be okay to test it on."

Once his hand was on the door, Cornelius poofed out of existence and disappeared, the barrier returning to what it had been a heartbeat before it dropped completely and the door swung outward while Cornelius swore and hobbled out with three gremlins attempting to bite and claw at him.

"I *hate* gremlins!" he roared, and pulled out a small pistol from beneath his vest, blasting one of them in the head, sending it to hell and the others skittering away from him. He held his pistol up as he pulled another from a holster on the other side of his hip, grinning. "But I *love* killin' varmints."

A tidal wave of shrieks greeted me as I roared and sprang into the room with Mako bursting from my forearm to roar at the creatures before him.

"Now *that's* a critter!" Cornelius howled before he started blasting into the crowd of gremlins scurrying toward us, his rounds catching and killing the creatures with an accuracy I could only call Texan based on his enjoyment of the scuffle.

"Marcus, get me close!" Galaxy called over the screeching din of the gremlins. I called Reaper into my hand from my ring and summoned the shadows with my will, mentally calling the power of the Huntsman to myself.

My sword swooshed through the air, lopping the gremlins in half and I almost felt bad for them because they were innocent, but I couldn't let them get to Galaxy. Their corpses disappeared into the shadows that spread across the ground from Galaxy and her hunger returned tenfold, making me swing Reaper faster and harder to kill everything in my path.

A man attempted to sprint for me, his face shifting and becoming almost like that of a jackal but there was no Dominion in him, so when my sword hit him, his arm flew into the air and my boot caught him in the chest. His body flew backward as his blood splattered the ground.

The gremlins around my feet stilled and began to lap the blood off the wooden floor rabidly, cleaning it away. I shook the sword away from me and blood splattered onto the floor moving away from me. I'd kill a gremlin and the blood spray would cause the others to pause and try to clean it up.

"Corn! Shoot the ones further away and make it messy!" He didn't even bother to acknowledge me, just firing off into the distance near the bar where some of the other enraged patrons turned from each other toward us. "Get out of here if you need to!"

"Boy, I got all this ammo and no range—this is *great!*" He whooped and hollered before he roared, "Can I get a yeehaw?"

Something in front of me burst through the wall with an ungodly shriek that almost sounded like what he was asking for, but he grunted, "That ain't right," then opened fire on the queen of the gremlins herself, with Serpath on her left shoulder, belted to her neck like an accessory.

The rounds only made her pause as she came forward, small welts showing where he hit, but it was me she came for. "Get out of my city, filth. Trash! This is *my* kingdom!"

Serpath stared on in a daze, but she didn't look happy. Something was wrong with her. The aura around her was heavily influenced by the rage, but it wasn't right.

None of it makes sense, Marcus, Galaxy chided me mentally before her voice turned icy. *Now, get me to them so I can stop all of this.*

I grit my teeth and took another step before noticing the

pitch-black lettering over Queen Umpta's shoulder opposite Serpath that read, **Seething Hatred** and got an idea.

I closed my eyes for a nanosecond and reached for the bond that her hatred of me had created and yanked using Bond Thief.

She blinked and shrieked long and loudly for a heartbeat, but as she did, I read about my bounty.

Gremmy-gorp – You have stolen the bond with the Gremlins from Queen Umpta and will retain it for thirty seconds.

"That short a time?" I yelped in surprise, the gremlins around me shaking off the rage that had coursed through them mere microseconds before. "Fuck, get Queen Umpta and hold her down!"

The gremlins who weren't cleaning the floor of blood turned toward her as one, her crying, "No! I am the Gorp! Me! You belong to meeeeee!"

That last word turned into a cry of worry from her as the gremlins surged over each other like a tidal wave of hands, oddly-shaped ears and eager-to-please servitude to hold her down long enough for Galaxy and I to get to her and her sister.

The elven goddess reached out and touched both of them on their heads and the red aura of rage surged into her as she slurped it up loudly like an extra-long spaghetti noodle.

Once they were free of the influence, Umpta tried to sit up, but couldn't without help, but as soon as Galaxy was finished, the ability I had stolen went away and the Gremlins helped their gorp to sit up at last. "What happened to me? Who are you?"

She looked down at herself and the area around her. "Why are we in this disgusting place?"

"You've been led astray by a creature who wants to destroy your city," Galaxy explained as she backed away from the two women. Serpath still didn't move. "Stand and prepare yourself and your people to defend your home."

"Who are you to issue orders to a queen?" Umpta huffed,

rolling her eyes as she tried to get to her feet with Serpath still attached to her. It took some doing.

I stepped into full view, still wearing the armor of my station and growled, "The patron goddess of the Wild Hunt, and your last line of defense against this creature. Obey."

Her eyes widened to the point that I thought she was going to attack us again, but she just nodded her head. "As the Huntsman and his goddess wish, so shall we serve."

I turned to find Cornelius standing there with his thumbs hooked through his belt loops as he watched. "Y'all got another varmint you're fixin' to go at?"

"A much bigger one, Corn." Galaxy grimaced, focusing as her eyes unfocused. "And she's nearing the city as we speak."

CHAPTER TWENTY-THREE

The gremlins had their orders and, with Merlin's help, the Wardens had assisted in a mass suggestion as to what was going on.

"The news reported on a massive sand storm that threatens the city!" one of the Wardens screamed from the truck that he rode down the street in. "Get indoors and close all your windows and blinds to help keep the sand out!"

When it looked like the suggestion wasn't holding, the gremlins would come in with handfuls of sand and throw it all around, sending the humans sprinting inside to wait out the coming storm.

The gremlins had also managed to destroy most of the internet with Cornelius and Kazmeer leading the way so that no one could access live feeds, cameras, or the net itself.

We would be fighting this creature on our own, and anyone who wasn't the Hunt would be a liability. We left the armor of our stations off for now, but I was ready to call it any time.

Queen Umpta and her slowly-recovering sister were livid that they couldn't do more, but they had no power over us other than having invited us here to stop this very thing from happening.

Merlin, Galaxy, Arden, Cassia, and Amabala stood with me as Mako paced up and down my skin in his tattoo form, impatient for the fight to commence despite us having enough time to set up a bit of a surprise for our coming guest.

"Are we ready to face this thing?" Cassia muttered, uncharacteristically worried as she thumped her metal mace on the ground to a rhythm only she could keep.

"Since when have we gone into a fight fully prepared?" Arden snorted and rolled her eyes. "We have treasure hunting to go do after this, since we need to kick this thing's ass and then go find one of my family members, I'm going to say that we had better fucking be."

Merlin grunted, "So inspiring."

Arden grinned. "I know."

A presence slid across my mind like a chill and I muttered, "Commence the Hunt."

Our armor covered our bodies and the strength of the Huntsman flooded me as Galaxy stepped into my shadow and the creature appeared, clearly annoyed.

"Bold of you to stand against me, traitor." She huffed and crossed her arms, staring at me specifically. "Do you honestly believe Garellia will be able to keep me from killing all of you?"

"I think you'll have a shitty time trying it, but if you want to fuck around and find out?" I held out my hands and roared, "Then bring your ass on down here!"

On the cue given, a single shot rang out as Galaxy's Dominion surged from her body to grab the creature in the air above us.

The shot clocked her in the forehead and dazed her for a second as the Hunt launched itself in unison into the sky at her, with spells slinging and rushing toward her.

She snarled, suddenly back to herself, and pulled something from thin air, breaking it. Her body went incorporeal for a moment, the spells washing through her with no effect, and she sneered. "You have no hope against me. But fine. Let us see how you do against this."

She sped down at us with a roar and slammed her ghostly body into mine, and I expected her to just slide through to go to the others. Instead, she was gone and I was too. I stared up at a darkened sun with light flooding a desecrated and barren void that felt so empty yet volatile at the same time.

"Welcome to the Null," the creature hissed at me with a grin in her tone before she appeared twenty feet in front of me, arms out to her side. "You told me to get my ass on down to you. Here you are, traitor."

I grimaced, taking stock of myself, now unarmored again. I could move, for sure, and I wasn't injured, so I had to find out what was going on and fast or this could get ugly. "You keep calling me that. Why?"

"It's what you are." She smiled her reptilian smile and stared at me. "We reached out to you at first, to try to help you attain your power as is right and return our prey to her place, but you scorned us and sided with her."

"I'm not whatever you are." My voice was angry and I felt the rage, but it was so much less than it was before. As if something here was forcing it to flee from me, and I could see the red haze surrounding her building. She was doing it.

"No, you are a lesser version of the Vorna, your bloodline polluted by centuries of intermingling with humanity." She sneered at me and waved her hand at the sky as whatever blocked the sun began to move. "Here she is, the first goddess, our Garellia. The one who opened the Null to the universe and began the end."

"What are you talking about?" I started to look for an opening to attack her and found nothing, even as a behemoth block began to move and form a woman in flowing robes who looked just like Galaxy in her elven form. She raised her arms and stretched, then looked at the blank canvas of the universe before her and clapped her hands three times.

Each clap reverberated along the entirety of my being and

as I watched her, I fell to my knees. The stars in the sky exploded into existence from her and along her skin, then the suns and everything else burst into existence.

"Never gets old, watching her will the universe into being because she was lonely." The Vorna chuckled from closer than she had been a moment before. I clambered to my feet but she didn't attack. "Your bloodline is Vorna. You may not look like me, but you *are* like me and the others. We hunted her for millennia untold and while she always sent us back to our home here in the Null, we never stopped escaping and hunting her."

"Why?"

She looked at me and shrugged. "It is our purpose. When she left the Null, she released us from our prison." She motioned to a figure with a large helm and a fleet of ships behind him, massive hands reaching into the stars. "Some ignored her and sought to remake the cosmos in their image by consuming world after world. Others like myself sought to contain her to keep her from remaking the universe. Others chase after her because the desire for power is great."

"She could do well remaking the universe," I offered calmly, remembering that she could siphon away my anger to feed herself with her sliver of Galaxy's Dominion.

"If she could, why did her oldest and strongest children rise up against her and imprison her on a planet with no intelligent life?" the Vorna countered, then paused and corrected herself. "With no intelligent life, *at the time*."

"What?"

"Which part confused you, lesser intelligent being?" She raised a ridged eyebrow.

I growled, and struggled to keep myself in check against her and spoke through gritted teeth. "What do you mean about her children rising up against her?"

"I don't know what happened." She seemed blasé about it now, waving her hand as if it didn't matter. "What I do know is that you have a choice to make. As a Vorna, you are drawn to power and it is drawn to you. Knowing what you are, you can awaken the Vorna blood within you and join us in keeping the gods and goddesses in check. Keeping the universe as it is until the end comes."

"How would that work?" I asked, trying to feign interest. "If I'm Vorna, how would I fight a god? The only reason that Garellia was contained by you is because she was weakened, right?"

She snorted and shook her head. "We took her from where she was and stole her Dominion, as all Vorna are capable of doing. We could devour the gods if we truly wanted to. It is why War was one of the most feared Vorna in this existence."

"*Was?*" I raised an eyebrow.

She looked uncomfortable and admitted, "He fell because he grew too complacent with his power."

I nodded as if I understood and asked, "So, how do I awaken this Dominion stealing blood?"

"You take some of mine." She lifted her forearm and made like she was going to slide a claw over it, then stopped. "*After* I can be certain you don't mean to betray me."

I frowned, how was I going to do that? Blinking, I shrugged as if it didn't matter to me. I was in a soul space of some kind, right? Like when I entered my body, or where Galaxy kept herself? I could use magic there. Could I use it here?

She stared at me and I grew a bit more uncomfortable under her scrutiny. Was she reading my mind?

I decided to try something that I had been meaning to try on Galaxy. *AHHHHHHHHHHHHHHHHHH!*

She didn't even blink.

Okay, not reading my mind. Cool. "How can you be sure I won't betray you?"

"I'll read your mind." She smiled and took a step toward me. "You will kneel on the ground and I will place my hands on your head and rifle through your memories and mind. Once I am certain that you can be trusted, I will give you my blood."

Fine. "Okay. You've convinced me." I took a step closer to her and knelt, saying, "If I can take revenge for the things she's done to me and the others because she's never been mortal, then so be it. Then I can take vengeance on the other gods for their persnickety natures."

She chuckled to herself and I put my head down, hoping she wasn't going to try to cut my head off, but if this was going to work for me, I needed to have a little 'faith' and let her believe I was earnest.

Her clawed feet appeared in my view and her clawed finger-tips dug into the side of my head. "Do not fight me, traitor, I will know if you mean to do anything. I will be reading your mind."

I tried to nod, but she dug her claws in a bit more, drawing pinpricks of blood. "Stay still."

"Okay." I stayed still and focused on the memories I wanted her to see. The invasions of privacy that had embarrassed me. The others. The times she was drunk on power and ordered us around.

She began to hum and her tail slapped the ground in time. As soon as she was deep into whatever memories she was in, I roared mentally like I had to see if she was reading my mind and stabbed upward with my right hand.

Fingers covered in Hoarfrost pierced her skin as I shoved her backward and stood.

She hissed and so did I, her clawed fingers bloody and dripping. I held my hand up and grinned. "Thanks for the donation."

"No!" She lurched forward as I licked my fingertips and the ice on it. The slushy blood tasted off, almost rancid as my tongue brushed against it, but it called to something within me that raced to the fore.

Ice slid up my arm as she brought her arm down toward mine and barely chipped it.

She was right. *I am Vorna…* I grinned. *But I'm also more.*

Her eyes widened as she screamed, "Submit or I will kill you."

"Try me." I smiled and whispered, "Commence the Hunt."

Even in this farce of a place that had begun to feel like home, the Mantle came to me at once by my call and covered me in my armor, my ice arm now wreathed in black shadow.

She tried to attack me again and I saw something that made me grin like a mad man. Over her shoulder, a bond had appeared that read, **Unadulterated Loathing.**

I thought about using Bond Thief, but instead, I called Reaper from my ring and readied myself for her onslaught. She radiated her red aura and her Dominion washed over us both, and I was laying on the ground, suddenly looking up at Cassia and Galaxy as they pushed against my chest and Cassia's mana assaulted me.

"Hey, what's going on?" I grumbled and Galaxy's eyes widened as she threw herself down on top of me without a care.

"She knocked you off Mako and we've been trying to revive you. Are you okay?" Cassia lifted me and Galaxy both physically off the ground so that she could be closer to me, and I grunted.

"Yeah, but where is she?"

"This isn't over, traitor!" the Vorna howled at me as she stood on the ground more than a dozen feet away, her fists clenched at her sides. "I'll find you and kill you myself. Then I'll take Garellia and put her back in her hole as we should have done together."

Cassia lifted her hand and another shot rang out, pegging her once more in the head as she started to fade, making her grimace and glare in the direction the shot had come from.

I shot a Bolt at her and she deflected it easily enough, so I cast Embodiment and threw myself at her from behind while she was still material and she fluttered out of the way, slamming her tail into my hips and stomach hard enough to launch me into the ground.

Concrete split and shattered under me, a couple of my ribs snapping from the impact. Cassia roared and another shot rang out, catching the Vorna in the shoulder as she moved to try to avoid the shot again.

Rather than meeting the pissed off oni head on, she faded from sight and the presence of her stolen Dominion faded as well.

"Ouch." I wheezed, finally able to relax a bit. Then the pain flared. "Ope, nope, don't relax."

"What the fuck happened to you?" Cassia floated into my now-swimming vision.

"Bones might be setting wrong, heal first," Galaxy ordered her and looked over me. "You did it again. You did things that I can't see in your memories."

"I'll tell you about it, don't worr—*fuck!*" Healing my ribs had been especially painful as Cassia had to lift me off the ground to get to the breaks in the back, the bone grinding along the fractures.

"Don't worry about it." Galaxy held up my book that Merlin had given me and tapped it. She opened it and began to read.

"You smell different, Marcus," Amabala growled at me, her eyes becoming slits. "More like that thing."

"There's a lot to chat about," I managed before hissing at the pain that still burned in my back, glad for the book. "Fuck, why does it hurt so badly?"

"Because a fall like that woulda killed a normal feller." A voice I had only heard on the phone made me chance a glance back at Kazmeer. "You took quite a spill, I reckon."

While her smile was comforting, she wasn't exactly what I was expecting with toting a big ass rifle like it was nothing. Her hair was middling-sized and cropped to the side a bit so that one side hung just a bit closer to her collar bone than the other. She wore simple clothes covered in a bit of dirt. They consisted of overalls along with a shirt that said, 'Give me pie, or give me death!' Her easy demeanor was charming. And this was who kept the ornery cowboy in check?

I grunted, chuckling to myself, then chanced a smile that

made me wince as I tried to look a little further back at her. "Ah, good shooting there, Tex."

She grinned, swinging her sniper rifle up and onto her shoulder. "Ya think?" Her grin only widened when Cornelius appeared next to her with an equally large smile on his face. "Fancies my shootin', Corn."

The other gnome snorted and rolled his eyes. "Have to be plumb dumb not to, you're a better shot'n me!" He laughed and it made me relax a bit as the pain in my ribs and back subsided some.

An ungodly screeching drew my attention, and a ball of black and white easily larger than Kazmeer reared up behind her, the beast opening its jaws wide with a feral widening of the eyes that *screamed* it was about to attack.

"Georgie, I swear to that there goddess, you tempt me one more time—I'll fix you but good, you trackin'?" She lifted her chin and stared straight up into the honey badger's face with a glare that would have made a drill instructor proud. "Try it. Your supper will go to the goats, you sack o' crap."

Cornelius fell on his ass with a howling laughter so loud that I worried it would attract an attack as the honey badger called Georgie made himself as small as possible to appease the tiny woman.

"Thanks for the contract, Hoss, but we better get." Kazmeer whistled and winked at her man as things began to get a bit more active with our surroundings. "Come on, Corn. We got Sketti and Pie to get ready for."

Both gnomes disappeared in a poof that made me jealous.

Wardens flooded the area and blue flashes of light kept anyone who could have been watching us from being too in the know as a group of them strolled up to us like they owned the place.

"They tend to think they do, Marcus." Galaxy snorted at me and I rolled my eyes. "Merlin, would you liaise for us?"

"Certainly." The chimera Warden stepped over to the others as Galaxy and Cassia helped me stand. Merlin began to try to explain things when one of them pushed straight past him and pointed a wand directly at my face.

Feeling better, I just stared at him as he issued his orders. "You will come with us and be interviewed, then you will be tried for negligence and, depending on our Ventricle's judgement, you will be leaving our city. Come—right now. Do *not* even think of doing any sort of magic. You let that thing escape and now we have to clean up *your* mess!"

"You're going to want to get that thing out of my face." I sighed and he just shoved it closer. So, I did what any self-respecting Marine with a weapon in his face would do.

My hand moved so fast that I barely registered my palm hitting the wand so my fingers could close around it as my left foot slid forward and I pivoted. Tugging his arm over my shoulder and thrusting my hip backward, I *flung* him away from me, but managed to retain his wand.

I looked at it, the solid piece of wood that it was and shrugged. "Mine now."

The other Wardens raised weapons of varying types and suddenly Serpath stood in between all of us. "By the authority of the High Table Council, I hereby place my protection on these people for the crisis that they *did* manage to avert."

"Our Ventricle—" The second eldest of the Wardens began, but when Serpath hit him with a level glare, he shut up.

She continued to stare at him for a moment before she spoke plainly and calmly, but with the threat of jobs lost in her tone. "Owes me a favor or twelve, and I will deal with Samuud if he so desires, but you will leave *my guests* alone."

He looked like he wanted to say something, but when Arden, Cassia, and I stepped closer to her, they acquiesced and bowed out, collecting their injured friend from the ground and dragging him away with them.

"Did you keep his wand?" Serpath stared at me with a raised eyebrow.

"Yup." I crossed my arms and stared at her. "Your other half under control?"

"She's... adjusting to her new abode as we speak." She sighed and put a hand to her forehead. "We need to talk about what you found. Everything. Come."

I looked at the others. *Do we trust her?*

Cassia shook her head, Galaxy passing along, *Not as far as we could throw her other half. But if it stops the deaths and saves the Table, we need to see what is going on. For now, at least. All else will have to come when it does.*

I nodded and we began to follow her to wherever it was that she was going to take us.

While we walked, I couldn't quite help the sinking feeling in my gut that told me that I needed to know where the other Vorna had gone. With her out there, doing whatever it was she was going to be doing, there was no way for me to know if we would be safe.

CHAPTER TWENTY-FOUR

We arrived at the High Table in Cairo only a short while later, the streets still quiet as the Warden Orders had been divvying out orders to have citizens wait in their homes until the 'attack' and damage could be assessed. They would have to actually make it look like there was an attack on the city of some sort and then assign blame.

Once we arrived, we went up a set of stairs that reminded me of the Columbus Branch. Looking at the hallway, it was almost exactly like it, with an eerie sense of déjà vu as well.

She opened the painted white door at the end of the hallway and the office was much more prim and proper than Uncle Yen's, but it was set up the exact same way as it was in his.

"I can see the recognition in your eyes." Serpath sighed as she sat at her desk and steepled her hands. "All of the High Table bars have their main offices set up this way as a means to assist in easy transition from one branch to another."

I frowned at that. "Transition?"

"Inter-branch travel," Cassia explained, then added as she nodded to the council woman, "The branches are all intertwined through the main tree. Having their offices set up this way makes it easier for those with access to travel from branch to branch to transition quickly. If we had access, we could have gone from Columbus to Cairo in a matter of minutes, but we don't have access and getting it is an act of council approval."

"And, unfortunately, few on the council are certain what to make of you as of right now to approve that level of mobility for the new Wild Hunt." She sighed once more and frowned to herself as she appeared to be in thought. "And now that I know what has happened under my very nose, I'm afraid I have no choice but to recuse myself of my leadership role and throw myself at the council's feet."

I was wondering if anyone else was going to say anything, but when no one did, I awkwardly cleared my throat and offered, "If you want, I can speak to the council on your behalf and let them know that it was an *actual* monster with a Dominion causing her to do this."

She nodded once. "I appreciate the offer, but I am just as complicit as she was due to our connection. I should have known that she was doing this with how needy she had been lately and with always feeling so full lately. I just chalked it up to her having stuffed herself as she always does, but not like this. Never like this."

She sniffed and tears began to fall down her face, but she bit her bottom lip and shook her head, refusing to cry in front of us. She waved her hand over the desk and a large suitcase appeared. "This is the payment that I promised. I will also write a letter of recommendation to the council on your behalf, stating that all of the damage was on me, and not on your negligence in any way, shape, or form."

I was about to say something when Merlin spoke up. "Did you know about the bugs that we found in our rooms?"

My eyes widened and Cassia actually grunted in surprise as the smaller woman looked at him in surprise and said, "The what?" She blinked and clarified, "There were bugs in your room? Does anyone eat them?"

He shook his head and said, "No. The listening devices that we found planted in the room after our arrival. Did you know anything about them?"

He made a small motion with his hands and suddenly Amabala paid more attention to the small woman on the other side of the desk.

She looked horrified, and anyone would have taken that shock as a sign of something, but she slammed her fist on the table. "How long?"

That shocked me, so I asked, "How long *what*?"

"How long into your stay did it take you to realize you were being watched? Who did you interact with?" She had a crazed look in her eyes as Merlin reached out a hand for her to take and she did, her eyes glazing over. She frowned and blinked, her eyes moving as if she were seeing things. "I *knew* it!"

"So it wasn't you?" Arden pressed and the gremlin-like woman just shook her head as she stormed around her desk and threw her fists into the air as if she were going to scream.

Then she did, long and loud, to the point where Amabala had to cover her ears to protect herself. "They were watching you! In *my* territory?" She seethed, her breath making her small chest heave violently. "The audacity. The *nerve*."

"The unmitigated gall?" Arden offered helpfully, only to be rewarded with a dour glare from all of us.

"Someone set you all up to take the fall somehow, or knew what was going on and they had you tapped and me as well, likely." Serpath stared around the room then grunted in disgust, lowering her voice to the point where it should have only been just audible enough for all of us as close as we were. "You cannot fully trust the council. While they have their uses, they have their own agendas as well. It would be best if, while in your position, you maintained a distance from them if possible."

"Can you tell us which ones are the worst?" Amabala asked hopefully.

Serpath turned her gaze to the cheetah woman and simply said, "All of them."

I closed my eyes and muttered, "Great." I growled to myself. *Does this mean that all of them are corrupt, or just self-serving and manipulative? Uncle Yen knew all this, and he tried to warn us. What did he have to deal with to give him this insight?*

"This does not mean that you cannot still continue to be of service to the various branches of the High Table, Marcus," Serpath scolded me softly. "It just means that you need to exercise a bit of restraint when working with the council."

As she said that last thing about it being a *bit* of restraint, she spread her hands as far as she could and raised her eyebrows suggestively. I cleared my throat to cover a soft chuckle at the memory of my drill instructors doing something similar to get our attention when something was truly important. "I see."

She grabbed the suitcase and held it out to us, staring me in the eyes. "For services rendered. They may say a lot about me, but I always repay my debts." I took the suitcase and she nodded once. "I'll have your letter of recommendation finished later today. As of this moment, you are no longer on loan to the High Table Cairo Branch. Oh, and before I forget…"

She looked at all of us and smiled. "I'm proud of all of you for coming back from Grestal stronger and without losing anyone. It takes serious strength and skill to manage that." She shook her head and sighed. "And without any outside intervention at that. You should all be extremely proud of yourselves."

I blinked. *Was she not who sent that guide to get us out of the city in Grestal?*

Galaxy's voice echoed through my head. *I don't believe she was. If that is the case, we have another mysterious benefactor and the plot thickens. Best not to say anything about it for now, everyone.*

Serpath stared at us all, a small smile stretching her already thin lips farther. "Humble, too. Good."

I took the suitcase from her and let it hang at my side for a moment before offering her my right hand to shake. She took it and I squeezed lightly as I said, "We don't know where that thing is. If she comes back, you call us or send some kind of alert however you can. Have a spotter looking out for if things get too weird to call us too. And I was serious about coming to testify for you if I can."

She nodded without a word and then finally let go of my hand and said, "Okay." She stood back from us, and pursed her lips. "I can protect you from the Wardens for a little while longer, but it may be better if you were to leave the area for a few years. Is there anything else you needed here? I assume you didn't stay in the quarters I paid for?"

I shook my head before answering her first question. "We left some of our things there so we could fool the watchers into thinking we would return, if you could collect them and send them back to us? We do have something to do, but it's outside the city. I assume you can offer us protection to the point where we leave the city limits?"

"You would assume correctly. Once you leave the city, my protection will wane, but I will take great pleasure in retrieving your effects for you." She frowned to herself and scratched her ears before grunting. "Watch yourselves in the sands. I can keep some from you, but the gods rule those sands out there, and they can be a bit fickle."

"We'll be careful," Arden replied easily, knowing we would be hunting down her family if we were staying in the area. "And we'll avoid any runaway gods if we can, as well."

I shrugged once and wondered if we might run into Anubis, or someone else. I mean, Odin himself had come to speak to me and had even clued us in about Dominions. Which had been fortuitous. But things weren't adding up to me about something.

"Serpath, the way your other half was taking apart the bodies is pretty... specific." She blinked at me and waited as I formed the rest of the thought before continuing. "Is there any rhyme or reason to that?"

"I thought that it had been her jealousy?" Arden frowned and turned from Serpath to me curiously. "Why bring this back up?"

"Because my former nurse, Kali, had been murdered in a way that was similar to this, but also different." I frowned and closed my eyes, trying to remember the way that it had been done to her. "Tongue and fingers taken. Defensive wounds…"

I scratched my head. "Sorry, it's not enough to add up. Not really."

"You said Kali?" Serpath asked curiously and turned around. "I knew someone called that. She had been here years and years ago. Give me a moment."

She waved her hand and a cabinet appeared beside her desk. "Cabinet, search, Kali-non-goddess."

The cabinet opened after a moment of us watching it in near silence, the clicking of the lock as it opened surprising us as a file slid out and into the woman's open palm.

She flipped it open. "She was then a private first class in the army, medic of sorts, and had been here for vacation. We tried to recruit her to our medical staff, but she had Normie family that she was concerned about."

My stomach may as well have had a permanent house in the bottom of that floor with how it dropped as she said that. She had been a supernatural creature. And she had been near me after I had found Galaxy.

I blinked and looked at Galaxy. "Did you know?"

She shook her head. "I was barely conscious at the time. I lived through you, Marcus. There was no way for me to know if you didn't. My concern at the time was gathering mana to recover."

"Do you think it could have been a creature like the one that came to Cairo hunting for Galaxy?" Merlin asked quietly, carefully broaching the subject.

"They're called Vorna, and there's really only one way for us to find out." They all looked at me and I sighed. "We need to go and take a look at her and the area." I turned to Arden and lowered my voice. "But we have somewhere to be."

It took us the better part of the rest of the day to get closer to the small blip on the map that signified where one of Arden's family members could be.

When we finally arrived, the sun was lowering in the sky and the sands under us were the same as so much of the rest of the desert that surrounded us. It looked like there was solid earth beneath it, but there was no real way to be completely certain until we touched down.

"There's nothing here." Arden sounded worried as she spoke, disappointed even.

Rocky burst from the thick bracelet on Merlin's forearm and began to sniff around the sand, kicking up dust as he went. After three minutes of watching the creature work, he stopped and sat at the edge of a dune and looked back at Merlin.

"He says there's something beneath the sand, but it's not stable." He frowned and looked at the fox for a heartbeat before saying, "It's like a house or something, but it's on the precipice of an underground cliff into a chasm. The only reason it hasn't fallen yet is because there's a layer of dense earth around this area."

"Can we get into it?" I asked softly and his frown deepened a bit.

"Not without risking the structural integrity of the ground keeping the sand out of the area." He scratched his head as the fox opened its jaws and a grinding sound like stones colliding emanated from it. "That makes sense, but it's going to be a lot more difficult than just doing it that way, Rock."

"What did he say?" Arden rushed over, a maddened light beginning to shimmer behind her eyes. "Can we get in there?"

"We can, but we'll have to work our way through the earth about a half a mile or so away and then walk to it from below." He scratched his head. "With what Serpath said about gods being out here, I just don't know if we have the extra power we may need to expend if we have to fight and what we need to get to this one right now."

She crossed her arms and pouted, before growling, "What,

the golem could feel something down there under the sand moving around? We went into a literal temple and fought a gremlin queen in the same *fucking day*, Merlin. We're right here, how can we not go down there right now?"

"Because we can't be sure that it's safe, Arden," I answered before the boy mage could open his mouth in retort. "Both for us, and for that place that could potentially hold one of your family members."

"He did sense things down there. Things made of earth," Merlin interjected as she went to round on me, her hair beginning to burn and rise from her chest and shoulders with her temper flaring. "Sure, we might be able to take them, but that's not saying that they couldn't just bring the roof down on all of us and send that house tumbling into the abyss."

Arden frowned and blinked at the boy, but he pressed on. "Arden, I understand wanting to have your family back at any cost, I do. I wish I could bring mine back. But I can't." He took a steadying breath and whispered, "I can't even remember their faces. I'm not going to let your family rot and waste away in those bottles. I'm going to find them with you, because I care."

"All of us do." Cassia grunted and stepped closer so that she could rest her hands on Merlin's shoulders.

"But we cannot go in there half-cocked and expect things to play out well." He pointed to me. "The only reason that Vorna didn't kill us when we first found it was because it had something out for Marcus and something against Galaxy. It was strong enough to. The second time, we got lucky having back up. This time? We go into the unknown with the cards stacked against us in a way that I can't see being limited by happenstance."

He ran his hands through his hair and sighed, realization setting in. "We go in there, there's too big a risk that the place will fall if a fight breaks out. I won't risk that. Not for you or anyone else here."

Arden's hair went inert as soon as he finished speaking, tears streaming down her cheeks as she muttered, "Thank you." She sniffed, shaking her head. "I'm sorry. I can't stand being so close but finding out that it's not possible."

"It's possible, we just have to do it *right*." I scratched my head and looked around. "Merlin, Cassia, is there a way that we can get all of this sand above the place moved out of the way? Like, clearing us a path to it or something?"

"We could, but it would take a long time." He cleared his throat. "Earth magic and sand aren't exactly the same."

"Wait, you can't just A-T-L-A that shit? Like Toph?" Arden raised an eyebrow.

"This isn't a cartoon, Arden." Merlin sighed.

Cassia grinned. "A *high-class* cartoon, Merlin, put some fucking respect on that." She shrugged and looked at Arden. "But no, it won't work like that. Sorry."

"Do we know anyone who can move a shit ton of sand out of the way?" I scratched my head as they all shrugged. "Is there some way we can bolster the crust under the sand? Make it thicker?"

Both Merlin and Cassia looked to be thinking it over, Rocky yipping in his stones-clashing style of communicating. Cassia finally grunted and said, "We could do it, but again—it would take a while. We would be here the majority of the night just doing the outer portion of it so that the center doesn't fall in, why?"

"I was going to say if it's strong enough, we cut a hole in the center to send one of us in." She shrugged as if that was a viable route, but spoke no further on it. "So either way, it's time intensive."

It was irritating to think of the various scenarios and options available and unavailable to us. Either it was go in guns blazing and see if the earth creatures below would cause the ceiling to collapse just to kill us, or try to make sure that the crust below the sand was strong and stable enough to send me in. Or hell, even Arden herself.

"Can you send Rocky in so that he can send you a clear mental picture of it? Do you have the ability to do that?"

Amabala asked finally. Merlin frowned and when he was about to speak, she clarified, "If you can do that, Galaxy can show it to me from you and I can use that to maybe make a portal?"

"Then that means that we would be without the ability to get out of here swiftly." I grunted and shook my head. "Our mobility is what will keep us safe."

"Marcus, have you forgotten what the Huntsman can do already?" Galaxy raised an eyebrow and suddenly the bonds between all of my friends and myself flared to life.

I grinned. "Then never mind me, I'll just go with the good plan."

Amabala grinned broader than I had ever seen her grin go and we started to plan.

CHAPTER TWENTY-FIVE

Focus, Marcus, Galaxy coached me for the sixth time in as many attempts. *Feel the bond between the two of you and dive through it. All you need is the spark of portal magic from her and you'll be set.*

I mentally rolled my eyes, eliciting a physical flick to the back of my head from Cassia that made me want to snarl several creative curses at all of them.

This had been so much easier with the others because their power was so much more readily believable. Tearing a hole through the fabric of reality to deposit matter taken from one place to another was so alien that it may as well have had acidic blood and a tongue with teeth.

That was… creative. Galaxy sighed inside my head.

I delved into my bond with Amabala and reached as far as I possibly could to see if I could glean anything from her. She was right *there*! So close that I could reach out and touch her face with my fingertips as she focused on opening herself to me so that I could borrow her power.

Once again, as soon as my mind touched hers, the alien nature of the power evaded my grasp. I growled and narrowed my gaze as I roared, *"Fuck!"*

A hand rested on my wrist softly as Amabala gripped me and ordered me gently, "Calm down." She turned to Galaxy. "Can you take some of *my* memories and show them to Marcus so that he can understand what my power feels like?"

Galaxy blinked at her, then looked to me. "If the two consent to it, I can do that." *Is that better, to ask both parties first?*

"Sure." I huffed and nodded quickly. Amabala ducked her head once and closed her eyes as Galaxy stepped into me and did what was expected.

Suddenly, I was Amabala, but somehow also not. Warm in the radiant plains of Grestal near the portal that the Matron had left us all by. Our litter mates bullied us, so we went closer to the portal that the Keeper guarded, watching the haziness of it building slowly and dissipating only to reform as someone stepped through.

It was a wizard of some kind, and their staff glowed amber as flames rolled forward and sliced through the man that guarded the portal to the Eastern Plains, and we couldn't keep our surprise from making us squeak before covering our mouth.

The mage looked our way and sprang forward toward my hiding spot only to be distracted by someone else coming through the portal. Each entrance, there was a soft fluctuation that you might feel when the bass of your car rumbles, or haptic feedback from something.

Memories sang through me again and we watched in rapt horror as the mage hoisted one of our siblings into the air and she burst into flames.

The other children were able to hide and keep quiet long enough for the warriors from Malarna that had been stationed near the area to watch over us arrived and attacked.

The other children blamed us, the runt, for giving them away and beat us mercilessly to the point where we almost never returned to the city unless directly ordered. We found more portals than the others ever could have, and it was easier for us to feel them.

All the times that we had been near them, they were plainly visible.

The first time we opened a portal to assist our new friends had been so exhilarating. There wasn't the *tearing* that most would associate with making a portal. The nuance of what we did was creating a path. From one plane where we existed, to the next where we could exist.

I slammed back into myself and suddenly felt like I had as much insight into all of this that I could have ever needed, but I couldn't help staring at Amabala as she bashfully watched me.

"You think you can manage it?" she whispered and looked away before glancing back to see that I was still staring at her.

Rather than just saying what I thought, I reached out and pulled her into a hug and muttered, "That wasn't on you."

She snorted. "I gave up beating myself over that long ago." She was lying. I could feel how she felt in the memory. She had nightmares about that moment. About the beatings the other children had given her. Hiding from them as they hunted *her* in the plains to exact revenge for their lost litter mate.

I pulled back and punched her shoulder softly, grunting. "Just because someone else dished out the beatings doesn't mean that you didn't sit there and take it because you thought you earned it." She stared at me a moment longer before looking away.

"I think we managed to get enough of a visual from Rocky to try this, are we good?" Merlin cleared his throat to get my attention and said, "You ready to try?"

I nodded and, with Galaxy helping, Rocky's vision of the area below the ground below us in several different shades of brown and orange.

"That's how he sees?" Merlin nodded at me and I looked to Amabala. "Is that sufficient for this?"

"I think so." She shrugged and looked uncomfortable. "I've never tried it this way. I would be cautious of doing it myself anyway."

I nodded at that, understanding how she would feel about it.

I reached out to her through our bond and this time it was vastly different. I could feel the ability she had and grasped it, pulling it through the bond into myself.

Portal Creation – Build a bridge through space and time to another place that you, the caster, have been, or have seen. Half Mana.

It takes half your mana? I looked over at Amabala. "It takes half your mana to make a portal every time?"

She nodded, then frowned as she opened her status screen, and her eyes flew open wide. "I've unlocked a new portion of my spell tree for portals!"

"What is it?" Cassia and Arden blurted in unison as they bum rushed her to try to see her screen.

Arden was the one who read the notification out loud after Amabala shared it with her. "Blip, caster can use this spell to instantly transport anywhere within one hundred feet. And the mana cost is super low for how much mana she has!"

"Oooooh." Cass grinned and prodded the cheetah woman with her finger. "Do it real fast. Come on."

As soon as she went to press her finger into the woman's chest again, Amabala just appeared right behind her and kicked her in the rump, making the rest of us laugh as Cassia whirled on her wildly. "We got our rogue!"

"She's so the rogue," Arden agreed with a grin, then turned to me. "Time is wasting, Marcus. You do this for me like you said you would, I may knock off a few things I'd ask you to do for me in order to discuss financing with that accountant for you."

"I planned to anyway, but I'm not going to say no to that." I grinned and focused on the image that I had Galaxy place in my mind before building my portal.

Amabala perked up and looked down, her eyes wide. "I can feel it." I would have laughed, but instead the others filed through with me following behind.

There was no light in here until Arden lifted her hand and flame began to build in the air over us like a miniature sun in a ring of water. "No heat, that way there's no eating the oxygen in here." She smiled at me. "I remembered this from the testing grounds for the Mantle."

I nodded and the light cast over the area was enough to see what was in front of us.

The house was... simple, and I was about to voice as much when Cassia beat me to it. "Are we sure this is where the bottle is?"

"The map says it's here." I shrugged and thought on it a moment longer. "Unless it's actually in the abyss over there."

"Let's not put that into the universe, shall we?" Arden gasped and lifted her hand into the air. "Something just moved over there."

True enough, a lumbering, wobbling creature of sand and mud lurched out of the darkness into the light and Cassia smacked it so hard that the explosion of earthen materials covered her and even some of us.

"Hell of a swing there, Sandy Sosa," I growled at her playfully.

"You go in and get it, Marcus," Arden commanded and tilted her head toward the darkness. "We can keep these things busy while you're in there."

I rolled my eyes. "Why don't *you* go do it, Arden, and I'll take your place?"

"Jinn can't touch the bottled, Marcus," she shot back with a hiss. "If we do, we can be sucked into the bottle and end up enslaved ourselves."

"That means I'm out too." Merlin shrugged apologetically.

"I want to fight," Cassia growled as I looked to her.

I didn't have a problem going into the place, it was just annoying being the one to do everything.

"I'll go." Amabala smiled at me. "I'm light and fast."

"And also a prime target for anyone who wants to fuck us over." I grunted, stepping forward and taking her wrist in my hand. "Let's both go."

Galaxy stayed where she was with me in my mana sea and

watched as we both marched forward. The sound of shuffling sandy feet drew the others' attention and we had to focus on getting in and out as swiftly as possible.

The simple home was so austere and without adornment that I wondered if maybe this had been a servant's quarters or something. Looking around, I muttered to myself, "There's no way it could be here. No one would have access to wishes and still live in a place like this. There's no fucking way."

Wisp flared in my hand and cast light around the room as I scanned. Finally finding something that shimmered in the light. It looked like one of those cartoon lamps and honestly, I worried about touching it, but grabbed it anyway. The dust that cleared from it as I picked it up revealed a small skeletal hand still clasped on it that turned into dust as the support fell away.

We returned to the others who were busy fending off the earthen creatures when Amabala called, "We got it, let's go!"

They turned toward us as one of the creatures let loose a rumbling scream and threw itself forward. Amabala had the portal open as Cassia and the others sprinted through it, me jumping through after them as sand began to cascade down toward us.

The portal closed with about two to three hundred pounds of sand washing over our feet in a wave that sent me and Amabala crashing into the others with a "Woah!"

Cassia stood firm, but Merlin and Arden both ended up on their backsides with us, sand pouring out of their clothes. I glanced up and around, finding that we stood in a familiar alleyway beside the High Table Columbus Branch just between the bar itself and the gym where we all worked out.

"This is going to take me *forever* to clean out of my fur!" Amabala whined as she looked down at herself in defeat.

"The bottle?" Arden's tone was worried, but she spoke in a way I hadn't heard in some time.

I lifted it and the light hit it, shimmering slightly with a silvery sheen as I moved it to where she could see it. "You want to let it out here, or do I have to make a wish first?"

"No wishes!" Arden bellowed, then blinked and looked to be taking control of herself. "Wishes shorten our lifespans."

I opened my mouth, then stopped and stared at her, recalling how badly she had taken me making wishes before when we had fought that other jinn. Finally, she said, "Yes, that was part of why I was trying so hard to stop you—you were inadvertently killing him and putting yourself in danger."

"Oh." I frowned and stared at the lamp in my hand. "So then how do we get them out of the bottle?"

"We can drain the magic from the bottle," Merlin proposed with a hand on his chin. He grimaced then spit out some sand.

"No, the magic that makes the bottle impervious to destruction belongs to the jinn inside." Arden frowned and stood up. "The only way I know to free her is to make a wish, but the amount of lifespan it takes is... different for each jinn. If she's been used a lot, there's a chance that she could be on her last legs."

"How do you know that the jinn *is* female?" I raised an eyebrow at her as I looked at the lamp in my hand.

"The shape of the bottle and the material." She pointed at it, the curves of the bottle from the handle to the spout and silver filigree with golden inlays. "Male jinn are put into more masculine looking lamps while this one is more feminine."

I shrugged and blinked at that, but she was the expert here. "So, what do we do, just wait to free her until we know for sure what's going on?"

Arden stared at the lamp in my hand and the battle within her raged. "There is nowhere perfectly safe for her to reside in there without being in danger or within easy reach of someone who could make wishes. We should just... risk it."

"Okay." I took a deep breath, then asked, "How do I avoid hurting her, or myself, for that matter?"

"The complexity and desire behind the wish is what will drain the lifespan the most." Arden sighed and closed her eyes, eyebrows knitting together as she fought to try to recall something. "Open-ended interpretations are how jinn will capitalize on a wish to kill you and gain their freedom."

"Like wishing for a mountain of gold and they conjure it above you so that it lands on you and crushes you to death?" Cassia offered helpfully.

"Or when you say, 'I want a million bucks,' and they summon a herd of enraged and confused deer to trample you to death," Merlin added excitedly.

I blinked and threw up my empty left hand in exasperation. "Great! So now I have a grammar Nazi and a rules lawyer to compete with. Anything else I should know?"

"That you don't have to be the one to make the wish?" Cassia held her hand out to me and flexed her fingers expectantly. "Give me the lamp, Marcus."

I pulled it into myself as she stepped closer, almost as if I didn't want her to take it. I didn't. It was my responsibility to lead and to make sure that the risks were on my shoulders. She would be putting herself at risk. I loved her. I couldn't allow that.

"Marcus." She spoke softly as she looked me in the eyes. "This is the one time—*the only time*—I do not want you to fight me." She closed her eyes and muttered, "Allow me to help my best friend for being honest with me before. I owe her this."

I put the lamp into her hand and grunted, "Okay," before stepping back and leaning up against the wall in the alleyway. "But should we take this somewhere a little less out in the open?"

Cassia looked to Arden who nodded, then led us into the gym area. Those inside working out stopped and stared at us as we traipsed sand onto the nice flooring and sighed. Keith's voice came from the back of the room, teasing, "Hey, did you leave some at the beach? How come we weren't invited?"

Merlin turned and flipped him off and several of the shifters guffawed as Keith howled, "Awww! Come on, little buddy, it ain't so bad to shuffle the sand off. Someone bury your nerdy ass?"

Cassia snorted and Merlin rolled his eyes muttering, "Fuck that guy," venomously under his breath.

I just chuckled and rolled my eyes as we ended up in one of the sparring rooms off the hall behind the gym floor. As we stood around waiting, Arden wrung her hands and watched her oni best friend.

Cass took a deep breath and released it as she rubbed the lamp with her free hand.

Heat filled the room swiftly, followed by a cloying scent of cinnamon and rhubarb pie. I blinked and asked Galaxy, *Is everyone else getting the sensory overload?*

Yes, they are. But no one else smells rhubarb pie. Why are you so weird?

I grumbled and watched as a half-formed woman appeared in front of Cassia, her hair a flaming mirror of Arden's, but instead of being long and flowing like water, it was short and spiked, almost like a campfire as it rose from her head.

Her features were a lot like Arden's as well, though she floated on a ghost-like tail of amber energy.

"Hello, Master." She bowed at her waist before popping up and glancing around the room. Arden stood behind her and sniffed, but the new jinn just ignored her in favor of her new master. "Your three wishes are my command. Tell me, what is your heart's deepest yearning?"

Cassia stared at the woman for a moment, apparently taking too long, because she started to open her mouth to speak to her, but Cass just held a hand up to silence her.

This drew a hardness to the jinn's gaze as she leaned back and waited, careful not to show any more disdain than she already was.

After about three minutes of awkward silence and Arden staring stricken at her sibling some seven feet from her, Cassia spoke with absolute authority and confidence, "My heart desires your freedom to be with your sister and reunited with your still-living family, with no ill intent toward you, me, those I care for, or the property we stand in and near—I wish you your freedom."

The captive jinn sneered and bowed at the waist. "As you wish, Master."

Heat rose in the room once more and my body temperature rose with it. *Something is wrong. She's cooking this room, but the wood and everything else remains untouched. Marcus, you have to do something. Cool the others with your bond.*

I didn't have time to think about what she had said and threw all of our bonds wide open and cast Hoarfrost along them, my body cooling swiftly to something a little more manageable.

I blinked and suddenly she stood there in front of me with her eyes locked on mine. "That's no fair."

"Jara—no!" Arden roared as her sister's fist slammed into the side of my head and sent me careening into the wall hard enough to fracture the wood and several of my ribs along with it.

I blinked as I tried to get back to my feet and the others prepared to pounce on her, the chains that appeared around her throat, wrists and hips flaring to visibility before shattering into millions of pieces and the heat died down enough that my fading spell left us all colder than we had been.

"What the hell is your problem?" Arden snarled as she grabbed her sister's arm and whipped her around. "Cassia's wish was damn near perfect!"

Jara's disdainful expression changed to one of outrage. "Damn near isn't good enough, is it, *Ardent Flame?*" The now-free jinn grabbed her sister by the throat, the last words from her mouth a taunt. "Do you honestly think I'm going to be caught being bottled again when I just got free simply because someone is wearing my sister's face?"

She whipped her arm back, clearly about to launch Arden into the wall too when Cassia appeared in front of her in her Yang form, her eyes flaring. "You need to cool off."

Jara froze where she was and a ghastly sigh squeezed from

her throat as she began to pale from her eyes outward and her whole body turned to stone.

"What the *fuck*, Cassia?" Arden whispered as the larger woman yanked her from her petrifying sister's grasp. Jara stood there in the same pose that she had been on, her right arm cocked back to throw her sister and her face a look of horror.

Cassia blinked and shut her eyes, blood dribbling from the corners of her gaze as she hissed in pain. "She was going to attack you, all of us. I couldn't let that happen, but I couldn't hurt her either. So I turned her to stone with my gaze."

"Where the hell was that when we were fighting the Vorna?" I growled half-heartedly, Merlin helping me stand as my ribs knit back together. Damn, always the ribs lately.

"The range is limited and I have to have them looking me directly in the eyes when I use it so I don't accidentally get any of you with it." She hissed again and rubbed her eyes with the butt of her hands. "Galaxy, why isn't it going back to normal?"

Galaxy stepped out of my shadow in her elven form and touched the sides of her head, whispering, "Don't open your eyes. I'm checking." Galaxy closed her eyes and grunted, biting her lip. "That's no good."

"What?" Cassia growled back.

"I hope you have a damn nice pair of shades, because they're... not going to return to normal for a while."

Arden gasped. "What the hell is that supposed to mean?"

Galaxy took a deep breath and held her hands out as if to calm the other women down while she explained, "Kind of like Marcus and his healing and allergy to silver is a lycanthrope thing, right?" We all nodded, so she waved her hand to Cass as if presenting something. "The party now has someone whose ability is that of a basilisk. So since she used the ability, the ability changed her like Marcus' healing and allergy gave him the scent of a shifter. Now, her eyes are like that of a basilisk."

"*How could you have not known that was going to happen?*" Cassia snarled and took a swipe at the woman, her right hand lashing out only to hit the air as Galaxy stepped aside.

"I warned you all that it was like a lottery of sorts." She sighed and held up her hands as all of us began to speak—shout—at her at once. "I can cure it!"

"Then why don't you?" Amabala asked softly, hers the only voice that hadn't been raised.

"Because doing so would eat into my Dominion, and with the Vorna out there waiting to strike, can we really afford for me not to be able to challenge her while it recovers?" She didn't look thrilled about it either, if I knew her well enough at all. As she turned back to Cassia, she spoke aloud, "Yes, it means that you won't be able to look anyone in the eyes. But we know someone who might be able to help us keep you safe enough to be around other people, and I mean to contact him personally."

"He's dangerous, Galaxy," Merlin warned. "He might hide behind half-truths and say that he won't hurt us if we stay out of his way, but the second we become a threat, he will end us."

"You speak of Zeke?" Cassia frowned and moved her face toward Merlin, the boy mage flinching as if she had flagged him with a loaded weapon.

"Yes," Merlin answered simply. "We should try to get Obrin to do it instead."

"We can try Obrin, but getting to him and back would take Amabala and you out of the picture for a time and that's time we could be spending doing other things." Galaxy stared at the boy for a moment, then acquiesced. "Very well, gather what supplies you think you will need and go to him. If you have a way to contact him without venturing into Grestal, then I would suggest that you do so in order to save yourself the trip."

Merlin ducked his head once and turned to the cheetah woman. "Come on, Amabala. Let's get this."

"Get what?" Amabala turned to leave with him, confusion washing over her face as she looked around. "What is there to get?"

I almost laughed at her missing the point of it all, but there was just nothing right about it as I watched Arden stare at her best friend in shocked worry, then glance even more worriedly at her petrified sister.

"We can put her somewhere safe, Arden," I offered her softly. "Whatever we have to do. Then we can turn her back and get her some help in dealing with what she's been through. I'm sure there's a reason that she attacked us all, and it's probably a good one."

"She was never all that nice to begin with, but I would have thought that being freed and reminded that she had living family to be with would have been enough to at least keep her in our good graces." Arden reached out and stroked her sister's stone cheek tenderly, then pulled her hand as if the woman would come to life and bite her. "Or us in hers."

"Don't let that get to you, Arden." Cassia grunted and flopped onto the ground with her hands over her eyes once more. "We have no idea what she was forced to make into reality. Better to keep her safe for now, then get her the antidote as soon as we can focus on her getting back to normal."

"Is there a back to normal for someone like this though?" I asked gently, not wanting to seem like I was contradicting myself purposely. My ribs still ached even though they were actively healing and making me hungrier.

Arden shrugged, then her shoulders fell. "There was a time when I was freed from my lamp that I had a real... bad run in with the world of Normies, and it wasn't what a lot of people would consider normal. You remember the plagues in Egypt?"

I blinked. "Was that you?"

She shook her head. "No. I plagued a small village in the outskirts of a country that no longer exists *because* of me. I rained blood down on them, literal fire storms for a while. Burned their crops. Killed livestock. I was angry, bitter, and more than a little pissed off."

Cassia snorted. "A little? I seem to recall you telling me about the time you lassoed a man you caught doing the deed in his neighbor's barn by the junk and paraded him through town before setting fire to him."

"That was just because he wasn't a good person, but I digress." She turned her gaze back to me. "The point is, we're all a little enraged when released, but this was different. She attacked even with the wish in effect. I don't know why the magic let her go even then."

That bothered me too, but it was Galaxy who answered. "She harbored no ill intent toward anyone in the room or the place." She stretched a bit then stared up at the taller statue of a woman. "She must have thought she was doing us a favor by trying to kill all of us. Like we were beneath her. She did mention something about being bottled again, though. Which I find curious."

"Sometimes a jinn will be inadvertently freed by a wish or a trick and someone else nearby will recapture them and bottle them," Arden explained. "She also said that they had used my face, I wonder what that could have meant."

"Probably an illusion." Cassia grunted and rubbed her eyes before slapping the sides of her head like she was trying to wake herself up, then sighing with relief as her healing energy filtered into her head. "That's a little better. Can someone get me some thick material or something to put over my eyes? Keeping them closed takes way more focus than I thought it would."

"Yeah, let me go see if Kenshi has anything you can borrow." Arden stilled and then muttered, "I'll break the news to him. I know how much he hates it when people hide their eyes from him."

She nodded as the jinn left Cass, Galaxy, and I behind. I awkwardly asked, "You okay? Is there anything I can do to help you?"

"Look me in the eye and tell me it will be okay?" She raised an eyebrow at me suggestively and I had to laugh. "No, I made a decision and I'm paying for it. Too bad it's not one I can turn off and on like I wanted."

"We'll get it sorted out. And we'll make sure to take care of you in the meantime too." Arden came back in as I finished speaking with Kenshi in tow, the worried-looking oni springing around the jinn in front of him to get to his sister a little faster.

"Sissy Cass, what happened?" Kenshi, the normally unshakeable oni hell fighter who cut me to shreds in our training with the blade, sounded genuinely shaken up.

"I'm okay, Bubba Kenshi, just some magic gone awry—nothing I can't fix eventually." She sighed as he ran his fingers and palms over her face like he was checking for wounds. "I really wish I could show you that I'm rolling my eyes right now, Kenshi."

"Do not sulk," Kenshi growled at her and continued his check before finally nodding to himself, letting his hands drop. "I bring blindfold."

"It better not be the one that smells like feet." Cassia snarled and started to open her eyes, my hand flying in front of her face to stop her looking at her brother.

"Not feet, incense." Kenshi grunted and presented a deep gray cloth to her, then paused and realized she couldn't see it. He grunted again and grasped her hand, placing the cloth there and said, "Helps focus."

"Smells more like feet than it usually fucking does." Cassia groaned as she tied it around her eyes.

CHAPTER TWENTY-SIX

Merlin and Amabala were gone, trying to find a way to reach Obrin. This was nearly impossible, so they had to make the trip to see him in Grestal with more than six two-liter bottles of pop and even some chips to sweeten any deal that he might offer them on top of actually taking currency he would respect.

That left the rest of us to our own devices back at the Table. In an effort to distract herself, Arden took the money that we hadn't bothered to count from Serpath to talk to our potential investor-slash-loan officer for the lair.

Are you seriously going to call it a 'lair,' Marcus? Galaxy groaned in my head as she played video games upstairs. *I'm researching, you know that.*

I snorted. *It's fine to want to relax and unwind after all that, Galaxy. Get it in now, though, because we're leaving to go to Maryland in the morning to investigate Kali's death.*

She groaned and cut off our communication so that she could focus on her game and I decided that I wanted to blow off some steam at the bar and maybe get a drink or six, besides being hungry to beat the band.

Finding out that I was something more than just a vanilla

human even before having found Galaxy was... weird. And now it was affecting Connell too. I had tried to get ahold of them, but Luca and Aeslyn's phones just went to voicemail and there was no response via email either.

The bartender on shift, a nice young lady named Milith'ra, poured me a shot. "You look like you need it."

I chuckled and nodded my head. "Rough few days, and they're not over yet either."

She laughed. "Know how that goes. You wanna order something special?"

"A Golden Dragon, Mili." Lucifer's voice drifted over my shoulder as he sat next to me. "Hello again, Marcus. How are you?"

I grinned. "Luce! How's it going, man? I'm... alive."

He grinned back boyishly with his nearly gaunt features delighted for some reason. "I can say that I am mighty glad that's the case." He held out a hand as if to shake mine. "I've been meaning to reach out and thank you."

I blinked at him, genuinely confused. "Thank me?"

"Yes, see, you saved Maze, my new puppy." He pulled out his phone and showed me a photo of one of the demon dog puppies laying on a large red pillow on a massive bed. "I love her so much."

"Oh, so you took one of them?" I smiled as he showed me a video of the tiny thing sneezing and setting his duvet on fire. "Oh!"

"Isn't she precious?" the man gushed and looked over to Mili. "Have you seen Maze, Mili?"

The bartender laughed. "You showed her to me yesterday! But I bet she's still cute as Hell."

Lucifer snorted. "Look at her dad, of course she is."

Mili brought over the drink and set it on the table before me with a flourish. It was a pale golden colored drink in a cocktail glass and it smelled deeply of oranges. "Oh, this smells great."

"Before you try that, would you like anything to eat?"

My mouth literally started dripping saliva as I thought

about the burgers the cook would make for me. "Yes, get the cook to make me a special combo please."

She winked as she replied, "Sure thing, but try the drink now, and tell me what you think."

I picked it up and took a sip, the flavors all biting at me at once, heavy alcohol content in this one. Mili saw me pause to process and explained the drink. "Two parts Galliano, Triple Sec, and orange juice, with one part Baileys Irish Cream rather than fresh cream. So, what would normally be called a Golden Dream thus becomes a Golden Dragon with the extra bite of more booze."

"Excellently explained, Mili." Luce tapped the bar where his card was, and where she produced a large glass of what looked like sweet tea. "Oh, you bad girl, giving me this."

"What is it?"

He chuckled and took a sip. "A simple pleasure, Mili's Tea." He sighed and waggled his eyebrows. "Won't tell anyone what's in it, and she only makes it for a select few patrons and I just so happen to be one."

"You're one of two, Luci." Mili snorted and rolled her eyes. "And it's only because I'm madly in love with you."

He preened a bit. "I know."

We drank and talked about some of the things that had been happening, but I kept the details of events in Cairo vague to protect him from the Vorna. I didn't know if he had any kind of Dominion, but I'd sooner keep him safe as a friend. My food soon came and was it ever as good as I could expect. We kept talking while I ate even as Lucifer declined food of his own. His loss, if you asked me.

After a bit, I begged to be excused, a little tipsier than I wanted to be despite the wonderful burger and beer batter fries, but overall in a much better mood. I returned to my room to find Cassia and Galaxy still gaming. "Any word?"

"Arden returned about two hours ago and said that he didn't want to talk stocks for once, but his exposing her to cryptocurrency has awakened her ire and she wants to punch you in the junk." I rolled my eyes at her as she snickered that last phrase.

"Sounds like Arden. Any actual news?"

"With the three million dollars we earned from Serpath, it would go a long way toward paying for something adequate for our needs." She paused her game and glanced my way. "How are you feeling?"

"Fine, why?"

"You don't *feel* fine." She frowned at me and stepped closer. "I know that you're concerned for everyone, especially Cassia, but the High Table is strong enough to resist those who would seek us out and we will be growing stronger still for it."

A noncommittal shrug from me quieted her. *It's not just the Table and everyone else I'm worried about. I'm also worried about me and Connell. What does this Vorna blood mean for us? I mean, he's telling me his magic is consuming things and sometimes he benefits. That sounds like your magic, right? Not Vorna.*

She answered out loud, Cassia pausing her game to listen in as well. "The Vorna are different from each other as well. None of them are the exact same. It is concerning that he can see screens at times, though, and I have no power over him. It makes me wonder if the Vorna have access to the same source of power I do."

"Do you know what that source is?" Cassia asked hopefully, excitement lacing her voice. "Have some of your memories returned?"

Galaxy narrowed her eyes in thought. "Somewhat? Hearing the name 'Vorna' brought back memories and emotions that I was concerned about at first, but with everything that she told you, Marcus, I've been able to piece together that they are a sort of counterbalance to me, it seems."

"All power has to have an equal and opposite force to contend with?" Cassia raised an eyebrow. "I thought that was bullshit."

"It may not be so at the cosmic level." Galaxy grinned

widely. "I *did* spawn the known and unknown universe, after all."

"Brag much?" I grunted and threw a pillow her way. It hit her in the chest and she tossed it back. "So the Vorna are your opposite. How is it that I could be your host if that's the case? My blood should have been anathema to you."

"It should have, but it wasn't." Galaxy shrugged and scratched her chin before snapping her fingers. "It may well have been your blood that made you a viable host in the first place. I can't believe I didn't consider that."

"Can you access my power as a Vorna?" She blinked in surprise, eyebrows rising as she stared at me. "I take that as a no?"

"Take it as an I wasn't sure." She frowned and began to pace in front of me, Cassia looking around, then remembering what was going on with her eyes just before glancing my way. "Your blood and power could be the reason that you can steal the abilities of your enemies or those with a strong enough bond to you."

"You really think that could be it?" I asked, hopeful.

She nodded and grinned. "If you meet that Vorna again, you might be able to steal her piece of my Dominion from her."

"Should he?" Cassia's voice was tinged with worry. Galaxy and I both looked her way and she must have worried when no one answered. "Can't see—use your words."

"Oh." I grunted and said, "Sorry. Can you explain that thought?"

"He's technically mortal, right? Even with Vorna blood in his veins, his body might not be able to contain the power of a Dominion, right?"

"That… isn't an entirely wrong thought, Cassia. Thank you for bringing that to light for me to dwell on." Galaxy stepped closer to the larger woman and smiled as she rested a hand on her shoulder. "You are very smart for someone who only thinks about fighting and fighting."

Cassia grinned, then nearly shouted, "Hey!"

We all laughed together as Galaxy leaned down and kissed her on the forehead. We had to get some rest for the flight we had to catch in the morning.

———

I woke up in the morning to a knock on the door, Galaxy laying on my side since Cassia didn't feel comfortable sleeping with us until she had something to keep her eyes covered so she didn't accidentally end up turning one of us into stone.

Galaxy yowled petulantly as she opened her eyes and muttered, "She's not here, Merlin!"

"I've already visited her and she's getting ready—our flight will be leaving soon. We need to go." He smacked the door twice and woke me up fully. "The flight will be first class, and I've already checked us in online. We can teleport there if we need to."

"We'll be ready in ten." I grunted and stood up, dragging clothes on as Galaxy laid there disappointed. I looked back at her and raised a brow. "You going to sleep in me?"

She growled, "Yes. I'm... tired."

That gave me pause. "Are you okay?"

She shrugged. "I feel alright, but I don't feel like myself."

"Is it having a fraction of your Dominion and knowing that there is more out there?"

"I hadn't thought about that." She sighed, then said, "It may well be."

"We'll get it back, so now that we know?" I turned toward her and pulled her toward me to give her a kiss. One that I felt that she needed. Exploring her mouth the way I deserved. We had been through so much lately, and I hadn't had the time to truly show her that I appreciated her and all she did for us.

Her hands found their way onto my back and her fingertips dug into the muscles there as she mentally told me, *I do what I can because I care. But with my Dominion returned to me, I could do even more still.*

I knew that. But I kissed her more. Now *I* needed this.

She finished our kiss and moved back, eyes half-lidded, and muttered, "Cass deserves this too. She and I both will need a good scrap soon."

From the hallway, I heard Arden bellow, "Come on!"

"She's just upset that she's not getting any." I grinned, then yelled back, "Go say hi to Masonai."

"Oh, I will!" She swore some more and finally huffed, "Let's go!"

I grinned and watched as Galaxy's clothes melted away, leaving her bare as she laid back on the bed, then she grinned back as her fresh clothes appeared on her body.

"Let's get to the airport then." She smiled and stood, her elven form melting away to her beautiful human form. "Before I send them and have us wait here."

I snorted at that and we were out the door and down the stairs in record time. Cassia greeted us with a rather nice pair of Oakleys. "Holbrooks." Cassia smiled. "Obrin broke my other pair trying to enchant them, but Merlin said that I have a way to send him items and requests now, so we should be okay."

"Wait, we what?" I rumbled at her and stared at Merlin.

"We made a box that will transport items back and forth." Merlin yawned, then smiled proudly. "Took a little bit and it was expensive for him, but we can send him a retainer fee for him to keep us at the front of any projects that he might have."

"So how big is the box?" Cassia frowned at him.

"Find out later, we have a flight to catch!" Arden snarled and pointed to a bleary-eyed Amabala. "You gonna be able to get us there?"

"I was there this morning and snuck in, let's just get to it." Amabala held her hands up and pulled them apart, pulling through space and opening the portal for us all to shamble through before doing so herself. Then she frowned. "This isn't right."

We were in the airport, certainly. But we were in a bathroom stall, the door open and a woman staring at us in shocked horror. Merlin held up his hands and his fingers wove through a spell just before a muted blue flash popped in front of her gaze. "We had the wrong bathroom and we're super sorry about that. Damn, silly Canadians."

He walked off as she scowled at us and let us through, Arden asking, "What the hell was that about?"

"She had a button on her bag about staying in Canada." He shrugged, and offered her a small smirk. "Figured she hated Canadians or something. It's really early and I haven't slept in a day or two."

"You can sleep on the flight." Cassia growled and put a hand on his shoulder protectively. "Then we will introduce you to an energy drink."

"Oh Christ." I wheezed as the oni shuffled him off and Arden began to try to talk her out of it all because of how much he and Galaxy enjoyed pop.

"I swear it's laced with magic or something." Galaxy smiled as she pulled a bottle out of her small bag and took a sip that made her smile. "Every time I take a drink, it's like I get a surge of mana."

"That would be the sugar." I grunted and shook my head.

She nodded with a soft smile and followed us to our gate. There wasn't a terrible wait ahead of us and it was easier just to wait.

"Why are we flying like Normies again?" Cassia wondered from behind her gaming magazine.

"Because flying massive distances like over states and the world takes a large amount of power that we can't afford to use right now with the Vorna out there doing who knows what." Galaxy's gaze flicked toward her and she nodded once. "This way we minimize our footprint and hide. You all haven't noticed the drain it puts on you to fly large distances yet because you just haven't yet, but it's there. My newly found memories tell me so."

"Makes sense." Merlin yawned and asked, "What if she has a way to track us?"

"What if grasshoppers had machine guns?" I grunted and his eyes shot open so that he could look at me and I shrugged. "You're worrying about something that doesn't make sense to worry about right now. We have a way to fight her, we just have to do it."

"It doesn't make sense to worry about the humans on this plane?" Amabala wondered for a moment, staring carefully forward as she spoke.

"I never said that." I grunted, then glanced over at her as she continued to stare ahead. "If it comes to a fight, we have it and can eliminate her before she becomes a true threat."

"At the expense of the lives here," Galaxy added, stepping closer to Amabala to put a hand on her shoulder. "She has a point, Marcus."

"There's not much we can do other than potentially save as many as we can if something like that were to happen anyway." Cassia frowned as she looked at all of the people bustling around us. "Can't be too careful for Normies."

I grunted at that, suddenly wondering why it seemed like I was the bad guy for knowing we could manage her, and decided to just keep my trap shut.

It's because it's not truly like you, Marcus. Galaxy was suddenly inside me and staring at me from across my mana sea. *Are you okay?*

I thought about it. Genuinely reflected on everything that we had been through in the last couple weeks. In the last year, I had been nearly killed, injured in an ambush that almost killed me *again*, was forced to leave the only life I had known to come to a place I barely knew with my nearly-estranged uncle to work in his bar. And all of that after intense physical therapy with a woman who was now dead.

In the last two weeks alone, I had learned that my son was half Fae, monsters, myths, and legends existed and thrived, and magic was absolutely real. I had found and fought the thing that killed my brothers and sisters in that temple after becoming the mythic Huntsman, met my son for the first time, and had made friends with the *literal* devil.

And through all of it, I had forged bonds with important people. But even more importantly, I was tired. Maybe I needed some rest.

I think you do as well. Galaxy suddenly stood in front of me and hugged me. *I think we all do.*

I opened my eyes and Cassia stood there grinning at me. "You can join us in Japan in a few months."

My eyebrows shot up. "I can?"

"He can?" Arden almost fell over as Cassia regarded her with an odd expression. "You've been looking forward to this trip for more than a year, Cass. It's all you talked about before, and you were so happy it was the two of us. Are you *sure* you want him coming?"

She nodded and offered me her hand. "Yeah, I'm sure." She grinned. "He needs to meet my sister and mother anyway. And we could all use a little break, don't you think?"

"I do." Merlin yawned again and stood up. "I need to move. Amabala, come with me to the bathroom?"

"Sure." She stood and looked down at me where I sat to wait for the plane. "I wasn't challenging you, just making sure you were thinking of everything."

I smiled at her and held up a hand. "I'm not mad. Just need time to really get myself back to normal."

She nodded and walked off with Merlin, leaving the rest of us to wait on the plane together.

CHAPTER TWENTY-SEVEN

"I mean, I'm glad that we were able to get the first class seats, but did they have to be this close together?" Arden harrumphed again as the plane taxied down the tarmac toward the runway.

"Not everyone is seventy-five percent leg like you, Arden." Cassia snickered as the jinn woman gasped at her from across the aisle and swatted at her half-heartedly. "Just relax and enjoy it."

Arden rolled her eyes and began to swipe through the screen on the seat in front of her so that she could find something to watch.

I stared out the window as the world around us moved. Flying in planes had always been one of the things I had loved. Watching the take off had been the most fun thing when I was a kid and would go on vacations with the family. Maybe I should give my mom a text or a call some time?

We hadn't really spoken much since she had found out about Connell—not that I'd tried to hide it or anything. She was just the prim and proper sort when it came to children and a parent's place and duty to their children. She hadn't believed me that I had wanted to be there for him and that I had done nothing wrong to drive Aeslyn away.

Maybe she would have forgiven me by now.

Deciding to do it when we landed, or maybe even later on after we got home, I watched our flight take off and let the gentle noise of the aircraft and the noise around me lull me to sleep.

"Marcus!" Galaxy shouted and I woke to her struggling with the Vorna in the middle of the aisle as people screamed all around us. The plane was still flying and the way she struggled was not gentle.

I tried to stand and get to her but my seatbelt wouldn't let me move.

Something shoved me and I lashed out with my arm and caught something, cracking knuckles, and blinked. That made no sense.

As I blinked again, I opened my eyes and found Cass staring at me with her hand wrapped around mine. "Marcus?" She stared at me some more from behind her glasses, making it impossible to see her basilisk eyes. "Do you need to fight?"

I cleared my throat and shook my head, my mouth suddenly drier than the sands of the desert that we had been in not just a day ago. "No. What happened?"

"You slept through the flight and now we've got to get off the plane." She watched me for a moment, then lowered her voice. "What happened?"

"I had a dream about the Vorna attacking and having Galaxy."

I am okay, but I do not remember seeing this dream. Are you okay?

I'm fine. A breath of air rushed from me as I stood and got off the plane with the others just as the hair on the back of my neck stood on end and a thrill flew down my body.

My eyes flicked from one corner and side of my vision to the other as I cast my gaze around as quickly and frantically as I could. Something was wrong.

A Dominion, but this one isn't mine. Some god is nearby, and it's hurt.

"Galaxy, lead us to it," I ordered and my shadow lengthened until Galaxy flew from my legs as a raven, fluttering out of the doorway to my left and onto the tarmac and toward the flight line.

We followed her out and onto the concrete below, me shouting, "Merlin, take care of the memories?"

"Got a limited number of times I can do this without more components, so we need to figure it out sooner rather than later." He sprinted forward into the controlled chaos that was the mess of planes and began his spell as people shouted at us to return to our aircraft.

"Commence the Hunt!" I spoke with feeling as Mako burst from my shadow and surged skyward, the blue flash behind us painting the sky even though it was the day and the wind whipping around my ears acted as a barrier for Merlin's forced explanation of the happenings here.

"How far out is it, Galaxy?"

Not far, flying. We will need to get there quickly because whatever this thing is, it's losing. She flapped on and finally said, *Badly.*

We flew for maybe five to ten minutes as fast as we could until Galaxy hissed, *We're here! And the Vorna is as well.*

I lowered my gaze toward the park we flew over and the scene was grizzly. A massive beast tore into the Vorna with the trees acting as a screen for it, but the Vorna didn't look too put out.

Honestly, it looked like it was having fun.

"Behind us!" Amabala shouted and a screech pierced the air. I whipped around in my saddle of shadow to find yet *another* Vorna almost identical to the one below save for the massive curled horns that came out of the sides of its head. The longer I watched, the more it focused on closing in on the cheetah woman as she rode in her armor from the Hunt.

Galaxy, watch out for the others and listen for my signal. I'm going to jump on that thing because it doesn't know me, yet.

Be safe, was all she said back.

I snorted and tugged on the bonds between myself and Cassia, praying I was gathering some of her strength as I leaped from Mako's back and toward Amabala.

She happened to notice me just as I was within a few feet and a cloud of smoke burst from her as she moved to the side several feet with her new ability. The Vorna's clawed arm slid through the smoke and nothingness a heartbeat before I entered the cloud of smoke and slammed into its upper body.

He clawed and spat, because I somehow knew it was a male Vorna, but I was already jamming my foot into his hip and wrapping my right leg around him to stab at him with my oni belt knife. The first time I'd really had a chance to use it, but with it being right there and easier to keep a grip with, I had a better time with it than with my sword.

That same sort of heat-like sway began to build over his skin as I stabbed and worked the blade, my mental shout to Galaxy as I stabbed again getting her attention.

She and I both activated Bond Thief as she blocked his Dominion with the sliver of her own, and my knife bit deeper into his collarbone as he continued to manually fight me off.

His fingers dug into my wrists and he pushed with all he had as his wings flapped and fluttered in the air behind him. "Traitor!"

"Fuck you!" I snarled back, letting go with my left hand to slap the back of my right as hard as I could to drive the weapon back into him while my ability tried to find a purchase inside him. Blood splattered outward as he shoved the knife away again and some of the warmth flecked my cheek and lips as I grit my teeth and tried to push back using Physical Buff. Thankfully, it gave me the strength I needed to nick the artery on the side of his neck, a small fountain of blood catching me in the neck and cheek.

Something clicked and slid into me and I grinned.

Slivered Dominion obtained – effect unknown, owner—

I didn't have the time to read the rest as the bastard shrieked in my ear and tried to bite me, driving forward into a dive toward the fight below.

Let him go, Marcus. You need to make sure that you can at least fall away from that fight.

Nope! I grimaced and stabbed once more. *I've got a plan, just keep the other one from using her Dominion.*

I could feel her nod as she focused her attention on the Vorna attempting to bite into the god that it appeared to be fighting against.

We were closer now, and I could tell that something was going on in my opponent's mind because he just tried to attack me and hold me closer, like he wanted to smear me on the ground and attack me with his pal.

Not going to happen, big'un. I slid my belt knife along his armpit and used that brief flare of pain as an out to kick him away from me and toward his friend as hard as I could while casting Embodiment. I used the spell to appear between the fighting Vorna and the god while summoning Reaper from my ring. "Now, Galaxy!"

Galaxy's Dominion and my stolen one meshed and kept the female Vorna glued to the ground as her friend slammed into her and shoved her forward onto my blade.

I was so sure of my victory that her tail slamming into my shoulder and tossing me away from both of them while leaving Reaper in her surprised the hell out of me. I smashed through the first tree and the second caught me in a way that really torqued my back, but the Mantle managed to keep the majority of the damage from kicking my ass too badly.

I growled and climbed back onto my feet so that I could stomp back toward her and my weapon. She pulled the blade from her hip and the wound closed slowly, but her partner fell to the ground with a gaping hole in his chest and blood seeping from multiple wounds and the light in his eyes draining away.

"You'll pay for that." She snarled and lunged toward me as I did the same toward her.

I waited until she was about six feet from me before I pulled my Silvaero and unloaded mana-covered rounds into her, the rounds still just pinging off her chest and hips as she came forward with my sword in her upraised fist.

Cassia and Arden landed on her with cries of fury, Galaxy still pressing on the Vorna with her Dominion to keep the Vorna from using it.

My stolen sliver of Dominion that you reclaimed is mine now, but if she kills that god, she's going to be able to claim his whole one. We need to protect it!

"Amabala, Merlin—get that god out of here." They looked torn at the prospect of leaving us to fight on our own so I bellowed, "Now!"

The Vorna's eyes opened wider as she realized her prey might escape, so she roared and flung Cass aside so hard that she took out two trees. Arden had to keep whipping her with a water and flame-style cord of elemental power to keep her away from the other two as they tried to help the god out of the fight.

The Vorna spat as the flaming whip slashed her cheek and grabbed the water one, tugging on it as she set her footing and flung Arden into the air like she was a fish on a line.

She let go of the magical weapon and turned toward her prey, only to get a round to the back of her fucking dome. I had my rifle out and started to sling even more mana through it, hoping that I could distract her enough to make it harder for her to focus on Merlin and Amabala. If they could get the god out of here, then we had better odds of beating her with her power dampened.

She ignored the bolt-like round that I had fired at her and kept walking as Cassia and Arden returned to try to even the odds, Mako jumping down in front of her to try to keep her bogged down, but even without her actual magic, she was stronger than she had been before.

"Someone is coming!" Amabala screamed as she fell to her knees, her hands flying to her head as she curled into a ball. "Portal! Portal!"

A doorway of sorts opened and power roiled through it.

The growing, familiar feeling of a Dominion in use raged across the area as a new figure I didn't recognize walked through. It was covered head to toe in massive armor and looked more beast than man, almost like that of the god laying nearly unconscious on the ground in front of it.

The figure stared at the scene in front of it and a thrill ran down my spine as the slits that could have been for its eyes turned our direction. Even the Vorna stalled in its steps as the figure strode confidently forward and grabbed the god on the ground, turning to walk away, a thick but stubby tail covered in armor swaying behind it.

"No!" The Vorna snarled and bolted forward, shouting, "That's my prey!"

The figure let go of the god and turned, lifting a hand almost lazily to grab their attacker out of the air and slammed her into the ground so hard that it created a crater that she lay in, twitching and stunned.

The figure grabbed the god once again and walked back into the doorway that had opened without so much as another glance back in our direction, then it closed and the presence was absolutely gone.

Get her before she gets back up, guys—go go go! I roared through Galaxy, the figure still making me a little jittery. I shook my head as she gave me a mental shrug and found myself reaching for Reaper on the ground, using the shadows to call it back to my hand by some form of an accidental miracle.

I was running low on mana with all the mana I'd used to try to shoot her, but I had more than enough to cast Arcane Infusion, wreathing the blade in ice and Hoarfrost at the same time. The others watched the area that whatever that had been disappeared into in shock, unmoving.

The Vorna lay on her back, still staring up at the sky in shock, her wings broken as they bent under her back at odd angles and her weird tail lay limp in the crater. She didn't even look at me until my icy sword stabbed all the way through her heart and Galaxy burst from my shadow to devour the other corpse.

She coughed, blood welling into her mouth and gurgling from the wound as she wheezed, "Traitor. We will find you. More will come." She took a deep rattling breath as her hand clasped my ankle. Her voice broke into my mind. *More will come now that she has some of her Dominion. We won't stop until we kill you all.*

My nose wrinkled as I growled and twisted my sword in her chest, lowering my voice so that only she would hear it. "They can come and damn-well try. I'll kill them all."

My sword lifted and this time I stabbed with every ounce of my strength into her throat and chin, splitting her head in half with it.

Galaxy joined me and ate her, then sat on the ground in a sort of meditative state, leaving me to check on the others.

Arden sported some broken ribs while Cassia shared the same in addition to a broken femur, but other than that, they were well enough. Amabala had stayed curled in the ball that she had made on the ground and it was so hard to just get her to talk. She had nothing more to say to any of us and no matter how much we pressed, we couldn't get her to talk at all, or unclench.

Merlin just stood there near her with a confused and concerned look on his face, but when I had finished trying to talk to her for now, he stared at me and said, "Who could that have been?"

I shook my head. "No clue, but whoever they were, they had a Dominion, so they must be a god, right?"

"Or another Vorna?" Galaxy asked as she opened her eyes where she sat. "I have three slivers of my Dominion back and I feel more... whole than I have in quite some time."

"I can imagine." I grunted and motioned down at Amabala. "Can you help?"

Galaxy nodded and closed her eyes. Amabala started to

rock back and forth before slowly unclenching herself. She relaxed to the point that she had passed out and began to snore softly. When she was no longer in any jeopardy in my mind, I spoke softly as Galaxy stared at me weirdly. "What was that all about?"

"She felt the fabrics of reality, space, and time bend and shift in ways that terrified her to her core," she explained, turning her now-unnerving gaze to the sleeping woman at our feet. "It was so powerful and sudden that it took her to the first time that she had witnessed death and kept her there. It wasn't hard to get her back and put up a safeguard, but that was… intense, to say the least."

Cassia growled, "Anyone else feel like we got cheated out of the final boss fight?" Arden nodded and Merlin just stood there silently staring at the ground. "What's wrong?"

"They just grabbed her and slammed her into the ground so hard that it broke her, and were able to take a literal god through a portal that scared a Keeper so badly she began to babble and freak the fuck out." Merlin ran shaky hands through his hair and let go of a shaken breath. "What—who—was that?"

"Someone we don't want to fuck with yet." Arden harrumphed, then looked at Cassia and me. "I feel like that could well have been a cutscene into a later boss fight that we are *horrendously* under leveled for."

"Speaking of levels." Galaxy snapped her fingers and we now had two very nice new levels to mull over how to spend. "I would recommend hunting more Vorna if we want to keep beings like that out of our business. They are *very* experience rich, and after all the fighting earlier, gave you more than a full level together."

She looked at me again and this time when she spoke, there was nothing nice about it. "Kali was murdered by that Vorna, the male, because he was looking for me. She had my scent on her because I was siphoning mana from the area and that meant her too, even if I didn't know that she was a real thing yet."

She looked down and muttered, "I'm so sorry, Marcus."

I looked down, angry that I hadn't been able to really make the bastard suffer for doing that to the woman that had helped me relearn how to take a step longer than a damned shuffle.

The thought alone was enough to make me want to scream and rage, but Galaxy was right. We needed to hunt more and get stronger. But we couldn't do that safely just yet.

"How do we break the news to my sergeant major?" My voice was soft as I spoke, but I looked up and stared into everyone's faces. "He's expecting some kind of conspiracy, and I have nothing to give him."

"We can make him think it was actually an animal," Merlin offered helpfully. "We can go and do it ourselves, or I can reach out to the military Wardens and let them know to wipe his memories of the attack and say that her death was a tragic animal attack and the animal was killed."

"Wait, the military has Wardens?" I raised a brow at him and he nodded. "Where? How?"

"They were added in as a rank." He shrugged. "Their title is even in their name. Chief Warden Officers? I know you all call them 'warrant' officers, but it's just a way to blend in. Don't you ever wonder why all of them are usually badasses in their fields? It's not purely because they're just the best, it's magical."

"God damn it." I cursed again under my breath for not knowing more. "We're going to all sit down and go over this shit so that I'm not constantly surprised about this stuff. It's a little grating."

"Oh, the crayon eater decided to use a big boy word, do we have cookies?" Arden chuckled as I leveled a murderous glare in her direction. "Too soon?"

I lowered my chin once and she nodded in return, muttering, "Sorry."

"Let's make that happen, Merlin, and see if they can do it,

or at least set it up so that I can. I'll go and mourn as I can and then from there we can head home. We should likely check in on Serpath and what's happened with the High Table Council too."

CHAPTER TWENTY-EIGHT

Sergeant Major Espinoza didn't take the news that Kali's death had been ruled an animal attack well, but knowing the beast that had done it was dead and buried went a long way toward quelling the rage within him.

We sat at the enlisted bar on base, the sound of bowlers behind us fading as he spoke to me at the end of the bar over his fifth beer. "Brandt knows what's going on, and now I do too." He looked at me, his eyes still puffy from what he called a fight, but I knew that the news had fucked with him and he'd cried. Couldn't blame him. "There were orders from on high to go and investigate that place, but when pressed about it, no one seems to know where or who they came from exactly. There's only so much that I can dig without raising any more suspicion, and now there are people who won't even look my way because they know I'm hunting something down. Shit ain't right, devil."

"No, it's not," I added and ordered another beer to add to my own growing pile. This wasn't really doing it for me, but it was on his tab and I wasn't going to take advantage. Not the kind of thing I'd do. Not to him. "But we can still keep digging until we figure it out. I guess I've got some contacts I didn't know about, and leads that I could work too. I'll keep you in the know if I can. We should both continue to lay low for a while longer. You get orders to anywhere else?"

He shook his head, "They want me to retire, but I'll be the next goddamn Archibald Henderson before I let that happen. I need to know what happened to our men. I'm not going to let them put me out to the farm just yet."

That made me snort. "I can't imagine a tough sonofabitch like you getting tossed out."

He grinned wolfishly. "They don't have the fuckin' balls, Bola." He took another drink then slapped his money down on the table. "Got PT in the morning, gotta keep the privates sweaty and tired." He raised an eyebrow at me that elicited a guffaw out of me before he held out a hand. "Keep me informed, Bola. And be safe."

I nodded and shook his hand. "Of course. Ooh-rah."

"Semper Fi, devil." He clapped me on the shoulder and left the bar. I left a nice tip and left the bar to find the others nearby. One of the Warrant Officers that had been responsible for wiping Espinoza's memory gave a decent report of what they had found at the scene, and how it had affected everyone.

"The residual leavings that they had come across were unlike anything that they had ever seen. It drove one of the Army privates insane. Had to put him in the brig to keep people safe." He stared at me. "So you're the new Huntsman?"

I nodded and he just grunted. "Figures it would be a Marine of all fucking people." He held out a hand for me to shake. "Better you than some others."

I shook his hand and he continued his report. "We were able to scrub the area of the influence but not before it drove him mad, so if you have a way to help him, we would appreciate it. Otherwise, we may have to put him down."

Galaxy nodded. "Which way is the brig?"

He pointed in a direction and she was suddenly off in raven form. It took about twenty minutes of us standing around and shooting the shit to get any word, but when she returned, she smiled and said, "He's better now. Don't release him just yet, but it's safe to be around him."

The Warden nodded and left us with a "Thanks."

Amabala took us home to Arden's, and I called Uncle Yen.

On the fourth ring he picked up. "You all okay?"

I frowned. "Yeah, what's up?" I waited and heard him speaking to someone. "Uncle Yen?"

"They said there was an attack and that another god has turned up dead." He sounded worried for us and came back a second later. "People are scared, Marcus. They're worried it's the Hunt."

"It's not, Odin cleared us himself." I grunted as I ran into one of the massive tigers on my way outside. "Damn it, kitty, move!"

The tiger grumbled at me and swatted before moving and Uncle Yen asked point blank, "*The* Odin? The All-Father himself?"

"Yes."

"Come in." He sighed. "I have news and I don't want to speak over the phone anymore."

I nodded and remembered I was on the phone. "Be there soon."

Galaxy, tell Cass I'm borrowing her SUV.

"She knows." Cassia spoke over my shoulder and unlocked the car. "Let's go. I need to check on my staff and friends."

"She broadcast it to us live," Arden answered me before I could even ask about how they knew. "Merlin and Amabala are going to stay behind to get things settled for her; she's still out of it. Galaxy told us to go and leave them to her."

I just shrugged tiredly and got into the SUV. It felt like as soon as we were on the road we had arrived at the Table. As we came in, there were four guards at the door, two in the doorway on the inside and two outside.

The feel of the bar was intense. People stared at us as if we could be the enemy, and it wasn't a good feeling. Especially after learning everything that I had about myself.

"Anyone staring at us got a fucking problem?" Cassia challenged, her hands balling into fists at her side as she swept her covered gaze around the room. "We just got back from killing the things that kept our friend captive for eons and it was *not* a very satisfying fight. So if you wanna come over and fucking get some—I'm so far down, I might as well be a fucking Aussie."

One of the guests chuckled and Cassia's head snapped to the side as she looked to see who it was, but they stopped.

Uncle Yen dropped down the stairs and came toward me with a small wand in his hands, and as soon as he pressed it toward my chest, Arden and Cassia were stepping in front of me. "What are you doing, Yenasi?" Arden growled.

"Checking for Dominion." He hissed and shoved both of them aside. When the wand didn't glow at all, he sighed. "He doesn't have any."

"He would if Galaxy was inside him." Cassia crossed her arms over her chest. "We've recovered slivers of hers." She watched his confusion grow and said, "Yes, Yenny, we know what it is, and hers was stolen from her. We've recovered some, and we think we might know who is killing gods."

"Who?" he barked. "Who is it?"

"We don't know *who* or *what* they are," I corrected them all, then addressed the room, "But we've seen them and they are wildly powerful."

"Did you fight them?" someone hollered and the crowd grew louder. So loud, in fact, that we couldn't answer and be heard.

"Shut up!" Uncle Yen bellowed, quieting the room, his concern growing. "Did you fight them?"

I shook my head. "We would have been hopelessly—hilariously—out of our depth. This thing took one of Galaxy's captors and cartoon Bam-Bam'd her ass so hard into the ground it broke her. It had been a hard fight for us, Uncle Yen, but we could have won against the captor with all of us together. But they made her look like a fucking bug, and walked off with the injured god dragging behind them."

Yen stood up straight and sighed, and began to pace the room back and forth. Then he finally raised his head. "The High Table Columbus Branch hereby extends safe passage and housing to all of its godly friends and patrons. I will speak to the council and see if they will do the same for our friends around the world, but until then, do not travel alone and do not go anywhere near where the other gods have been taken. It's not safe."

The commotion returned as he turned on his heel and stalked up the stairs to speak to the council, I presumed, but I followed along. He heard the stairs creak behind him and turned on me. "I don't have more time to talk, Marcus. There's a lot to prepare, and I need to speak to the council."

"I was wondering if you had heard of what happened to Serpath?" He shook his head and I frowned. "If you hear anything, will you tell me?"

He nodded. "Of course, kiddo." He turned around and then stopped and faced me once more. "I'm proud of you for knowing your limits. Not a lot of people would have stood by while something like that took place if they had power like you. That was smart. Real smart. Gonna need my bartenders back, son. Can I count on you to help out?"

I nodded. "I'll start back tomorrow and Cassia, Arden, and I can wait a little longer before we go on vacation to Japan."

He nodded. "Good idea. Just lay low. Real low."

"Will do." He turned as I spoke and all but sprinted to his office.

I turned around to head back down to the girls and let them know what was going on. We could wait for a while, but we wouldn't be idle at all.

While we 'laid low,' we would be going to Grestal to hunt and level up. And maybe sometime soon we would be turning our sights on the potential god killer. But who knew when that would be, and we still needed to settle the not-so-small matter of getting a house to make our lair. It would take time. All of it would.

But all I knew was that time was something we had for now, and the new Wild Hunt would be putting it to damn-good use if I had anything to say about it.

Of course you do, Marcus, Galaxy purred through my head. *You're the Huntsman.*

ABOUT CHRISTOPHER JOHNS

Christopher Johns is a former photojournalist for the United States Marine Corps with published works telling hundreds of other peoples' stories through word, photo, and even video. But throughout that time, his editors and superiors had always said that his love of reading fantasy and about worlds of fantastic beauty and horrible power bled into his work. That meant he should write a book.

Well, ta-da!

Chris has been an avid devourer of fantasy and science fiction for more than twenty years and looks forward to sharing that love with his son, his loving fiancée and almost anyone he could ever hope to meet.

Connect with Chris:
Facebook.com/AxeDruidAuthor
Twitter.com/JonsyJohns

ABOUT MOUNTAINDALE PRESS

Dakota and Danielle Krout, a husband and wife team, strive to create as well as publish excellent fantasy and science fiction novels. Self-publishing *The Divine Dungeon: Dungeon Born* in 2016 transformed their careers from Dakota's military and programming background and Danielle's Ph.D. in pharmacology to President and CEO, respectively, of a small press. Their goal is to share their success with other authors and provide captivating fiction to readers with the purpose of solidifying Mountaindale Press as the place 'Where Fantasy Transforms Reality.'

Connect with Mountaindale Press:
MountaindalePress.com
Facebook.com/MountaindalePress
Twitter.com/_Mountaindale
Instagram.com/MountaindalePress

MOUNTAINDALE PRESS TITLES

GameLit and LitRPG

The Completionist Chronicles,
The Divine Dungeon, and
Full Murderhobo by Dakota Krout

Arcana Unlocked by Gregory Blackburn

A Touch of Power by Jay Boyce

Red Mage and
Farming Livia by Xander Boyce

Space Seasons by Dawn Chapman

Ether Collapse and
Ether Flows by Ryan DeBruyn

Bloodgames by Christian J. Gilliland

Threads of Fate by Michael Head

Lion's Lineage by Rohan Hublikar and Dakota Krout

Wolfman Warlock by James Hunter and Dakota Krout

Axe Druid,
Mephisto's Magic Online, and
High Table Hijinks by Christopher Johns

Skeleton in Space by Andries Louws

Chronicles of Ethan by John L. Monk

Pixel Dust and
Necrotic Apocalypse by David Petrie

Henchman by Carl Stubblefield

Artorian's Archives by Dennis Vanderkerken and Dakota Krout